The queen lifted a bejeweled hand

and pointed at Brenna. "Look at her. Her hair tumbles wildly about her cheeks and shoulders, and spills down her back in a tangle of curls. Her traveling gown and cloak are dusty and wrinkled. And is that blood upon her gown, Morgan?"

Morgan flushed uncomfortably. "Aye, Majesty."

"Her blood?"

"Mine."

"You subdued her with your sword?"

"She attacked me with a knife."

"This small female managed to wound Morgan Grey?" The queen's eyes danced with unconcealed humor. "Can it be that the man who subdues entire armies cannot control one woman?"

Dear Reader,

This is it, what we've all been waiting for. The month when history becomes twice as exciting and twice as romantic. Thanks to popular demand, Harlequin Historicals are increasing from two to four titles per month, starting now!

Our four books this month span the globe from the deserts of the American Southwest to the Scottish highlands as we bring you stories by some of your favorite authors.

With *The Silver Link,* Patricia Potter brings to life the early days of New Mexico in a poignant story of love and deception between a Spanish beauty and an American army scout. Heather Graham Pozzessere, in her eagerly awaited *Forbidden Fire,* takes you to turn-of-the-century England and to San Francisco on the eve of the Great Earthquake of 1906.

Contraband Desire by Lucy Elliot is a triumphant love story of devotion and hope set in Tennessee during the dark years of the Civil War. And finally, be sure not to miss Ruth Langan's *Highland Heather,* the next book in her series of adventuresome tales of the Scottish MacAlpin clan.

We hope you enjoy all of our historical romances. And whatever you do, don't forget to look for four Harlequin Historicals each month from now on, and join in the excitement!

Yours,
Tracy Farrell
Senior Editor

Highland Heather

Ruth Langan

Harlequin Books

TORONTO • NEW YORK • LONDON
AMSTERDAM • PARIS • SYDNEY • HAMBURG
STOCKHOLM • ATHENS • TOKYO • MILAN

Harlequin Historicals first edition February 1991

ISBN 0-373-28665-1

HIGHLAND HEATHER

Books by Ruth Langan

Harlequin Historicals

Mistress of the Seas #10
Texas Heart #31
Highland Barbarian #41
Highland Heather #65

Harlequin Books

Historical Christmas Stories 1990
"Christmas at Bitter Creek"

RUTH LANGAN

traces her ancestry to Scotland and Ireland. It is no surprise, then, that she feels a kinship with the characters in her historical novels.

Married to her childhood sweetheart, she has raised five children and lives in Michigan, the state where she was born and raised.

To Aubrey Langan Bissonnette
And to her proud parents, Carol and Bryon.

And, of course, to Tom,
Founder of the dynasty.

And the beat goes on.

Chapter One

Scotland, 1562

The sudden, shocking silence of the tranquil summer afternoon alerted Brenna to danger. It was as if a cloud obscured the sunshine. The birds disappeared from the trees, their chorus abruptly cut off. Even the insects seemed to stop all movement, all buzz and whir and hum.

Seventeen-year-old Brenna MacAlpin withdrew the dirk from her waistband and hissed through her teeth to her younger sister, "Return to the castle. Now."

Though fifteen-year-old Megan often rebelled against orders, she recognized that tone of voice. Danger. There was no time to question. She did as she was told and ran.

Within minutes a sea of men and horses swarmed over the rim of the hill. Sunlight glinted off shields of polished silver and hammered gold. The raised standard bore the crest of the hated English soldier known as the Queen's Savage, Morgan Grey.

The man riding the ebony stallion was garbed all in black. Even his hair and eyes were the color of Satan. Wide shoulders strained the seams of his gleaming sable tunic. His body was lean and hardened from years of battle.

The young woman saw everything, yet she was aware of nothing but the tip of the sword pointed at her heart.

"God in heaven, Brenna. We are under siege. Run,"
Megan cried over her shoulder.

Brenna MacAlpin was acutely aware of her younger sister racing toward the security of the castle walls. But she
could not move. She was frozen to the spot. It was not fear
for herself that held her, for she had lived her whole life with
war and death. It was Megan's life she worried after. She
would die rather than see her younger sister harmed.

She closed her eyes a moment, willing the fiery little
Megan to safety.

The man's voice was low, menacing. "It is not my intention to harm you. But if you do not drop the knife I will be
forced to run you through."

"Aye." Her voice was equally low as the knife slipped
from her fingers. "That is the way of the English."

His eyes narrowed at the carefully contained fury in her
tone.

Brenna saw Megan slip into the shadows of the castle
walls. Without realizing it, she let out a low sigh. She could
face death now. Her sister was safe.

She lifted her head and met the dark stare of the stranger.
"Finish the deed. I have no fear of you, nor of the death and
destruction you bring with you."

The horseman found himself staring down into the face
of the most bewitching woman he had ever seen. Her brow
was smooth, her complexion flawless. Her nose was small,
her lips pursed in anger. Thick black hair fell in waves to
below her waist. Such a tiny waist, he noted. Her figure was
lush, inviting. Her breasts rose and fell with every measured breath. But it was her eyes that held him. Eyes the
color of heather. At this moment they glinted, not with fear,
but with proud, haughty defiance.

"My men and I have not come here to attack your people. My queen, Elizabeth, has sent us on a mission of
peace." He chose to ignore the sneer his words brought. "I
desire only that you take me to the castle and present me to
your leader."

"For what purpose?"

He shot her a look that had caused men from England to Wales to cower and beg for mercy. Yet the lass merely faced him, her violet eyes blazing, her chin lifted.

"I shall discuss my business with your leader. Now walk ahead of me." He slid from the saddle and pointed his sword menacingly.

He missed the smile that touched the corner of her lips as she turned away. But he could not fail to see the way her slim hips swayed as she strode, head high, spine rigid.

"Alden."

At his call, a ruddy-cheeked man with a thatch of straw-like hair separated himself from the others.

"You will see to the men."

Within minutes his men fell into procession behind him.

When they reached the castle doors, a shout went up from within the fortress. The impenetrable doors were instantly opened to admit the young woman and the swarm of men who followed.

"They are wise not to fight," the Englishman muttered. "We have them greatly outnumbered."

"That is not the reason they submit," Brenna countered. "They do not fight because they know I would be harmed if they did."

"Is the life of one insignificant woman so important to them, I wonder?"

She did not respond.

He turned to a stooped old man who hovered near the door, and his voice rang out with authority. "Summon your leader."

The aged keeper of the door turned a worried glance at the young woman, who shook her head gently before turning away. With a sly look the old man hobbled up a flight of stairs.

Ignoring Morgan Grey, the young woman crossed the room and paused a moment to warm her hands before the fire. Then she turned.

Her tone was low, her words softly spoken. But there was no mistaking her calm assurance as she said, "I am the leader of my people. I am Brenna, the MacAlpin. These men follow my orders. And you and your men," she said with quiet authority, "trespass in my castle."

Brenna MacAlpin. It took Morgan Gray a full minute to recover from the shock of her pronouncement. This mere slip of a girl was the leader of the MacAlpins? He had heard of her, of course. Many an English soldier had returned from battle with stories of the MacAlpin woman who led her clan. But he had pictured a giant of a female with a man's muscles, wielding a broadsword and straddling a horse bareback. He had surely not expected this delicate creature who would look more at home with needle and thread, and servants offering her tea and scones.

"If that be true, why did you allow us inside your castle? Did you not realize that you would be even more vulnerable once my men were within your fortress walls?"

Brenna motioned to old Duncan MacAlpin, who strode forward, sword drawn. His white hair was in sharp contrast to his tanned, leathery skin. Though stooped with age, his arms still showed muscles honed through years of hard labor.

"Ye will do as I command." His voice rasped like the creaking wheels of an ancient cart. "I order your men to surrender their weapons, or I will give the order for my men to advance."

Morgan Grey threw back his head in laughter. "Am I to tremble in fear of this old man?"

"Nay, my lord," Brenna said softly. "'Tis the sight of your men surrounded by mine that will convince you to show Duncan the proper respect."

Thunderstruck, Morgan turned. Behind each of his men stood a Scotsman, armed with both sword and dirk. And standing with the men was the small, slim girl who had raced to the safety of the castle when he and his men had approached. Though her hair was the color of spun gold and her eyes were tawny, there was no mistaking the similarity of features. She had to be sister to the woman who called herself leader. Instead of the calm, almost serene presence before him, the lass had the fiery look of a warrior.

The English soldiers also turned and found themselves facing armed guards.

"So." Morgan turned back to the woman. "I see I misjudged you."

"A dangerous mistake. State your business, Morgan Grey, before I lose my patience."

"You know of me?"

"Aye." Her eyes narrowed. "They call you the Queen's Savage. But Elizabeth of England is not my queen. And here in Scotland we do not fear you."

He took a step toward her. Instantly Duncan raised the tip of his sword to Morgan's tunic, at a place just above his heart.

"Old man," Morgan said through clenched teeth. "If my mission were not peaceful, you would already lie in your own blood."

"Ye will step back from the Lady Brenna."

Morgan's hand tensed by his side. He longed to thrust his sword into the arrogant man's heart. Yet he admired the spirit of the two who faced him, despite the fact that they were nothing more than a doddering old fool and a fragile, helpless female. Still, he had his orders.

Ignoring Duncan he withdrew a scroll from inside his tunic and handed it to Brenna with a slight bow. "I bring a message of peace from my queen, Elizabeth of England. She bids you receive my men and me in friendship and allow us to abide with you a few days. It is my queen's wish that these wars between our borders cease and that our citizens learn to live in peace."

"And if we lower our weapons, will we not find a knife in our backs? Or worse," Brenna said softly, "will we wake to find our castle looted and our horses stolen?"

"Nay, my lady. If we desired your horses we would have taken them. And if we desired your castle, we could have easily laid siege and conquered you in battle. I would remind you that my men outnumber yours five to one. The ones you see here are but a small portion of the rest who await my orders just outside your castle walls."

Though her face did not change expression, he saw the quick flash of realization in her eyes. The hills had been black with men and horses. Yet only a hundred or so had followed him inside.

"Why does your queen now seek a truce between our people?"

Morgan's lips curled in a hint of a smile. "My queen is cousin to your queen. Mayhap they grow weary of dissent."

What he said made sense. Possibly. Or was it only that she wished it so fervently?

The Scottish clans who lived along the border between England and Scotland had suffered for generations because of the tensions between their two countries. As leader of a Borderer clan, Brenna had tasted war from the moment of her birth.

She studied him quietly. "How long do you wish to abide?"

"A day or two. No more."

She nodded. "Your men will sheathe their swords. If any weapon is drawn against one of my men, it is drawn against all."

Morgan's hand curled into a fist at his side. She was so cool, so regal, he couldn't decide whether to bow, as though in the presence of royalty, or throttle her within an inch of her life.

"Aye, my lady." He turned to his men. "Sheathe your weapons. Let no man raise a hand against another while we partake of the MacAlpin—hospitality."

She heard the note of sarcasm in his tone.

He turned toward Brenna. "My men will see to their horses first."

"My servants will prepare food and lodging."

"We are most grateful, my lady."

She gave him a curt nod and turned her back on him, crossing the room to stand with her men. "My servants will see to your comfort."

She paused beside her younger sister and touched a hand to her arm. Cool amber eyes, like those of a fox, appraised Morgan Grey before the young lass sheathed her sword and followed her sister from the room.

How different they were, Morgan mused as he turned toward the fire. The younger one looked as feisty as his young page before battle, nearly trembling with energy. But it was the older sister who filled Morgan's mind, crowding out all other thoughts. She was so haughty, so controlled, she might have been born to royalty.

He glanced at the tapestries lining the walls of the great hall. One central figure caught his eye. One man, from whom all the other figures descended. There was no mistaking the likeness of Kenneth MacAlpin, the first great monarch of Scotland. Morgan moved closer and studied the intricate needlework, tracing the lineage. It appeared that that infuriatingly regal air had been bred into the woman, Brenna, through the generations.

His lips curved into a smile that was laced with danger. Morgan Grey had always enjoyed sparring with royalty. And winning.

Chapter Two

Morgan Grey leaned a hip against the doorway and watched as his men eagerly filed into the great hall. Behind them came the Scots, their weapons put away, or at least hidden from sight beneath their tunics and capes.

Though there were two armies within the castle walls, the castle did not seem overcrowded. A giant fireplace at either end of the hall, filled with crackling logs, took the chill from the room. Tapers set in sconces along the walls cast a warm glow. The men's heavy boots scraped along the floor as they took their places at long wooden tables, scarred from generations of use.

The English soldiers sat at one end of the hall; the Scots at the other. The room echoed with the sounds of rough language and coarse laughter, as the men, enemies for centuries, self-consciously took the measure of each other.

Abruptly the crowd became subdued as the young women entered the hall. Morgan's eyes narrowed as he focused on the leader of the two.

Brenna's gown was deep lavender velvet. It hugged her firm, high breasts and tiny waist, then fell in soft folds to the tips of her kid slippers. The wide sleeves were inset with ermine and tapered to narrow cuffs. Her dark hair had been braided with ribbons and fell over one shoulder in a cascade of ebony and silk.

The girl behind her was gowned in pristine white. A cloud of yellow hair drifted around her shoulders like a veil. With her slender figure, she could be mistaken for a much younger lass. But there was nothing childlike about the way she openly studied the soldiers filling the room. Her misgiving about these foreign intruders was obvious.

While the two walked to their position at the head table, the Scots soldiers remained standing at attention. The English soldiers, surprised at the respect being shown, followed suit.

"My lord." A young servant approached Morgan. When he glanced at her, she timidly lowered her gaze. "My lady asks that you sit at her table while you sup."

He gave her a curt nod and followed. When he reached the table, the two young women looked up in greeting.

"It occurs to me that I have not yet introduced you to my sister. Megan is the youngest of the MacAlpin clan."

He bowed over the girl's hand and was aware of the way she cautiously appraised him. When he took her hand in his and brushed his lips over her knuckles, he felt her flinch.

"There is no need to fear. I carry no weapons, my lady."

Brenna saw the way his lips curved into the hint of a smile. But her younger sister was not amused.

"That is wise, my lord. For I was not prepared to trust the word of an Englishman."

She touched the hilt of a dagger at her waist.

His eyes narrowed.

Brenna put a hand on her sister's arm to still her words, then turned to soothe the tension of the man beside her. "We are not accustomed to entertaining English soldiers in our home."

"It is a new experience for me as well, my lady."

"Please." She was eager to keep this meal from erupting into open warfare. "Let us take our places at table."

As Morgan took the seat indicated, his thigh brushed Brenna's. Their gazes locked, his amused, hers angered.

He saw the cool disdain in her eyes and looked away. It was obvious that the Lady Brenna would do her duty and entertain him, even though she found it distasteful. He would also abide by his queen's wishes and tolerate the situation, though laying siege to this ice maiden's castle would have been more to his liking.

Brenna took a deep breath to calm the fluttering of her heart. Though she gave every appearance of being in control, her nerves were strung as tightly as the strings of the lute that lay in her sitting chamber. There was something completely unsettling about the man beside her.

"Have my servants seen to your comfort, my lord?"

"They have." He accepted a tankard from a serving wench and drained its contents before setting it down. The damnable woman made him uncomfortable, though he could not say why.

When a servant approached with a platter of fowl, Brenna offered the first serving to her guest. She watched as he took the food and broke it into several sections. How big his hands were. What strength lay in his fingers. She felt a tremor along her spine and wondered why such a thought had crept into her mind.

"None for you, my lady?"

"I..." She felt herself blushing. "I fear I have little appetite this evening."

"I am ravenous." Morgan helped himself to a second serving. This was followed by trays of venison, partridge and salmon, as well as thick-crusted breads still warm from the oven. Morgan savored every serving. Each time his tankard was emptied, it was immediately refilled by a hovering servant.

When at last he was finished, he leaned back with a sigh of contentment. "You are a most generous hostess, my lady."

Brenna had barely touched her food. Yet she had actually enjoyed the way Morgan indulged himself. There was something oddly satisfying about seeing a man eat with such lusty enthusiasm.

"Do you do everything with such zeal, my lord?"

"Everything that is worthy of doing." He turned his gaze fully upon her. "My youngest brother died from a fever when he was but ten and five. With his last breath he fretted that he had not yet lived. Never would he have the chance to lift his sword in the name of his queen. Nor journey to distant lands. Nor bed a woman."

Seeing the color that flooded Brenna's cheeks, Morgan realized that the female beside him, though leader of her people, was probably much like that lad. He discreetly changed the subject.

"Your keep is well fortified, my lady. I find it hard to believe that the old man who stood at your side this morrow is your first man-at-arms."

"Old Duncan stood at my father's side from the time the two were lads. His loyalty is deserving of my respect."

"An old man's loyalty will not stay an enemy's sword, my lady."

Her eyes flashed before she responded in a carefully controlled voice. "For hundreds of years my people have lived in the path of English, hungry for our land. Your people covet what we have—rich, fertile hills and sleek, desirable cattle."

"Not to mention your women."

She heard the hint of laughter in his voice, and her tone hardened.

"Do not cross words with me, my lord."

"Would you rather we cross swords?"

"Do you think me some pale English lady, who would grow faint and swoon at the sight of a sword? The MacAlpins, though peaceful by nature, have been forced to become a warrior clan. And as leader of my people, I would not hesitate to take up the sword against anyone who threatened mine."

Morgan felt grudging admiration for the woman's spirit. Still, her attitude rankled. "Forgive me, my lady, if I remove myself from the fray. Now that my men have been admirably fortified with food and drink, I will see that they withdraw to the quarters you have so generously prepared for them."

Brenna watched as he pushed away from the table and strode across the room. There was an arrogance even in his movements. At a single command his men followed.

From his position at the table, Duncan waited for her signal. Brenna nodded and he assembled his men. While the English slept, he and the Scots would keep careful watch. In MacAlpin Castle, the word of the English was worthy only of scorn.

As the English soldiers cleared the room, Brenna felt herself relax for the first time in an hour. It was impossible to be at ease in the company of Morgan Grey.

The cool evening air was fragrant with the delicate scent of heather. Clouds scudded across a half-moon, throwing the gardens into shadow.

Brenna pulled the cloak about her and walked among the carefully tended hedges. She was troubled by the presence of the English, and especially Morgan Grey. His reputation had preceded him. He was no mere messenger, carrying a missive from his queen. The man was legend, not only among his own people, but among those he had fought, as well. His name caused armies to tremble. From Scotland to Wales and even across the Channel to Ireland, the Queen's Savage was a man to be feared.

He was much more than a soldier, however; he was a titled English gentleman. Among the political factions dividing England he was a leader. His father had been one of King Henry's closest advisers. The English queen, Elizabeth, trusted Morgan Grey as she trusted few within her circle. And, in fact, if rumors were to be believed, he was one of the men being considered as consort for the queen.

Knowing all this, Brenna had still not been prepared for the man himself. His mere presence was daunting.

She heard the sound of footsteps and turned, her hand on the dirk at her waist.

Morgan's voice was hushed in the darkness. "Forgive me, my lady. I did not mean to startle you." When he recognized the glint of metal, his voice lowered. "I know of no English lady who would arm herself for a simple walk in the garden."

"Then your Englishwomen are most fortunate, my lord. May they never have to fear an attack from those who would take what they do not wish to give."

Once again he was startled by the anger in her tone. "If you do not trust me, perhaps the stalwart Duncan should be at your side."

She couldn't help but smile. "Duncan and his Mary are most surely asleep by now. With the arrival of your men, he was forced to put in a full day."

"And what of your safety, my lady?"

Her smile grew. "I do not think you will spend even one minute worrying about my safety. But just so you understand..." She inclined her head. "My men walk the perimeter of the garden, as well as all the castle grounds. If a single night bird should call, they will note it. Despite the presence of English soldiers within these walls, my men will see to my safety."

"You need have no fear." As she started to walk, he moved along at her side. They passed a planting of roses surrounded by rows of wild heather, and he was reminded of the woman beside him. She was as delicate as a single rose petal. But her words were as sharp as any thorn. She appeared as cultured as the rose, and yet as wild as the heather.

"Have you read the missive from my queen?"

"Aye." Brenna bent her head to inhale the wonderful perfume from a perfect red rose. "The English monarch declares that yours is a peaceful mission. But peace has long eluded our people. She does not say how she hopes to unite our borders.''

''It is the queen's belief that if the lands bordering our two countries could be united, the bloodletting would cease. Elizabeth sends an emissary to your Queen Mary in Edinburgh to arrange suitable marriages that will ensure peace.''

''Marriage. To an Englishman.'' Brenna paused in the act of touching the flower and prayed that her hands would not tremble and betray her.

''Does that trouble you, my lady?''

Brenna forced herself to meet his cool look. Was that a hint of mocking laughter lurking in those dark depths?

With a flounce of skirts she turned away and began walking until she came to an arbor of vines and climbing roses. Unable to contain her anger, she turned on him.

''Why should it trouble me? Should I not be willing, nay, eager, to hand over my loyal people, my fertile lands, and the castle that has been in my family for generations in return for the ill treatment I am bound to receive at the hands of an English husband?'' Her tone lowered to a furious whisper. ''Should I not be overjoyed to lose all that I hold dear for the sake of peace between our countries?''

''And what about the unhappy Englishman who is forced into marriage with his enemy? Will the poor lout not be forced to watch his back each time he lies in his bed?''

Her eyes glittered. ''He will if he insists upon marrying a MacAlpin.''

''Such anger in one so young.'' The mockery was wiped from his eyes. His voice softened. ''What have the English done to you that you should bear such hatred?''

''My mother was killed at the hands of the English. For all that my sisters and I suffered, my father suffered a hundred times more. She was his reason for living. I saw the light go out of his eyes after her death.''

''I am sorry.'' Without thinking, Morgan placed his hand on her arm. That was his undoing. He felt a rush of heat that startled him.

At his touch Brenna drew herself up stiffly, fighting the feeling of panic that threatened to paralyze her.

"I must go." As she tried to pull away, Morgan caught her by the upper arms, forcing her to stay.

Her throat went dry. Like a cornered animal she looked around, hoping to spot one of her men. But the tangled growth around the arbor shielded her from their view.

"Unhand me," she said fiercely, "or I shall be forced to defend myself." She pulled the knife from her waistband and brandished it menacingly.

"I see that you are indeed no pale English lady. In fact, in England you would not be considered a lady at all. I know of no lady who would threaten a man with a knife unless she intended to use it."

"I fully intend to use this on you unless you retreat this minute."

Without warning Morgan caught her hands in a painful grip and twisted the knife from her fingers. When she lifted her free hand to push away, he caught it and dragged her roughly against him.

"There are few who have drawn a weapon against me and lived to tell about it." His words were choked with anger.

She stared at the knife, glittering dully in his hands. Her chin lifted in a defiant gesture. "Is this how your queen intends to bring peace to our borders?"

"Nay, my lady. Not like this." He dropped the knife onto the earth at their feet. "Like this."

Without warning he lowered his head and ground his mouth over hers.

He fully intended to punish her with his kiss, knowing how much she would detest being touched by an English soldier. He would enjoy humbling this arrogant wench. But the moment their lips met, all his intentions were forgotten.

God in heaven. Where had the fire come from? The heat that flowed between them was shocking in its intensity. And though he knew he would be burned, he could not pull away.

She was pliant and warm, and her breath was as sweet as the flowers that filled the arbor. The soft contours of her body seemed to melt against him. Her hands were balled into fists that she kept firmly between them.

Brenna held herself stiffly, fighting the reaction that shuddered through her at his touch. This could not be happening. Not with this hated Englishman. Yet even while she fought to resist, her body betrayed her. As his lips closed over hers, a tiny ripple of pleasure shot along her spine, leaving her trembling. Though she continued to keep her hands between them, with a will of their own her fingers uncurled until her open palms rested against his chest.

He pulled back, staring down at her as if seeing her for the first time.

Her eyes were wide with fear and loathing. But even as he watched he saw that there was another emotion mirrored in those depths, as well. Desire? Could it be the first tiny stirrings of desire?

He knew he should walk away. Now, before her guards became suspicious and decided to investigate why their leader lingered so long in the rose arbor. A disturbance at MacAlpin Castle could shatter the fragile peace that Elizabeth was trying so hard to establish.

While he studied her, his thumbs unknowingly made lazy circles on the flesh of her upper arms. God in heaven. She was stunning. Her dark hair had pulled loose from its comb and drifted like a veil around her face and shoulders. Her lips were pursed in a little mew of surprise. Though he knew he should resist, he lowered his head and gave in to the desire to kiss her again.

This time the kiss was the merest touching of mouth to mouth. His lips softened, moving slowly, lazily over hers, savoring the sweetness of her.

Brenna held herself rigidly in his arms, fighting the overwhelming feelings that threatened to swamp her.

Never before had her body betrayed her like this. Though she wanted to resist, she could not. Even though his hands held her as gently as if she were a fragile flower, she was imprisoned as if by arms of steel. The sweetest prison she had ever known. His lips were warm and firm, and as they moved slowly over hers, she felt a delicious tingle that left her limbs weak, her head swimming.

What had this man done to her? Why was she behaving in such an outrageous manner with this Englishman?

Every instinct told Morgan to walk away from this woman now, while he was yet able. And still he lingered over her lips. Such tempting lips. Why had it taken him so long to notice how perfect they were?

Without warning he drew her more firmly into his arms and took the kiss deeper. His mouth devoured her, searching for a release from the sudden hunger that gnawed at him. Her breath filled his lungs. Her lips seduced. Her breasts were flattened against his chest. He dragged her hips against his and heard her little moan as his tongue brazenly invaded the sweetness of her mouth.

This could not be happening. Brenna barely recognized the sound of her own voice as a moan slipped unbidden from low in her throat. When his tongue touched hers, she drew back. But the hands at her spine were strong, holding her even closer when she tried to resist. Damn the man! And damn this strange weakness within her that seemed to have robbed her of all strength to resist.

Tentatively she drew in the taste of him. Dark. Mysterious. And then, for one brief instant, she relaxed against him, savoring his magnificent strength.

The thought crept unbidden into her mind. He kisses the way he does everything else in his life. With such wild abandon, it is marvelous to behold, impossible to resist.

But resist she must, if she were to survive. Slowly, like one awakening from a dream, she surfaced and brought her hands to his chest.

He felt the pressure of her hands and struggled for control. Though he was a man of many appetites, it was not his way to force himself upon a woman.

Lifting his head, he stared down into her eyes.

"A man might be tempted to risk your dirk in his back just for sake of another kiss like that one, my lady."

With a mocking bow he scooped the knife from the dust and handed it to her. She snatched it from his hand and, lifting her skirts, ran until she reached the safety of the open portal, where old Bancroft stood awaiting her return.

Morgan stood very still, watching until she had disappeared inside the castle. With a savage oath he turned and strode among the hedges, seeking to exorcise the fire that raged within his loins.

His arms were still warm from the touch of her. His lips still full of the taste of her.

Chapter Three

Brenna stood in the shadows of her upper balcony and watched the movements of the figure far below. Unconsciously she touched a finger to her lips. A ripple of feeling coursed along her spine. She shook it off. How dare the Englishman kiss her like a lowly serving girl. Never before had a man dared to treat her in such a manner.

And what of her reaction? Even now she could feel the heat rush to her cheeks at the thought of the way she had melted into his arms. Just thinking about the way he had kissed her brought a weakness to her limbs.

She must get rid of this man, and soon, before he had time to cause any more havoc.

A tap on her door caused her to whirl nervously. At the sight of her sister, she let out a long breath of air.

Megan was taken aback at her sister's display of nerves. For as long as she could remember, Brenna had been the calm in the eye of the storm.

"I cannot sleep knowing the English lie within our castle walls."

"Aye." Brenna turned her attention back to the one who walked the garden paths. "It is the same for me."

Megan crossed the room and paused beside her sister. Following Brenna's gaze, she spied Morgan Grey. "Is that not their leader?" At her sister's nod, she said softly, "Why do you permit him to move about unmolested? What if he should open the gates and admit the rest of his men who wait beyond our walls?''

"He claims to be on a mission of peace from Elizabeth of England.''

"You believe him?''

Brenna shrugged. "I have not yet decided what to believe about Morgan Grey.''

Megan was puzzled by the inflection in her sister's voice. It was not anger she detected, but something not quite definable. "And how does England's queen hope to achieve this miracle of peace?''

"By arranging marriages between our people, especially those of us who are Borderers.''

"God in heaven.'' With a stricken look Megan caught her sister by the arm. "Does that mean that you and I would be forced to marry Englishmen?''

"Nay.'' Brenna's eyes narrowed at the thought of allowing her sister to be sacrificed in such a manner. As for herself, she was the MacAlpin. No one told her what to do. "I would pay any price for peace, save that one.'' Her voice softened. Her eyes took on a dreamy, faraway look. "I recall the way Father grieved after Mother's death. Theirs was a true and lasting love. As is the love our sister, Meredith, feels for Brice, her beloved Highlander.''

Megan nodded. "But no one expected her to give her heart to the barbarian.''

"It matters not that he was not one of us. Brice Campbell is devoted to Meredith, just the way Father was devoted to Mother. I'll not settle for less.'' Brenna's eyes burned with a determination that sent her younger sister's heart soaring with renewed hope. Brenna could be counted upon to stand firm in the face of danger.

"I swear, Megan, I'll give myself to no man until my heart tells me 'tis true love.'' She opened her arms and gathered the girl close. Against her temple she murmured, "We must remain true to ourselves and our people. And the English queen be damned.''

* * *

Morgan Grey awoke in a foul temper. He had slept badly, despite the softness of down beneath his head and the warmth of a cozy fire in the sleeping chamber. It was not down he needed. Nor a warm bed. It was the softness of a woman's body next to him. A woman slender of frame and beautiful of face, with raven hair and a voice that whispered over his senses. A woman like . . . Nay. He wanted no part of the Scotswoman. He wanted only to be rid of this place and the woman who fired his blood.

She was not at all the sort of female he would willingly seek out. He much preferred a plump tavern wench, all soft curves, with a boisterous wit and a lusty laugh. Or one of the many willing women at Elizabeth's court, who dressed to please the men and knew how to brazenly flirt. With that kind of woman there need be no fear of entrapment. They were seeking merely a few moments of pleasure. Love was not part of the bargain. That was why he enjoyed their company. He had no intention of losing his heart only to have it shattered. Never again.

He dressed quickly, then went to inspect the soldiers' quarters. Once there he took his time listening to the complaints of his men. Ordinarily he would have berated them for their petty quarrels. The food was not as tasty as English food. Their beds were hard. The horses were not being stabled properly. But this day he let them ramble on without reprimand. He found the company of his men far more inviting than that of the woman with whom he would be forced to break the fast.

When at last the men assembled for their morning meal, he had no choice but to accompany them.

Brenna stood in the center of the refectory, giving orders to one of the serving girls. She knew the exact moment Morgan Grey entered the room. Though she finished her command, she had no idea what she was saying. She babbled on, achingly aware of dark eyes staring at her with such intensity, she could feel the heat clear across the room.

She turned and acknowledged him with a slight nod.

"Good morrow, my lady." He cautioned himself to be pleasant if it killed him.

"I trust you slept well." She prayed her cheeks were not as flushed as they felt.

"Very well." He studied her gown of palest pink, the sleeves crusted with jewels. Her lush, dark hair was held back with pale pink netting. He had a fleeting wish to tear away the netting and watch her hair cascade down her back, loose and free. That thought brought an instant frown to his face. "Your accommodations are most satisfying."

So satisfying that he looked as if he had slept in a briar patch the entire night. "You will join me at the head table?"

"As you wish."

He walked beside her, then paused to hold her chair. As he bent forward he inhaled the fragrance of heather. Damn the woman for all her soft looks and polite words. Why couldn't she be a hag, with bad teeth and the scent of the stables about her?

"I trust you will be leaving for England this day."

"Nay." He saw the look that came into her eyes and began to enjoy himself for the first time since he had awakened. So she was eager to be rid of him, was she? "My men and I will tarry here for a few days longer."

"For what purpose, my lord?"

"To—assess the situation for the queen."

As a servant approached with a tray of food, Brenna felt her stomach lurch. A few more days of this man. How could she even think about eating after such an unpleasant bit of news? Why did the man have to sit so close? Just the thought of those hands touching her, soiling her, caused strange sensations deep inside.

Morgan broke the bread, still warm from the oven, into thick slabs and handed one to her. She watched as he spooned honey over his and tasted it. He gave a smile of pure pleasure.

"To a soldier who has been long away from his home, there is nothing more satisfying than good food." He noted that she had not yet eaten. "Taste, my lady." There was the hint of a smile on his lips. "Mayhap it will sweeten your day."

She took a dainty bite and prayed she would be able to swallow.

"Is your sister not joining us this morrow?"

"She was still abed when I came below stairs. She did not sleep well last night."

"A pity." His appetite had just sharpened considerably. Now if only he could cause the one beside him to sleep badly as well. But that was probably asking too much. She was too regal to ever lose her composure.

"A little mutton, my lady? Venison?" As Morgan filled his plate, he insisted on filling Brenna's as well. While he ate until he was sated, she nibbled at a piece of honeyed bread and left the rest untouched.

Morgan emptied a tankard of mulled wine and felt his blood heat. After such a repast, he could lay siege to an entire enemy stronghold. Or at least the enemy beside him.

He leaned back and glanced at Brenna. A drop of honey clung to her lip. Without thinking he touched a finger to the spot, then brought his finger to his tongue.

With a look of astonishment she watched him lick the honey from his finger.

He gave her a mocking smile. "Your lips made the honey even sweeter."

"You are too bold, sir. This time you go too far."

She scraped back her chair, nearly knocking it over in her haste to escape his touch. Without a backward glance she lifted her skirts and hurried from the room.

As she disappeared, Morgan's lips curved into a lazy, satisfied smile. So, he had managed to ruffle the lady's feathers. He just might enjoy his stay at MacAlpin Castle after all.

From his place across the room, old Duncan MacAlpin watched through narrowed gaze.

"Hamish." Brenna and Megan launched themselves into the arms of the tall, handsome youth who came to call midmorning.

Across the room, Morgan assumed a bored expression as he watched.

"What brings you to MacAlpin Castle?"

"Everyone knows that there are English soldiers camped about your lands. I could not sleep another night without knowing whether or not you were safe."

He took Brenna's hands and studied her carefully. Too carefully, Morgan thought. Like a lover.

"Have you or your sister been molested?"

"We are safe enough. But I am grateful for your concern. Come," Brenna said. "Meet the leader of the English soldiers."

As she led the youth toward him, Morgan noted the dull copper hair, and barely hidden beneath the plaid, the muscled arms and shoulders. The lad's skin was kissed by the sun, and displayed not a whisker nor a blemish.

"Hamish MacPherson," Brenna said with a smile, "this is Morgan Grey, who carries a message of peace from his queen, Elizabeth."

The two men studied each other somberly, each taking the measure of the other.

"Are you a messenger for your clan, lad?"

Hamish pulled himself up to his full height. He knew of Morgan Grey, called the Queen's Savage. All of Scotland did. But even his fierce reputation did not give him the right to be insulting. Especially in front of the MacAlpin women.

"I am the eldest son of Blair, leader of the clan MacPherson. We are pledged to the protection of our neighbors, the MacAlpins, against any danger."

"How noble." Morgan suddenly despised this youth, with his unlined face and ready smile. He'd bet a gold sovereign that the only MacAlpin this callow youth cared about was Brenna. "I assure you, I pose no threat to these good people."

Hamish smiled down at the woman beside him. "I am greatly relieved. I came prepared to do battle. You know I would die rather than see you harmed."

Brenna lifted her face to him and gave him a look of pure adoration. "I know, Hamish. That was good of you."

"Foolish, I would say."

All eyes turned toward Morgan.

"If you came prepared to fight my soldiers, you should have brought half of Scotland with you. One puny man would hardly cause us to change our minds, if we had come on a mission of war instead of peace."

The smile was wiped from Hamish's eyes. His hand went to the sword at his waist. Instantly Brenna caught his hand and twined her fingers in his.

"Pay no attention to this man's words, my friend. It is enough to know that you cared enough to risk your life for ours. My sister Megan and I are forever in your debt."

The youth caught her hand to his lips and stared deeply into her eyes. "Perhaps you and Megan could come to stay with my people until the English have gone."

Brenna turned in time to see the look of fury in Morgan's dark eyes. What a sense of power it gave her to know that she could rouse the Englishman's ire with such ease.

"That is most kind of you. But of course I cannot leave my castle unattended. Nor my guests." She gave what she hoped was her sweetest smile. "Come, Hamish. You must stay and visit a while. Perhaps you can sup with us this night and return to your own home on the morrow."

Hamish MacPherson was overjoyed. Never in his wildest dreams had he hoped for such tender treatment from Brenna MacAlpin. Always in the past, the young woman had treated him like a leper, holding him, like all the others, at arm's length. Perhaps she was more afraid of this Englishman than she admitted. It would seem that he had arrived just in time.

He puffed up his chest and allowed himself to be led to the great room. Once there, however, he found himself left alone with the younger one, Megan, while Brenna went off to her chambers.

It was not until midday, when everyone had gathered for a meal, that Brenna once more singled out Hamish for her attention.

Beside her, Morgan Grey seethed. The ice maiden, it seemed, had a fondness for pink-cheeked boys with broad shoulders and little between their ears.

"A rider approaches, my lady. He carries the standard of the English warrior, Morgan Grey."

Brenna looked up from her embroidery. Across the room, her sister and Hamish were enjoying a rousing game of cards. Though darkness had descended, the room was made bright by the light of the fire and the candles that burned in sconces along the walls.

"Does he ride alone?"

"Aye, my lady."

"Since he is a lone rider, allow him to enter."

The order was given. Scots soldiers lowered their weapons. The wooden staves were thrown, allowing the huge double doors to swing wide.

Brenna watched as old Bancroft, the keeper of the door, accepted a scroll from the stranger.

"He carries a message for his leader, Morgan Grey."

Brenna nodded and waited while a servant went in search of the man she had been avoiding all day. When Morgan appeared, she shot him a haughty glance before looking away.

Morgan scanned the words of the scroll, then looked up with a frown. "Was there nothing more?"

"Nay, my lord."

"Tell the men camped beyond the walls that we will leave at first light."

Brenna could scarcely believe what she was hearing. Though she carefully schooled her features to hide the excitement she felt, she could not help but give a sigh of relief as the soldier smartly saluted and turned away.

"You are leaving, my lord?"

He heard the note of eagerness in her tone and silently cursed her.

"Aye." He ignored Hamish, who had crossed the room to stand protectively beside Brenna. Morgan experienced such a rush of anger it puzzled him. Jealousy? That was impossible. How could he harbor such ridiculous feelings over a woman he didn't even like? "It seems the queen has need of me."

"You are returning to England?" At his nod she added, "I will immediately instruct my servants to prepare food for your journey."

"You are too kind, my lady. You need not hurry. We do not leave until the morrow."

"But there is much to prepare. The day begins early."

As she turned away he saw the relief lurking just below the surface of her composed features. She was overjoyed to be rid of him. If she could, she would see him gone within the hour.

Well, he thought, watching her retreating back, did he not feel the same way? He had resented this mission. Had resented wasting his time and his men on something so trivial as this Scotswoman. The time he had spent here could have been better spent subduing enemies of the Crown.

He made his way to the men's quarters and instructed them to prepare to leave at dawn. Then he made his way to his chambers and packed his few supplies.

From the desk, he picked up a tankard of ale, then glanced at the notes he had written chronicling the Mac-Alpin holdings. The Scotswoman was unexpectedly wealthy even by English standards. Brenna MacAlpin would make a fine bride for one of England's titled noblemen.

He walked to the balcony and stared at the darkened hills below. Brenna understood what the queen had in mind. And from all that he had observed, she would rather die than allow herself to be wed to an Englishman.

He swirled the contents of the tankard, deep in thought. She was an intelligent woman. More intelligent than most he had met. If she intended to thwart the queen's plans, there was a simple enough solution. Before he had a chance to reach England and present his findings to the queen, the MacAlpin woman could easily persuade one of her own countrymen to marry her. The oaf below stairs would need no persuasion. He was already a poor dog, eating out of the lady's hand.

Once wed, even the Queen of England did not have the power to rule against such a union.

God in heaven! In just the short time he had known her, he could already glimpse her devious little mind at work. It was what he would do in her place.

He downed the ale and slammed the tankard onto the desk. As a loyal servant of Elizabeth, he knew what he had to do. With the decision firm in his mind, he felt more lighthearted than he had in days.

This was not a personal feud, he assured himself. But that would not prevent him from enjoying a certain amount of personal satisfaction at the lady's discomfort.

To keep Lady Brenna MacAlpin from marrying another, he would have to force her to accompany him and his men to England.

Chapter Four

The sky to the east was still dark when Brenna awoke. With a light heart she climbed from her bed. At the first sound of her footsteps, old Morna, her maid, was at her side, helping her with her morning toilette.

"You be anxious, child."

"Aye. The English soldiers are leaving us this morrow."

"Thanks be to God. Their leader, Morgan Grey, is a fearsome man. He reminds me of the one who wed our dear Meredith."

"How can you say such a thing?" Brenna studied the old woman's reflection in her mirror. "Brice Campbell is a Scotsman. Morgan Grey is English."

Old Morna shrugged. "Aye. But there is a look about him. A bit of a rogue. If I were fifty years younger..."

"Are you daft?" Brenna stood and smoothed her skirts. "The man owes his allegiance to the English queen. That makes him our enemy."

"You spend an inordinate amount of time staring at your enemy when you think no one is watching."

No one except this old woman would ever speak so bluntly to the mistress of MacAlpin Castle. Brenna flushed clear to her toes, then reached for the door pull. "I have no time for your silly prattle. I go below stairs to oversee the food for the English soldiers' journey."

As she flounced away, Brenna fretted over the old woman's words. Perhaps she had spent a good deal of time staring at Morgan Grey. But it was only because he was a man who could not be trusted. It had nothing at all to do with the fact that he was indeed easy to look at.

Halfway down the stairs she turned and found Megan following her. The girl's face was wreathed with smiles.

"'Tis a day for rejoicing," she called, as she caught up with her sister and linked arms with her.

"Aye. Perhaps our lives can now return to normal."

The girls came to an abrupt halt at the bottom of the stairs. Morgan Grey stood near the main entrance, calling orders to his men, who were already carrying supplies to the horses who stood saddled and waiting in the outer courtyard.

"My ladies." He bowed and smiled charmingly.

Too charmingly, Brenna thought. This was a side to Morgan Grey that she had not previously witnessed.

"You are afoot early, my lord. It would appear that you are eager to be away."

"Every soldier harbors a longing for home."

"Aye. Then I will not delay your departure." Brenna turned away. "I will see to your morning meal at once."

He watched as she hurried away, followed by her sister. For a moment he stood very still as he went over his plan in his mind. Then, confident that he could carry it off, he returned his attention to the men and their supplies.

The meal was a lavish affair, and at last Brenna had found her appetite. With Morgan about to depart, she felt free to enjoy herself. He watched as she savored the thick slab of pork and bread warm from the oven. When she drank the hot mulled wine, she felt light-headed, and couldn't decide if it was the wine or the knowledge that she would soon be rid of this troublesome man.

Across the room she noted that Duncan's chair was vacant. She would speak with his wife, Mary, as soon as the guests were gone. The old man often had trouble getting out of bed these days. He had earned the right to his rest. Perhaps old Duncan could be persuaded to retire soon and turn over his duties to one of his sons. She hated to admit to herself that the Englishman had been right when he suggested that Duncan's loyalty was not enough to keep her safe. Her old friend would give his life for her. But that might not be enough. She needed one younger, more agile, at her right hand.

She turned aside the troubling thoughts. She would find a way to handle the matter gracefully, with no slight on Duncan's good name.

Hamish MacPherson was obviously delighted to be part of the festivities. Seated to the left of Brenna, he ate with relish and drank more than a little ale, until his face was flushed and his eyes a bit cloudy.

He paid special attention to his hostess, hanging on her every word. If the Englishman to her right was scowling, it mattered not to Hamish. Soon enough they would be rid of the scoundrel. And perhaps, if the fates were smiling, he could persuade Brenna MacAlpin to allow him to stay on another day or two.

When they had had their fill, Brenna and Megan led their guests to the courtyard, eager to bid them farewell.

"Safe journey, my lord," Brenna said, her eyes dancing. "You may extend my warm wishes to your monarch."

"You may extend those wishes yourself."

She thought she heard a trace of laughter in his tone. But his words had her puzzled.

"I fear you make no sense."

He crossed the distance between them and caught her by the arm. Surprised, she stared at the offending hand, then up into his dark eyes.

"You have but a moment to see to a wardrobe suitable for traveling."

"I do not . . ."

Her eyes widened. He saw the confusion, then the sudden, terrible knowledge at his next words.

"I fear I cannot bear to be parted from you. I insist that you accompany me to London, my lady."

She swallowed. "You cannot be serious."

"My queen has already petitioned her cousin in Edinburgh, my lady. She intends to have you wed to an Englishman. To that end I am sworn to obey."

"You cannot take me from my own home, my own land, against my will."

"You are wrong, my lady. I fully intend to do just that."

At Morgan's announcement, Hamish MacPherson unsheathed his sword. But before he could brandish it, Morgan's words stopped him. "Look around you, boy. If you but lift that sword against me, a dozen men will step forward to stop you. And the lady will see you lying at her feet in little pieces."

"At least I will have the pleasure of wounding you or perhaps even killing you first."

Morgan shrugged carelessly. "If you wish."

As Hamish lifted his sword, Morgan unsheathed his own weapon and moved so quickly the lad had no chance to defend himself. The tip of Morgan's sword pierced his shoulder. Blood spurted as Hamish's sword clattered to the stones of the courtyard.

"That is but a warning, nothing more," Morgan said between clenched teeth. "Know that if I had wanted to kill you, you would already lie dead at my feet."

Megan and Brenna rushed to assist the wounded lad.

Morgan Grey looked beyond them to old Morna, who stood on the steps just inside the castle doors, wringing her hands.

"Take your mistress upstairs and see that she is dressed in something warm and comfortable for the journey."

"Aye, my lord."

Brenna looked up from her place beside Hamish. "My men will never..."

"Your men will do as I command." He called out to Allen, his second in command, who came forward leading Duncan MacAlpin, still dressed in his nightclothes. The old man's face was flushed with embarrassment.

"Forgive me, my lady. The villains invaded my sleeping chamber. They are holding my Mary prisoner."

Brenna glanced up and saw the old woman standing stiffly on her balcony. An English soldier stood behind her. Morning sunlight glinted on the knife at her throat.

"So this is your mission of peace."

At Brenna's angry words, Megan pulled the dirk from her waistband and leaped at Morgan Grey. Instantly Brenna wrapped her arms around Megan, pinning her arms at her sides. It took all of Brenna's strength to contain the fury in the girl.

"He humiliates us, degrades us and threatens to take you by force. Why do you stop me?"

"Because I love you," Brenna whispered furiously. "Because I cannot allow my foolish trust of the man to cost the life of the sister I love more than life itself."

"If you love me, let me kill him."

"Nay." Brenna continued to hold her sister until the knife dropped from her fingers. Then she turned her into her arms and allowed her to weep out all her fears and frustration.

Morgan watched without emotion. When the girl's tears had been stemmed, he said quietly, "Go with your nurse. Dress quickly. We have wasted enough time."

With a last hateful look at her enemy, Brenna turned, keeping her arms firmly around her younger sister as the two followed Morna up the stairs.

When they were safely in her chambers, Brenna released Megan. Instantly the young girl flew into a rage.

"Why did you not permit me to attack that villain?"

"Megan." Brenna caught her sister by the hand. "I implore you to listen to me. You are a very brave lass. And I love you dearly. But you and I are no match for a man like Morgan Grey."

"How can you calmly allow him to take you away from all you love?"

"I have no intention of giving in to that madman."

"But why..."

Brenna touched a finger to her lips. Both Megan and old Morna gave her their complete attention.

"Do you remember how we used to climb the castle walls when we were children?"

Megan nodded. "Mother used to say her heart stopped each time she discovered our little prank."

Brenna turned to her old nurse. "You must delay for as long as you can. When Morgan Grey finally loses patience, stand back and force him to break down the door. That should give us enough time to climb down and cross the River Tweed. Once across, we will make our way to the Highlands."

"And the safety of Brice Campbell's protection," Megan said with sudden understanding.

"Aye." Brenna began stripping away the filmy gown she had worn to celebrate the retreat of the English. "Hurry, Megan. We must dress quickly and be on our way."

"You have no horses, lass," Morna moaned. "How can you go all that distance on foot?"

"Once in the forest we can enlist the aid of the Highlanders. They know of our relationship to Brice Campbell. They will come to our aid."

"They are a strange breed, lass. They would just as leave kill you as help you."

"Not if we explain that we are running from the English. They do not forget old grudges. Besides," Brenna said as she pulled on a heavy woolen cloak lined with ermine, "I would rather die in Scotland at the hands of the Highlanders than in England at the hands of Morgan Grey."

"He would not kill you, lass, only hand you over to his queen."

"Aye. To be wed to some hated Englishman. That would be worse than death."

When at last the two young women climbed over the balcony and began making their way down the uneven stone wall of the castle, old Morna stood watching, her lips moving in prayer.

"Godspeed," she called. She lifted tear-clouded eyes to scan the forested peaks in the distance. Safety was so far away. And yet it was their only chance to elude the man who waited below to steal away her beloved mistress.

The English soldiers allowed old Duncan to assist Hamish in stemming the flow of blood from his shoulder. While they worked, Morgan Grey paced the courtyard. He had originally intended to go with Brenna and see to her hasty arrangements. But after witnessing the emotional outburst of her younger sister, he had changed his plans. He would allow them a few minutes alone. There was much they would have to say to one another.

His men stood beside their horses as the sun climbed higher in the sky.

Morgan cursed this peculiar trait in women that caused them to take hours to do what a man could do in only minutes. What was the damnable woman doing? Packing the entire contents of her wardrobe? He glanced around. How many additional beasts would it take to transport all that she was bringing?

He would be firm. He would personally inspect every trunk and insist that she leave behind all except the most necessary items. Like all women, she would weep and wail and beg to be allowed to take all her silly frills to England. But in the end he would prevail.

He paced again, the length of the courtyard and back. He had been patient long enough. Exasperated, he charged through the doorway and up the stairs.

"I can give you no more time, my lady," he called through the closed door. "We must leave before the sun grows any higher in the sky."

He paused and listened. There was no sound from within.

He pounded a fist on the door. "My lady. We must leave."

Once again there was only silence.

He frowned. What trickery was afoot?

"Old woman," he shouted. "Are you inside?"

He placed his ear to the door and listened. No sound issued from within.

"Alden." Alarmed, Morgan ran to the top of the stairs and shouted for his second in command. "Bring your strongest men. And a log with which to batter down this door."

Hamish and old Duncan watched with sudden interest as several of the English soldiers hurried inside. The rest of Morgan's men grew tense. They listened to the sounds of pounding as the log was thrust again and again until the massive door gave way.

Morgan strode through the open doorway and stared at the old woman who huddled against the far wall.

"Where is your mistress?"

The old woman trembled.

He strode across the room until he towered over her. His voice was low with rage. "You will answer me. At once."

In a quavering voice Morna croaked, "She has gone to the Highlands, where she will be safe."

"The Highlands. How did she escape this room?"

The old woman pointed to the balcony. Astonished, Morgan stalked to the railing and stared down.

"How can this be? There is no rope."

"My girls never needed a rope," the old woman said with a surge of pride. "From the time they were wee lasses, they were able to climb the castle walls by placing their feet and hands into the notches made by missing stones."

Morgan swore savagely, then turned to his second in command. "Alden, choose five of your fastest horses and riders. They will accompany me to the Highlands. You will lead the rest of the men back to England."

In a low tone, so the other soldiers couldn't hear, Alden whispered, "You dare not follow the woman to the Highlands, Morgan. You've heard the rumors. An English soldier would never survive those savages."

Morgan's mouth was set in a hard, tight line. The tone of his voice left no doubt of his intentions. "I go to the Highlands. Or to hell and beyond. It matters not to me. But this I know. I shall return to England. And when I do, the woman will be with me."

Chapter Five

Within the hour, Morgan and his five men pushed their mounts forward into the cold waters of the River Tweed. They climbed up the far embankment, then began the slow ascent into the rugged hills.

A thick wall of forest closed around them. Somewhere nearby they could hear water rushing, but they could not see it. As they continued to climb, the sun was blotted out by the tall spires of ancient timbers.

They beheld a strange new world of soft glens and gentle fells. Craggy mountain peaks glinted high above them, some of them wreathed in clouds.

They spoke in whispers, as if they were in some ancient, hallowed cathedral. Their ears became attuned to the sounds of nature around them, and they became enraptured by the chorus of birds and insects.

To a man like Morgan Grey, born and bred in the cultured life at the English court, this primitive forest presented a new challenge. He had fought many enemies on their own soil. But he had heard that the Highlanders fought like no other soldiers ever encountered. They were rough giants, exposed to a way of life so harsh, so rugged, they could overcome their opponents by sheer size and determination alone.

He cautioned himself to savor the beauty of his surroundings without relaxing his guard. He had but one goal

here. Find Brenna MacAlpin and carry her off to England,
he hoped before he encountered a band of Highland clansmen.

When at last he found the pair of small footprints in the
soil, he gave a tight-lipped smile. The footprints belonged
to Brenna and her sister. Of that he had no doubt. The
prints were no bigger than his hand. And he had spent an
inordinate amount of time staring at the lady's ankle and
foot.

"They are headed that way. Toward that distant peak."

He climbed into the saddle and urged his mount into a
trot.

Night fell early in the Highlands. It was soon too dark to
follow the tracks. Besides, Morgan's men were feeling tense
and edgy. Even their beasts were skittish.

"We will rest the night here," he commanded in low
tones.

As he pulled his cloak about him for warmth, he found
himself wondering about the women who ran from him.
Had she thought to bring warm clothes? Did she and her
sister have enough to eat?

One of the soldiers brought him a tankard of ale. He
drank gratefully, then cursed the way his mind was working. Damn the woman. By now they could have been
halfway home. Let her starve. Let her freeze. But let her remain alive, he prayed. At least until he caught up with her.
So that he could have the satisfaction of wringing her lovely
neck.

Brenna drew her sister into her arms and wrapped her
warm traveling cloak around them. As they snuggled deep
into the hay she offered a prayer of thanks for the Highlander who had piled the dried grasses in his field for the
livestock. The hay, mixed with heather, made a cozy bed.

"Do you think the English dared to follow us?" Megan whispered.

"Aye." In her mind's eye, Brenna saw the fierce face of the English savage. "Even the Highlands would not stop that man once his decision has been made."

"Then we should not stop to rest." Megan sat up. "We should keep running until we reach the safety of Brice Campbell's keep."

"Hush. We can go no farther in the darkness." Brenna drew her sister down beside her. "But do not fear. Even the English must rest."

"But what if this Highlander finds us in his fields?" Megan shivered. "I cannot rid myself of the old fears of the Highlands."

"I know. But they are part of our family now. With Brice Campbell wed to Meredith, we have nothing to fear."

"Unless we are in the field of one who is foe to Brice."

That thought had already occurred to Brenna. "Sleep," she whispered. "I will keep watch."

As the moon slipped beneath a bank of clouds, Brenna strained to peer into the darkness. It was not the Highlanders she feared. Even those who were foe to her sister's husband. There was only one to be feared this night. The Englishman who would separate her from all that she loved.

The thrill of the hunt was invigorating to a soldier like Morgan. He awoke quickly, his mind sharp, his thoughts clearly focused on his goal. This day he would have his victory. He could already taste it.

He led his mount to the trail of prints made by a small, feminine boot. The trail disappeared into a wooded glen. Before the first flicker of light touched the horizon, he and his men pulled themselves into the saddle.

"The men are hungry," his aide grumbled.

"As am I. But there will be time enough to satisfy our hunger when this task is behind us. We ride until we find the woman." He tossed his aide the dried meat that often accompanied the soldiers to battle. "Chew on this until your hunger is abated."

The grim-faced soldiers fell into line behind their leader.

They rode for nearly an hour before coming upon a Highland woman busy milking her cows. When she saw the English standard, she began to race toward the small hut in the distance.

"We will not harm you," Morgan called.

Ignoring his words, the woman ran for her life.

"Stop her."

As his men urged their mounts forward, he added, "But take care that the woman is not harmed. She must be made to understand that we come in peace."

Though she bit and kicked and scratched at the hands holding her, his men did as they were bid and brought her to their leader. She stood before him, sullen and silent.

"We seek two young women from the lowlands." Morgan caught the woman by the chin and forced her to look at him. "Did you see them?"

"I saw no one."

"And if you saw them, would you tell me?"

She shot him a look of defiance. "I would not."

"I thought as much." He nodded toward the small pen where the cows waited patiently before being turned into pasture. "Was there any sign of them in the animal shelter?"

The woman shook her head.

Morgan nodded toward his men. "See to it."

After a thorough inspection, the men returned to confirm what the woman had said. "There is no sign of them."

Morgan released his hold on the woman. "Then we search elsewhere."

"But what of the woman?" one of his men cried. "If you release her, we will have an entire Highland clan on our heels."

"Our fight is not with you," Morgan said sternly. "Or with your people. When we find the women we seek, we will be gone. Do you understand?"

She nodded.

As he pulled himself into the saddle, the woman spat at him, then turned and began to run for safety.

"'Twas a mistake to turn her loose," his aide muttered. "At least until we find the ones we seek."

"It is a risk we must take. I wish to show the Highlanders that I do not come to do battle."

"'Twill prove our downfall."

"Perhaps." Morgan's eyes narrowed as he studied the hay on the far side of the pasture. "Would women from the lowlands risk sleeping in the animal pen, so near their enemy?" He prodded his horse into a trot. "Or would they rather sleep in the open, where they could slip unnoticed into the forest at first light?"

His men followed as he rode toward the hay. Dismounting, he studied the slight indentation. "Did the Lady Brenna rest here perhaps?" He suddenly knelt and breathed in the scent that he knew to be hers, mingled with the fragrance of dried grasses and heather. Excitement rippled through him.

"She was here." He would never mistake the scent of her. It was already deeply imprinted in his memory.

He stood and pulled himself into the saddle, then studied the trail of trampled grass leading to the forest once more.

"She is close. I can sense it."

"One pair of tracks leads that way," a soldier cried.

"A second pair is headed there."

"Would the two women separate?" the soldier asked.

"Nay." Morgan smiled, remembering how calmly Brenna had faced his knife until her younger sister was safely inside the castle walls. The woman would do anything to save her sister. Anything except leave her to the dangers of this primitive environment. "It is a clever ploy to divide our strength and send us on a merry chase."

"Which tracks will we follow?"

Morgan shrugged. "It matters not. I have every confidence that they will come together at a prearranged destination."

As the soldiers moved out, Morgan was forced to admit a grudging respect for the Lady Brenna. In her place, he would have done the same. It would seem that despite her delicate appearance, she had the instincts of a soldier.

They followed a set of tracks as it wove through a forest of towering evergreen. The sky was obscured by the thick canopy of boughs. Gradually the woods thinned until they found themselves in a high, grassy meadow.

For a moment the sun was so bright, they had to shield their eyes. But as his eyes grew accustomed to the light, Morgan drank in the sight of a field of blue-violet heather that stretched as far as the eye could see. He was reminded of Brenna. The flowers were the exact color of the eyes of the woman he sought.

Far in the distance he spotted a slight movement. Had it been a Highland breeze rippling the flowers? Or could it have been a human form, taking cover beneath the heather?

Brenna broke free of the forest and entered a meadow abloom with heather. For a moment she stared around with a look of wonder. Not even the sense of desperation that drove her could detract from the beauty of her surroundings. How strange these Highlands were. One minute savage and primitive, the next so lovely they took her breath away.

At the far side of the meadow she saw Megan emerge from a wild tangle of shrub and thorn. So far their plan was working. They had skirted the woods from two different directions and had managed to come together again without mishap. Now, if the fates continued to smile upon them, they would reach the fortress of Brice Campbell by midday. Once there, no English savage could dare to touch them.

"Brenna." Megan lifted a hand as she spotted her sister.

Brenna returned the salute and opened her mouth to call out. Suddenly the words caught in her throat.

Emerging from the dark woods far beyond Megan was a horse and rider. Even from so great a distance, Brenna had no doubt as to his identity. God in heaven. Morgan Grey was already close on Megan's heels, like a wolf after a helpless fawn.

Several other horsemen followed their leader. Her sister's back was to the English. As yet, she had no idea that they had trailed her.

With no thought to her own safety, Brenna broke into a run, determined to reach her sister before the soldiers. With her breath burning in her throat, she spanned the distance between them and threw herself at Megan, dragging them both to the ground.

"What...?" Megan pushed against her sister, fighting to regain her balance.

"Hush." Brenna covered Megan's mouth with her hand, then came to her knees and chanced a quick glance in the direction of Morgan Grey.

"What is it?"

Brenna frowned and crouched low in the grass. "English. I count six of them."

"Have they seen us?"

Brenna shrugged. "I know not."

"But I was so careful to keep to the woods."

"These are soldiers, trained in the art of tracking their enemy. 'Twas not your fault." Brenna drew her sister close and pressed her forehead to Megan's. "Listen to me. And listen well. From this moment on we must go in separate directions."

"Nay." Megan clutched at her.

Brenna's whispered voice was unusually calm. It was the way she always dealt with danger. "We have no choice. We will crawl through the heather, always keeping that distant spire as our goal. There lies Brice Campbell. There lies safety."

"But why must we separate?"

"Because there are only six of them. If they divide, there are only three against each of us." She gave her sister an impish, engaging smile, meant to lift her spirits. "'Tis well known that three English against one Scots warrior would hardly make a fair fight. 'Twould take at least a dozen English soldiers to bring down a single Scotsman."

Despite their perilous situation, Megan joined her sister's laughter. "Aye. God help them if they find us." After a moment she sobered and clutched at Brenna. "I cannot leave you. You cannot make me."

"Listen to me, Megan." Brenna grasped her sister's arms and stared into her wide eyes. "I love you too much to see you sacrificed to the English."

"And what about you?"

"I am the MacAlpin. I order you to leave me."

Megan opened her mouth to protest, but Brenna whispered passionately, "Megan, my dearest little sister. I could die this moment and find eternal peace, as long as I knew that you were safe. Promise me that you will neither stop nor look back until you reach the safety of Brice Campbell's stronghold."

The younger girl studied her sister, seeing the pain in her clear blue eyes. There would be no defying Brenna's heartfelt wishes. Slowly she nodded. "I go. But only because the MacAlpin has ordered it."

Tears filled Brenna's eyes. "God go with you, Megan."

"And with you, Brenna."

Brenna watched as Megan flattened herself to the ground and began crawling slowly toward the distant forest. A gentle breeze ruffled the heather, making the field look like a sea of rippling blue waves. For long minutes, Brenna watched, willing her younger sister to the safe arms of their beloved oldest sister and her warrior husband.

She watched until she saw the girl run and hide herself in a stand of trees. Safe. Once in that wooded glade, Megan would never be found by the English.

Dropping to the earth, Brenna began to crawl in the opposite direction. If the breezes worked in her favor, the English would be unable to detect her in the heather. If the breezes ceased...

Brenna refused to allow herself to think beyond this moment. She would run, she would fight and she would die if necessary. But she would not allow herself to be taken to England.

Morgan studied the waving blossoms of heather and blinked, then studied them again. Had he seen a movement or were his eyes playing tricks on him?

As a soldier he had always relied on his instincts in time of battle. This time was no exception. Though he could not see the Lady Brenna, he could sense her presence. She was here. Of that he was certain.

He turned to his men. "Comb this meadow. Trample and pluck every blossom if you must. But do not return to me unless you have the women."

As the men fanned out, he turned once more and studied the place where he had first seen the movement. Urging his horse into a slow walk, he studied the ground. A body could easily hide beneath this lush growth. Especially a slender young body like Brenna MacAlpin's.

Ahead of him he saw the heather part, then flatten. As his horse moved closer, he caught a glimpse of small kid boot. The blood began to pump hot through his veins. Brenna. He'd known she was here. With a flick of the reins his horse leaped forward, and he spied a length of ermine-trimmed traveling cloak.

Morgan felt his palms begin to sweat. So close. She was so close. And yet...

The hood slid from her head, revealing a mass of tangled ebony curls. Brenna brushed a strand from her eyes and moved forward several paces before becoming aware of the thundering sound. Her heart? She paused and lifted her head to peer anxiously behind her. Her heart seemed to stop before beginning a painful drumming in her chest.

Dear God. Morgan Grey, astride a spirited mount, appeared even more fierce and threatening than she'd remembered.

"It is useless to try to run any farther, my lady." He slid from the saddle with an ease of movement that belied his great strength. "By this time on the morrow, we will have joined the rest of my men on their journey to..." His words faded as she let out a gasp and darted out of reach.

Lifting her skirts, she began to run. Morgan was surprised at her agile movements. Though small and delicate, she made quick strides through the field of wildflowers.

Her lungs ached from the effort to elude him. But though desperation made her strong, she was no match for the one who pursued her. His legs were long and lean. With little effort he caught up with her. His hand closed over her wrist.

She turned on him with a cry of rage. He stared in surprise at the jewel-encrusted hilt of the knife held firmly in her hand.

After his initial surprise, a slight smile touched the corner of his mouth. "Am I to fear one small woman and her puny knife?"

"It takes but one small dirk to spill a man's lifeblood, my lord. And I intend to spill yours this day."

As she lunged, he moved aside. The tip of her blade pierced his tunic above his heart, sending a stream of blood coursing from the wound.

With a savage oath he caught her hand and twisted it until the knife slipped from her fingers and fell to the ground. As he bent to retrieve the dirk, she struggled free of his grasp and began to run.

"Damn you, woman." Morgan sprinted after her. With one last burst of speed he lunged at her, sending both to the ground in a tangle of arms and legs.

Brenna lay beneath him, struggling to take air into her burning lungs. Morgan straddled her, his legs firmly pinning her torso, his hands holding hers above her head in an iron grip. The blood oozing from his wound stained the front of her cloak and gown.

"Let me up." Though she struggled bravely, she was no match for Morgan's strength.

"I am no fool, little wildcat. Until you sheathe your claws, you are staying right here, where I can keep you from attacking me again."

"If you insist upon taking me to England, I swear, Morgan Grey, I will attack you every chance I get." As she spoke she twisted her head from side to side.

For long minutes Morgan studied her. With her dark hair wild and tangled like a Gypsy's, and her eyes matching the heather that bloomed all around them, she took his breath away.

He caught both her hands in one of his. With the other hand he reached out a rough finger and traced from the curve of her eyebrow to the circle of color that suffused her cheek. "Oh, you are going to England with me, my lady. Of that I have no doubt."

He saw the way her breasts rose and fell with each agitated breath, and his own heartbeat quickened.

He wanted her. In some deep, dark corner of his mind the thought seemed to take shape, then forced its way to his consciousness. God in heaven. Where was the logic in it? In her bid for freedom she had inflicted pain, and would have killed him given the chance.

She was all wrong for him. He was a soldier, a man who had been to hell and back for his queen. She was a lady. Cool, serene, delicate. Nay, he corrected quickly. Far from delicate, as his wound proved. Worst of all, he was English and she was Scots.

His eyes narrowed. She was so lovely. More beautiful than any woman he'd ever known. And despite her regal bearing, he knew that beneath the ice maiden's cool facade, there beat the heart of a spirited woman.

He lowered his face until he was mere inches from her lips. He inhaled the warmth of her breath and felt his throat go dry. One kiss. While he held her imprisoned in his grip, he would allow himself one final kiss. And then he would have her out of his system.

With his tongue he traced the contour of her lips.

"Nay." He heard her quick intake of breath before she turned her head away.

Excitement rippled through him.

"Aye, my lady." With his hand he caught her face and held it firmly for his inspection. There was no fear in her eyes. Only defiance, and something else. Something—indefinable.

He bent his head until her breath mingled hotly with his, then crushed his mouth over hers.

Instantly the fire was there, raging between them. And though each of them tried to give it another name, its name was desire.

Dear God she was sweet. Her lips were as soft as a rose petal, as cool as a morning mist. He drank deeply and was instantly aroused.

At the first brush of his lips on hers Brenna forgot to breathe. Her hands, caught in his big palm, went slack. Without realizing it, her lips opened for him and his tongue met hers.

She was aware of the hard, firm body pressing hers into the soft heather. His hand left hers to caress her cheek, and though she fully intended to resist him, she moved against him like a cat.

This was what she most feared. This unnamed feeling that curled deep inside her and took over her common sense whenever this Englishman touched her. She did not want him, she told herself firmly. She could not bear the sight of him. But even while the battle waged within her, her lips gentled and softened, inviting more.

To hell with logic, Morgan thought as he crushed her to him. It no longer mattered whether or not they were wrong for each other. He would take the pleasure of her kiss while he had the chance. He'd lusted before, and lived. Still, as the heat flowed between them he was forced to admit that it had never before been like this. He'd never met the woman who could set him afire with but a single touch.

He lifted his head and looked down at the woman in his arms, his body pulsing with need.

His men spurred their mounts toward him, shouting that there was no sign of the golden-haired younger sister.

Brenna stiffened in his arms. Despite her fear and revulsion at being captured, she took comfort in the knowledge that at least Megan had escaped. With her sister safe, Brenna could face whatever torment lay before her, secure in the knowledge that Brenna remained free of the English tyranny.

With a supreme effort Morgan rose to his feet. Brenna rolled away from him and took in great gulps of air to steady herself.

Morgan glanced idly at the blood that seeped from his wound. He would carry the scars from this woman's touch long after he had delivered her to the queen. Delivered her, he thought with a sudden trace of disgust, to warm some other Englishman's bed.

Even that thought could not cool the fire that raged within him. Her taste was still on his lips.

He needed to return to English soil and the arms of a willing English wench. That would finally cool this fever in his blood.

Chapter Six

From her position of safety in the forest, Megan watched in horrified fascination as her older sister was dragged by the English savage and lifted onto his horse.

Brenna's head was raised in haughty defiance. Even from so great a distance, Megan knew that her sister's pride would permit no show of weakness. There would be no tears, no pleading for her release.

One of the soldiers could be seen tearing a tunic into strips and applying it to Morgan Grey's chest.

Wounded? Megan strained to see. Aye. The English savage was bleeding. The wound must have been inflicted by Brenna's dirk.

If only she had a longbow, Megan thought. She would pierce Morgan Grey's heart and have the supreme satisfaction of watching him fall to his death. Her fingers curled into a fist. Oh, for a sword. She would willingly take on the entire company of Englishmen to save her sister.

As the mounted soldiers formed a protective ring around their leader and his captive, tears of impotent rage spilled from Megan's eyes and coursed down her cheeks. "Forgive me my weakness, Brenna," she whispered. But the tears fell faster, blurring her vision.

God in heaven. Sweet, noble Brenna was being taken from her home. For as long as she lived, Megan realized, she might never see that beloved face again.

With a curse that would have made a soldier blush, she swiped at the tears with the backs of her hands. Pulling herself up into a tree, she watched until the forest swallowed up the company of riders. Then she climbed down and began to make her way once more toward her destination. If she could but find him, her brother-in-law, Brice Campbell, would know how to rescue Brenna. He had an army of Highlanders at his command.

Brenna held herself stiffly in Morgan's arms and willed back the tears that threatened. As the horses' hooves trampled the heather, she felt her heartbeat keeping time to the pounding rhythm. Lost. Lost. All was lost.

They passed through the Highland meadow where she and Megan had spent the night in the haystack. Brenna prayed the farmer and his neighbors would rise up and resist the Englishmen who despoiled their countryside. But as she rode past, she saw only silent, sullen stares from the man and his wife and children.

When they left the Highlands behind, the horses' gaits lengthened. With ease they crossed the frigid waters of the River Tweed, then ate up the miles of lowland territory that separated Scotland from England. As they departed Brenna's homeland, she could no longer contain the pain and rage that coursed through her. To keep from crying out, she bit her lip until she tasted her own blood. But even that was not enough to hold the tears at bay. She bent her head, allowing her hair to swirl forward like a veil, and prayed that it would hide her weakness.

Home. Home. Ne'er more will I see you. Farewell to all that I hold dear.

With hands bound and head bowed, she wept bitter tears.

Morgan felt the shudders that passed through the slender body in his arms and knew that the woman was silently weeping. He had a sudden urge to draw her close against his

chest and offer her comfort. But he sensed that the regal
Brenna would prefer to grieve in private.

Why was he moved by her tears? Was she not, after all,
the woman who had driven her knife into his flesh? Had he
not reacted quickly, she would have pierced his heart.

He frowned. The little fool would soon discover that she
was going to a far better life than the one she left behind.
From what little he had seen of her life here, it was austere
at best. The court of Elizabeth was no dreary prison. And
the wife of a titled Englishman would enjoy a life of riches
beyond belief. Not to mention the pleasures of his bed.

At that thought he experienced a rush of annoyance and
berated himself for caring about what happened to this
woman. He reinforced his resolve. The sooner he got this
beauty to England, the better.

"One day soon all the pain will be erased from your heart,
ice maiden. Go ahead and cry."

His muffled words shocked her to the core, but not for the
reason he might have expected.

"I do not cry. That is for frightened children."

"Aye." A smile touched his lips. His voice warmed. "And
it is plain that the one in my arms is no child." His hands
came to rest at her rib cage, just below the fullness of her
breasts.

Instantly she stiffened. "I may be your prisoner, Morgan
Grey. But I will not be sullied by your touch."

His smile vanished. His tone hardened. "You had best
hold your tongue, lass. My temper is legend among my
men."

"Am I to fear you, then?" She turned her head until she
was facing him. "Have you forgotten that I am the Mac-
Alpin, the leader of my people?"

"I have forgotten nothing." Especially the color of her
eyes when she was angry. "In my land you are a woman
without title or power. You would be ill advised to incur my
wrath."

She sniffed and turned away to escape the danger she sensed in his dark look. "What more can you do to me? You have already stolen my most treasured possession, my freedom. My home, all that I hold dear lie back there, in Scotland. I vow, Morgan Grey, that I will escape you. And if I do not, I will stand and fight you to the death."

He brought his lips close to her ear. "If you push me too far, woman, you will feel the sting of my anger."

She shivered. But was it fear that caused the tremors? Or the nearness of this man?

She pushed away such thoughts. He was the enemy. She would remain alert and wait for the first opportunity to run.

As the horses continued at a steady pace, hour after hour, Brenna found herself lulled into a half sleep. Without realizing it, she leaned back against Morgan's chest and settled comfortably into his arms. In repose, all signs of tension were erased from her face. In the sunlight her skin gleamed like fine porcelain. Her eyebrows were slightly arched, her nose upturned. Her lips were perfectly formed. Her mane of coal-black silk drifted across Morgan's chest and lifted in the breeze, tickling his face. While she dozed, the man who held her was achingly aware of the prize he had captured. The prize that would be claimed by some nobleman in the Queen of England's court.

Morgan sensed Brenna's weariness. Signaling to his men he called, "We will stop and rest for a short time."

When he helped Brenna from his horse she pressed her hands to the small of her back and arched her body.

"'Tis a long time to be in the saddle if you are unaccustomed to it."

"Aye." She turned away, averting her gaze, when two of his men stepped into a stand of trees.

Seeing it, Morgan stepped close. "You would perhaps require a moment of privacy?"

She nodded.

"I will see to it." He strode away and spoke to his men. A moment later he returned. "You may walk into the woods unmolested, my lady."

She gave him a grateful smile, then lifted her skirts and walked to the place he had indicated. When she entered the dark forest, she turned to ascertain that she was indeed alone. Morgan and his men waited patiently beside the horses. She stepped behind a tree, then turned and peered once more at the soldiers. Three of the men were seated with their backs to the trunk of a gnarled old tree. The other two were talking in low tones to Morgan, who had removed his plumed hat and was mopping his brow. With a last glance at the sky, Brenna began running through the forest. She knew the direction she must take. North. Toward Scotland. Toward home.

Within minutes she heard the sound of someone shouting. Morgan Grey. By now he would have realized his mistake in trusting her. She began to run faster, determined to make it to the deepest part of the forest, where the branches grew so thickly together no light could penetrate. There she would hide until Morgan and his men were forced to abandon their search.

The sound of branches snapping behind her sent her into a panic. The Englishmen were closer than she'd anticipated. She pushed herself to the limit, until her throat burned from the effort. And still she ran, clinging to her last chance to escape.

The men were so close she could make out their words as they called to each other. In desperation she began climbing a tall tree. If the fates were kind, the Englishmen would not think to look up, and they would pass beneath her without notice.

The branches caught the hem of her gown, slowing her progress. With each painful step, the rough bark tore at her tender skin until her hands were raw and bleeding. But still she pulled herself higher into the tree. Standing on tiptoe, she reached for a high branch. Again and again she made a valiant grab for it, until at last her fingers wrapped around it and she drew it down. If she could pull herself to the top, they would never spy her.

As she began to pull herself upward, she felt a mighty tug on her ankle. She looked down, then let out a gasp.

"So, my lady. You like to climb trees? Perhaps your English husband will buy you a manor house in the country and have trees planted there to amuse you."

Though Morgan's words were spoken lightly, she could read the angry scowl on his face.

"Will you climb down, my lady?" His words frosted over. "Or will I pull you down, unmindful of your modesty?"

"Modesty be damned." She blinked back the tears of frustration that sprang to her eyes. A little more time, a few minutes more, and she would have been free.

Without a word she made her way down. Morgan's fingers remained locked on her ankle until she dropped lightly into his arms.

As his men clustered around them, he leaned close and whispered, "There will be no more moments of privacy, my lady."

"You cannot mean that."

His dark eyes flashed. "You have convinced me that you are not to be trusted. You'd best pray that you have no need for relief between here and the queen's residence, Brenna MacAlpin. For you are never leaving my side."

"That is uncivilized."

He flashed her a rare smile. "I never claimed to be otherwise."

"The Queen's standard flies at Richmond Palace, my lord."

Morgan nodded and urged his tired mount along the winding path of the Thames. Once their party reached the royal grounds, their weariness seemed to vanish. Unmindful of the grime of travel staining their tunics, the men assumed a stiff military bearing. They passed long columns of soldiers patrolling the vast forest surrounding the palace and entered a road wide enough to allow a dozen horsemen to ride abreast.

They rode in silence until they reached the entrance courtyard. At their arrival several servants hurried forward to take their mounts.

There was a commotion from within, and several elegantly dressed gentlemen surged through the open portal. Leading the way was Alden, Morgan's second in command. But instead of the drab garb of a soldier, he was dressed in the clothes of a titled gentleman, with satin breeches and fine tunic.

"At last," he called, hurrying to his leader's side.

Morgan slid from the saddle and unceremoniously dragged Brenna into his arms.

"What kept you, old friend?"

"The lady led us a merry chase."

"But, as always, you managed to prevail."

The two men shared a laugh.

"'Tis time to learn your fate, ice maiden."

"You would not take me to your queen like this. Without even time to refresh myself."

"Would I not?" Morgan gave her a dangerous smile. "And you look so fetching. Why, every nobleman at court will probably beg for the hand of my dirty little ragamuffin."

"Please, my lord. I cannot be presented to the queen in such a fashion."

He closed a hand over her arm and drew her firmly against him. "This is not a royal ball, my lady. And you are not here to be admired. Until the queen decrees otherwise, you are my prisoner."

She gave him a hate-filled look and tried to pull away, but his fingers closed around her arm in a possessive manner.

To the keeper of the door he called, "Announce me to the queen, my Lord Clive. I come at Her Majesty's request."

The old man nodded and scurried away. Minutes later he returned. "The queen will see you immediately, my lord."

As Brenna was hauled along beside Morgan, her throat went dry at the thought of meeting the Queen of England. If the rumors were true, Queen Elizabeth was a fascinating, beguiling, yet very shrewd monarch.

Alden cast a sympathetic glance at the woman being dragged roughly by his friend. "You could afford to give the lady a few moments to repair her toilette."

"You have not spent the last days as I have, my friend, or you would not even suggest such a thing. The lady cannot be trusted out of my sight."

One look at the hard set of Morgan's mouth caused Alden to hold his silence. He knew when his friend had been pushed to the limit.

More than a hundred people milled about the great room, many of them clustered, talking in low tones. When they noted the standard of Morgan Grey, the hum of conversation increased. The Queen's Savage was not a man who could pass unnoticed, even in a crowd.

When double doors were thrust open and a dozen or more gaily dressed men and women entered, all conversation ceased. The arrival of the gentlemen who preened like peacocks and the fawning ladies was the signal that the queen would now hold court.

Elizabeth walked alone, with no one to her right or left. Her gown was a dazzling midnight blue, with high ruffled neck and wide sleeves inset with jewels. The bodice was low, the waist tiny. A full skirt twinkled with hundreds of jewels, each one painstakingly sewn on by one of the queen's army of seamstresses. A magnificent tiara of diamonds and sapphires nestled in her red curls.

She moved quickly, as though in a hurry. Even after she was seated upon her throne, she seemed to radiate energy. With an expectant look her glance scanned the crowd. When at last she spotted Morgan Grey, a warm smile touched her lips.

"At last, my brave warrior, you have returned to your queen. Come forward and tell me what female's bed kept you from your queen's side for so long."

Brenna was shocked at the queen's crude remark. And even more shocked to see that the men and women at court joined in a chorus of laughter at Elizabeth's joke. She glanced at Morgan, expecting to see his famous scowl. Instead, his face was wreathed in smiles.

"Forgive me, Majesty, but someone must see to the business of the Crown."

"Are you suggesting that it was royal business that kept you away so long?"

"Aye, Majesty. If you recall, you sent me to Scotland to investigate the possibility of wedding one of your titled gentlemen to the leader of the MacAlpin clan, whose lands lie on the border."

"I recall much more, Morgan Grey. I recall that you bristled at such an assignment, suggesting that it was beneath your dignity as a warrior, and fit merely for a lackey. Yet this simple task has taken you away from me for too long. Did you not miss the sight of your queen?"

Morgan stepped closer, leaving Brenna encircled by his men. His voice warmed. "Aye, Majesty. I have missed not only your beauty, but your sharp tongue as well. There are few who can match words as my queen."

Elizabeth threw back her head and laughed. "I, too, have missed our duel of wits, my Lord Grey. I am truly pleased that you have returned. Now tell me the outcome of your journey to Scotland."

"The people are still mistrustful of the English, Majesty. And though I assured them that we came in peace, I could sense that they did not believe me."

"They had the word of your queen."

Morgan smiled at Elizabeth's sudden flash of anger. "Aye, Majesty. But I think you were wise in your decision to bind the two countries through an arrangement of marriages. We have lost many a good Englishman on the Scottish border.''

"The Highland chiefs,'' Elizabeth said dryly, "have already pledged their loyalty to me through the Treaty of Edinburgh.''

"Aye. There is that. But our borders continue to be plagued by outbreaks of fighting, Majesty.''

"So, Morgan, you suddenly approve of these arranged marriages.'' Elizabeth held out her hand and drew him close. Many women in the room watched the scene with interest. Morgan Grey was a handsome devil who caused more than a few female hearts to flutter. And the queen was as yet unwed.

"Tell me about this Scotswoman who leads her clan.''

"I will do better than that, Majesty. I will present her to you.''

He turned. At his command his men moved aside, revealing Brenna.

"Majesty, may I present Brenna MacAlpin, leader of the clan MacAlpin of Scotland.''

Many in the crowd gasped. At their reaction, Brenna lifted her head defiantly.

The queen appeared stunned for a moment before regaining her composure. "Can this truly be the leader of her people? In such a state of disarray?''

Brenna's cheeks went bright red, but she continued to meet Elizabeth's direct look.

The queen lifted a bejeweled hand. "Look at her. Her hair tumbles wildly around her cheeks and shoulders and spills down her back in a tangle of curls. Her traveling gown and cloak are dusty and wrinkled. And is that blood upon her gown, Morgan?''

He flushed uncomfortably. "Aye, Majesty.''

"Her blood?''

"Mine.''

"You subdued her with your sword?''

"She attacked me with a knife.''

The queen looked more closely at the woman who stood before her. Arching an eyebrow she said, "She more resembles an orphaned waif than a leader." She turned toward Morgan. "Is she truly the MacAlpin, my Lord Grey, or are you rivaling the Court jester?"

"I do not jest, Majesty."

"But why have you brought her here like a common prisoner?"

"Because she attempted to evade your wishes, Majesty. The Lady Brenna vowed she would marry a man of her own choosing."

"She did?" The queen's look changed suddenly, from one of disdain to one of sharp interest.

"Aye, Majesty. I was forced to track her to the Highlands. Once there, I decided it was in your Majesty's best interest to keep her with me until your Majesty decided her fate."

"She ran from you?" The queen studied the young woman before her. "This one small female managed to elude Morgan Grey? And to wound him in the fray?" The queen's eyes danced with unconcealed humor. "Oh, this is a fine joke. Can it be that the man who subdues entire armies cannot control one woman?"

Morgan's eyes grew steely.

"And you were forced to follow her to the dangerous Highlands?"

He nodded.

"How very interesting." The queen studied the way the two refused to look at one another. The emotions flowing between them were raw and savage. "And so you have brought her here against her will." The queen smiled slowly. "A very—wise decision, my Lord Grey, although my cousin Mary of Scotland would perhaps not agree."

Elizabeth addressed the woman. "You would choose your own husband?"

"It is the way of the MacAlpin."

At Brenna's harsh tone, there was a distinct silence in the room. Every eye was on the woman who sat upon the throne. Though small in stature, Elizabeth was every inch the queen. She tolerated no show of disrespect in her presence. Especially not from one who swore allegiance to another.

The queen turned toward the gallery of robed men who sat to one side.

Brenna's voice carried through the suddenly quiet crowd. "In my country, women are not chattel, to be bargained for. Nor jewels, to be worn for adornment. We are valued for ourselves. And since our lives are so deeply affected by the choice of partner, our voices are heard."

Though the queen's eyes flashed, her lips softened into a smile. There was an audible sigh through the crowd. Once more the queen's anger had been diffused.

"I would ask the council to pay heed to this Scotswoman. Your queen is not the only one who wishes to choose her own husband."

Morgan chuckled, low and deep in his throat. Beside him, Alden laughed aloud. Gradually others around the room did the same. The atmosphere became more relaxed.

Turning back to Brenna, the queen said, "What am I to do with you, Brenna MacAlpin? Shall I parade every titled Englishman past you, until you choose the one who piques your interest?"

"Nay, Majesty. The Englishman is not born who will win my heart."

"Is there, perhaps, a Scotsman who holds your heart?"

Morgan waited a moment, unaware that he was holding his breath.

"There is not. But I will not be bartered like a fatted calf."

The queen's smile suddenly faded. "I would advise you, woman, to beware of your sharp tongue. There is only one here who will decide your fate."

The queen saw the flash of fire in Brenna's eyes before she lowered her head. And though Elizabeth admired her courage, she would tolerate no show of disrespect.

"What of you, Morgan Grey?" The queen saw the way he watched the woman beside him. "Would you be willing to take on the unpleasant task of marriage to the unwilling lady?"

"Majesty." Morgan's tone was patient. "You are aware of my feelings toward the unholy sacrament of misery."

Many in the room laughed at his words.

"Aye. You are, I believe, the man who swore that marriage was the lowest form of slavery."

Alden swallowed his laughter and pointedly stared at a spot on the floor rather than face his friend.

In her agitation, Elizabeth got up from her throne and walked forward until she came to a halt beside Morgan and the woman. In a low voice she said, "I am more than a little surprised, my Lord Grey. And, I might add, disappointed. Since you dared to risk the fragile peace between our two countries and bring this—ragged woman here against her will, I declare that you are responsible for her until I find someone willing to wed her."

Morgan frowned. "I was merely following my instincts as a soldier, Majesty. I am convinced that this woman would surely have married one of her own countrymen before your plans could be implemented."

The queen sighed. "If you were not such a rogue, I would insist that you take your duty a step farther and wed this baggage." Elizabeth flashed one of her most brilliant smiles. "Of course, since you are descended from royalty, I had always thought you to be one of my suitors."

Morgan's eyes twinkled with teasing laughter. "If I thought I had a chance to win your heart, Majesty, you know I would pledge my own. But though we are true friends, I fear your heart lies elsewhere."

The young queen looked up into his handsome face and felt the familiar twinge. He was indeed a man who could start a fire in her blood, as he did, it seemed, in the blood of every woman in the kingdom. But they both knew that he was far too lusty a man to spend the rest of his life observing rules of protocol while his wife governed. Life at court had always been the part of royal life that Morgan Grey least enjoyed. Which was probably why he sought the battlefield.

Elizabeth looked from Brenna to Morgan. "'Tis said the Scots will need a firm hand if they are to be won over. And there is no firmer hand in all of England than yours. Also, there is no doubt as to your loyalty, my friend. But I suppose I cannot ask this truly supreme sacrifice. Marriage." She chuckled as if it were a great joke. "To this—untidy foreigner."

"I would rather face a horde of invaders without a weapon." Morgan's tone was crisp. "But ne'er fear, Majesty. You will find a solution to the problem. I agree that the woman will not be easy to marry off, especially when a suitable partner learns how difficult she is to subdue. She is devious, shrewd and cunning." He touched a hand to his wound. "Not to mention skilled with a knife."

Even while she shared a laugh with Morgan, the queen saw the look of anguish in Brenna's eyes and fought to ignore it. Did she not understand the lady's desire to choose her own destiny? But how many could afford such a luxury? She lifted her head regally. Not even one born to the Crown.

"You know I can refuse you no request, Morgan Grey. I am indebted to you a hundredfold for your loyalty. And so I will not command you to marry your prisoner. But, though I see the wisdom of bringing her here until a decision is reached regarding her future, I cannot ask another to be responsible for the lady. And since she is a woman of noble birth, I am reluctant to consign her to a prison cell until her future is decided."

"Aye. The Tower would be too harsh."

Brenna stood rooted to the floor, hearing their words echoing in her head. This could not be happening. While a hundred strangers watched with disinterest, her fate was coldly being decided without any regard for her feelings.

She clenched her hands tightly at her sides and bit her lip to keep from crying out at the unfairness of it.

Morgan glanced at Brenna. He chose to ignore the anger and fury in her gaze. Was there not enough anger in his own heart? He was a soldier, not a nurse. He had seen to his duty, and had brought the Scotswoman to England. Now he wished to be finished with her. He turned to the queen. "I cannot take responsibility for the lady. It is enough that I have brought her here to you."

The queen watched his eyes, reading the frustration he could not hide. "The lady is your prisoner—you are her jailer. Where you go, she follows. You bear sole responsibility for her."

"And if I go to battle?"

"Your battlefield lies here in England, for now."

"Then I pray, Majesty, that you decide the lady's fate quickly."

The queen could not resist a quick smile. "All in good time, my lord."

"You mean—" Brenna's voice was choked with rage "—I have no voice in my own destiny? I cannot return to my home? I must remain this man's captive?"

Morgan gave her an indulgent smile. "It seems you are fated to remain under my—protected care."

"Aye," the queen said quickly. "Take her and good riddance. Set her up in one of your households, Morgan, until I am able to arrange a suitable marriage."

Brenna heard no more. She felt the blood rush from her head, leaving her ashen. The queen's words faded until they were only a slight buzzing in her ears. The room began to spin in a dizzying rush. And as she slid to the floor, a soothing black mantle settled over her.

Chapter Seven

"Mon Dieu. Did you not give this poor child anything to eat during her journey to England?"

Brenna felt the press of a cool, damp cloth against her forehead and struggled to open her eyes.

Morgan's voice, deep with concern, was very near. "I tried to feed her. The damned female refused all offers of food."

"And did you allow her to rest, *mon cher?*"

"Rest? I am a soldier, on a mission for my queen. I expected her to keep up."

Brenna heard the queen's voice, low, regal. "Was she not given even a moment's privacy?"

"I foolishly offered her privacy. But only once. She bolted and tried to run home to Scotland. My men and I were forced to waste precious time chasing after her again. I tell you, the woman needs a firm hand."

"Be careful, Morgan Grey," the gentle French voice said, "that your firm hand does not break her into little pieces."

"I do not break easily." Brenna's throat felt parched. Her lids fluttered. Into her line of vision swam an unusual woman's face. Large, sensuous lips parted in a friendly smile. Almond eyes studied Brenna with concern.

"Ah. You are awake. You fainted, *cherie.*"

Brenna struggled to sit up. "Impossible. I have never fainted." The very thought of such a weakness was repugnant to her.

The woman placed her hand gently on Brenna's shoulder and forced her to lie still. "That may be so. But I have known a great many people who react violently to strange circumstances. Even the strongest woman must give in to the demands of her body, *cherie*."

"Who are you?"

"I am Madeline d'Arbeville, Duchess of Eton. And I am told that you are Brenna MacAlpin, leader of a Borderer clan in Scotland."

"Aye." Brenna gave her a grateful smile. "Thank you for your kindness. Where am I?" She glanced around at the sumptuous bed hangings.

"You are in my chambers." The queen leaned close.

In the queen's own bed! "Majesty, I did not mean to create such a disturbance. Forgive me for my weakness," Brenna whispered.

Again she struggled to sit up. This time it was Morgan who restrained her.

"Rest a while longer." His tone was gentler than he'd intended.

"Aye." The queen gave a conspiratorial smile. "Your little spell gave me the perfect opportunity to dismiss the court and free myself of all duties for the rest of the day. A rare thing indeed. Now," she said, linking her arm through Morgan's, "perhaps I can spend some time with you, dear rogue. We have much to discuss."

Morgan turned toward the figure in the bed. His eyes narrowed as he studied her carefully, noting with satisfaction that the color was returning to her cheeks.

"You will stay with Brenna, Madeline?"

"*Oui.* It will give us a chance to become acquainted."

Brenna watched as Morgan and the queen retired to a small alcove. Instantly a servant approached the two with goblets of wine. When the servant left, the queen and her loyal soldier bent their heads close in intimate conversation. Though they kept their voices low, Brenna was aware of the tension in their tones. Whatever was being discussed, it was obviously of utmost importance.

"Would you like to tell me about yourself?" Madeline asked softly.

Brenna shook her head slightly, afraid her voice would tremble.

"Then I shall tell you about myself," Madeline said in her charming French accent.

Brenna gave a grateful smile, relieved to be free for the moment from the scrutiny of Morgan and the queen.

"I am married to Charles Crowel, Duke of Eton. He is one of the queen's most trusted aides."

"You are not English."

"Non." Madeline gave a low chuckle. "That I could never pretend. Not with this accent. My home, until my marriage, was France."

"Do you not miss your home?"

"Oh, of course. But I go there often to visit. And my beloved brother and sister come to England to stay with me so that I am not nearly so homesick."

Brenna grew silent and turned to watch the queen and Morgan.

"So, *cherie,*" Madeline said, noting the direction of Brenna's gaze. "Already you have become the object of much speculation. How did you happen to get captured by that fascinating man?"

Brenna gave a wry smile. "There is no mystery to it. He overpowered me."

"No mystery?" The Frenchwoman handed the damp cloth to a serving girl, then began plumping the pillows about Brenna's head. "Morgan Grey does not capture women; he eludes them. He has managed to evade the snares set by every eager woman at court." She gave a knowing smile. "And, *cherie,* there were many hoping to ensnare him. Why, even the queen was rendered speechless when he presented you at court. I think, from the way he looks at you, that he desires you.''

"He does not desire me.'' Brenna's voice trembled with intensity. "He merely wishes to punish me.''

"Punish? But why?''

"Because I managed to spoil his plans and elude him, delaying his return to England. He has brought me here to see me wed to an Englishman, so that my lands and holdings will then belong to his queen.''

"And that is why he looks at you this way? I do not believe he brought you here to see you wed to another. I believe he would keep you for himself.''

"Marriage to any Englishman would be horrible. But especially to that one. He is a cruel, vindictive man.''

Madeline placed her hand over Brenna's. Feeling the tremors, she stared into her eyes. "Do not be misled by the name he carries. The Queen's Savage is a soldier of the Crown, notorious for his skill in the art of battle. It is well known that entire armies fear him. But he has never shown himself to be cruel or vindictive.''

"You do not know him,'' Brenna whispered, shivering.

"Though I am only in this country a few short years, I know him well, *cherie*.'' Madeline pulled the blankets around Brenna's shoulders. "He is a rogue, and a man of great appetite.'' She smiled broadly. "Great appetite. But I would trust Morgan Grey with all that I hold dear. He is a man above reproach.''

Brenna felt a welling of tears and turned her head away. Was there no one at court who would take her side in this? Was she truly doomed to remain a captive of a man she hated, and to lose forever her land, her titles and even her name?

"Rest, *cherie*.'' Madeline brushed the dark hair from Brenna's eyes, then settled herself comfortably in a chair alongside the bed. "I will sit here beside you while you sleep, so that when you awake, you will not find yourself among strangers.''

"Thank you." Brenna's lids fluttered as she blinked away her tears and struggled to focus.

The last thing she saw before she drifted off to sleep was the face of the lovely Frenchwoman who had shown her such kindness.

"There have been several—accidents since you have been away, Morgan." The queen's head was high, her chin thrust forward defiantly.

Now that the others were dozing, and the servants had been dismissed, she allowed her voice to rise.

Morgan barely managed to mask the alarm he felt. "Tell me about them."

"There was my personal groom. While riding a mount meant for me, the saddle fell, leaving him badly injured."

Morgan's eyes narrowed.

"Lord Windham suggests that the poor fellow lied to cover his laziness."

At the mention of the queen's trusted aide, Morgan's temper flared. "Windham is a fool. What else has happened while I have gone?"

"The royal carriage. A wheel came off on our journey here to Richmond Palace. No one was hurt. The driver insists that it was an accident. Still, my servant swore the carriage had been carefully inspected before our journey."

"God in heaven. Is there more?"

Elizabeth shook her head. "Nothing. Just—rumors."

"Give me names, Majesty. Who repeats these rumors?"

Elizabeth grew agitated. "I do not know the names. A whispered word here. A hint of something there."

He leaned close, his hands on his knees. "Whispers. Hints. These are not enough to call home an entire army. You are not telling me everything. You have heard something."

The queen suddenly stood and stared out the window, hugging her arms around herself. "I do not forget, Morgan."

"Forget what?"

"What it feels like to be marked for death." She shuddered. "From the time I was a babe, I have known that even those who should be closest to me might want me dead. My own father bastardized me, then reluctantly reinstated me to the order of succession. My sister, Mary, banished me to the Tower, and would have permitted my execution had any incriminating evidence been brought to bear." Her voice lowered. "And there was the mistreatment of my mother. Always I must live in the shadow of my mother's beheading."

"We live in a brutal age."

"Aye. A brutal age. All my life I have heard the threats, Morgan. And now the whispers begin again. Someone plots my death. I know it here."

She touched a hand to her heart and turned toward him. In the light streaming through the window behind her he saw, not a queen, but a young woman. And for one brief moment before she blinked, he saw the hint of terror in her eyes. Instantly he was on his feet, drawing her into his arms.

"I am not afraid, Morgan."

Her words were muffled against his tunic. With a wave of tenderness at her bluff, he clutched her to him and pressed his lips to her temple. There were few in the kingdom who would dare to take such liberties with their queen. But the friendship between these two had begun in childhood and had endured through hard times and good.

"I know that, Majesty. Throughout the realm it is known that you are fearless."

He continued to hold her until the tremors passed. When she was calm, she pushed a little away and lifted a palm to his cheek.

"I needed you here with me, Morgan. You must not leave England again."

He pressed his hand over hers. "I will not leave you. I will seek the source of these rumors. And I will uncover the truth about these accidents. But you must promise me that you will stay here, within these palace walls, until I have had time to look into this."

"I cannot stay confined in Richmond."

"If you must travel, I will be at your side. Do you understand?"

She nodded, and he saw the tension slowly drain from her.

At a sound across the room they both turned.

Brenna tossed aside her blankets, pondering what she had overheard. The words seemed to run together in her mind. Could it be that the Queen of England was truly in danger? Or had she merely dreamed it? Now that she was completely awake, she was no longer certain of anything. Brenna glanced at Madeline d'Arbeville, who was dozing in the chair. There would be nothing to be learned from her.

The queen walked toward the bed. From the coolly regal expression on her face, Brenna decided that she must have imagined everything. One glance at Morgan's closed expression convinced her. These two could have not been discussing anything more pressing than England's misty weather.

"So, Brenna MacAlpin. You are awake. How fare you?"

"I am fine, Majesty." Brenna pushed herself into a sitting position and waited until the dizziness passed.

Her hesitation did not go unnoticed by Morgan. In quick strides he was beside her, his hand grasping her upper arm.

"Not so fine as you pretend," Morgan said in low tones. "Perhaps we should tarry here at Richmond for a day or two before proceeding to my estate nearby."

Brenna stared at the offending hand, wondering if Morgan felt the tremors she couldn't hide. But if he took notice, he gave no indication.

"I think that is a fine idea," the queen said. She clapped her hands and a dozen servants appeared within moments.

From her position beside the bed, Madeline d'Arbeville started, then looked up in confusion. "*Mon dieu*. Is it possible that I slept?"

"That is what late nights at the gaming tables will do to you," the queen said with a laugh. "Madeline, we have good news. Morgan has consented to stay on at Richmond for a day or two."

Brenna felt a surge of hope. As long as she was not forced to be alone with Morgan at his residence, there was a chance that she could win a reprieve. What could he possibly do to her here in the queen's home? And perhaps the queen, given enough time, might be persuaded to allow her to return to her beloved Scotland without being forced into bondage to an English lord.

To the servants the queen said, "Prepare a suite of rooms for Lord Grey and his—guest."

The transformation in the queen was instantaneous. A warm smile touched her lips. Her eyes danced with merriment. "Oh, Morgan. It has been too long."

Morgan returned the smile. It pleased him to see the queen forget her worries, if only for a little while. "Aye, Majesty."

"We shall celebrate with a feast." Elizabeth cast a speculative glance at Brenna. "Have you any clothes besides those?"

"Nay, Majesty." Once again Brenna was reminded of her bedraggled appearance.

"No matter." The queen turned to a waiting servant. "Send a seamstress to see to the lady's needs."

The servant nodded and scurried away.

Orders were given. Servants hurried about, carrying news of their queen's latest surprise.

"Madeline, can you drag your husband from his official duties long enough to join us?" Morgan asked.

"*Oui*. He will be eager to see you, Morgan. He has complained of your long absence." Madeline lifted her skirts and curtsied to the queen. "By your leave, Majesty." At the queen's nod, she rushed from the room.

In no time, Brenna found herself being ushered from the queen's bedchamber. With Morgan beside her, she followed a servant along a wide hallway toward a suite of rooms. Several of Morgan's men trailed along behind them. Guards? Brenna wondered with alarm. Could it be possible that he would have her guarded here in the queen's residence like a common criminal?

The sitting chamber assigned them was a large room overlooking the queen's formal gardens. Through the open windows of the balcony drifted the fragrance of roses and lavender. Tapestries depicting the royal lineage softened the stark walls. The floors were covered with ornately woven rugs. Chairs and settles, many draped with magnificent animal hides, were drawn up before the huge fireplace that dominated one wall. A fire had been set to ward off the chill.

Brenna was pleased to note that there were doors on either end of the sitting chamber. These led to two separate sleeping chambers. At least, for the moment, she was not being treated like a prisoner. She would have her own sleeping chamber, away from Morgan's scrutiny. She noted no chains on the doors.

The sleeping chambers were nearly identical, with huge beds hung with elegant linens, and cheery fires set in the fireplaces. Tapers were lighted in sconces along the walls, adding even more light and warmth to the rooms.

When the servants finished showing them to their quarters, they quietly withdrew, leaving Brenna and Morgan alone for the first time since their arrival in England.

Feeling Morgan's narrowed gaze upon her, Brenna had a need to be busy. She moved around the room, dropping her traveling cloak on a settle, running her hand along the softness of a hide, stopping to study the intricately worked tapestry.

With her back to him she murmured, "How long do you intend to hold me prisoner?"

"Prisoner? My lady, you are an honored guest of the queen."

She heard the thread of sarcasm in his tone and stiffened her spine.

"Nay. I am a prisoner. Despite the fact that I am allowed a room in the palace, and wear no shackles, I am still not free."

"Would you rather be sent to the dungeons, my lady, until the queen finds a nobleman willing to wed you?"

She turned to meet his dark gaze. "I do not wish to be wed at all."

He gave her a dangerous smile. "You would shock the women at court with such words. They think of nothing except winning a wealthy husband. Or a wealthy lover." He seemed to pause a moment before saying softly, "I think there are many men who would be only too happy to take you as mistress, my lady."

His words caused a chill along her spine.

He did not move, but merely watched her. At last, when she could no longer bear his scrutiny, she turned and walked to the balcony, keeping her back to him.

A boat moved along the Thames, and she watched it with a heavy heart. Oh, to be on that craft, sailing away from here. From the clutches of this madman who had torn her world asunder.

She heard his footsteps and knew that he'd followed her to the balcony. His voice, low and deep, caused a little flutter in her stomach.

"'Tis a beautiful land, is it not?"

She refused to answer him.

"There is no lovelier sight in all the world than that of the sun seeming to rise clear out of the Thames and color the eastern sky."

"Then you have not seen a blue sky hanging o'er the Cheviot hills of Scotland, all silvery with dew." Her voice trembled, and she realized she was close to tears.

"You will see your land again." His voice was so near she was startled and had to force herself not to recoil.

"When?" She studied the progress of the boat.

"When you are safely wed and have declared your loyalty to my queen, you will be allowed to return often to your people."

"How generous of you, my lord." She turned on him, feeling all her fear and loathing bubbling to the surface. "When you English have succeeded in stealing my land, my crops and my cattle, you will send me back to watch my people starve."

"Little fool." Without thinking he grabbed her by the upper arms, as if to shake her. But the moment he touched her, everything changed. His words vibrated with intensity. "We are not your enemy. A wealthy Englishman has no need of your land, crops or cattle. It is not the queen's intention to take from you."

"Is it not?" She tossed her head and tried to push away, but the more she struggled, the more firmly he dragged her against him, until she found herself completely imprisoned in his arms.

Her breasts rose and fell with each measured breath. Her hair, wild and tangled, invited his touch. Her lips were pursed in anger.

Morgan was aware of his lie. Though he needed neither her goods nor her land, there was something he wanted from her each time he looked at her. And wanted it desperately.

"So you find my touch repulsive?" His lips hovered a fraction above hers. Their breath mingled, hers hesitant and a little afraid, his hot and simmering with excitement.

"Aye, my lord," she answered, though she did not try to draw away from the strong hands holding her.

"I cannot say the same." He moved his mouth along her temple, and felt her trembling response.

She struggled to feel nothing. Why were his lips so gentle upon her skin? Even the hands imprisoning her were as gentle as a caress.

"Do not do this, my lord."

He lifted his head for a moment, and she took in a deep breath, hoping to clear her mind. But before she could think, he lifted her hand to his lips in a courtly gesture. The merest brush of his lips on her fingertips caused another tremor.

He continued to hold her hand for a moment before running his fingers along her arm. He watched her eyes darken as his fingertips skimmed her upper arm, then traced her throat to her collarbone.

"You are a beautiful woman, Brenna MacAlpin. A beautiful woman whose family has strong traditions, is that not so?"

She tried to nod her head, but he reached a finger to her lips, causing her to go very still.

"I come from a family of many traditions as well. Unfortunately we have become civilized." His rough, callused finger traced the outline of her mouth until her lips quivered and parted for him. "There was a time when a member of the Grey family, seeing a beautiful woman with hair like a raven's wing and eyes the color of a field of heather..." His wicked smile alerted her to danger. "...would simply take her."

His mouth crushed down on hers, cutting off her protest.

At the first contact with his lips, she felt a rush of heat that left her trembling. A flame raced alone her spine, heating her blood, searing her flesh. His lips were warm and firm and practiced. Her lips trembled beneath his, then slowly softened, then invited. She would not have believed it possible to be taken so high by a single kiss.

A breeze blew across the balcony, billowing her skirts, lifting her hair, but it was not enough to cool her skin. She was hot, so hot, where he was touching her.

While his lips continued their seduction, his hand moved along her spine, drawing her even closer, until she could feel his body imprinted upon hers. She attempted to push him away. But even her hands betrayed her. They grasped his shoulders and she held on tightly to keep from falling. Surely her knees would buckle and her legs refuse to sup-

port her. She clung to him, hating the weakness in herself.
A weakness that she had not been aware of until she had met
this man. Though she claimed to detest his touch, she had
not the will to stop him.

Morgan took the kiss deeper. She tightened her grip and
clung to him with a fierceness that surprised her. What was
happening to her? Without soft words, without tender
touches, some primitive force seemed to have taken over her
will. Or perhaps it had taken over both of them, consum-
ing them with its intensity.

The hand at her back tightened perceptibly, drawing her
even closer, until she could feel his heartbeat inside her own
breast.

His lips left hers to follow the pale column of her throat.
She arched against him, afraid of the way her body was betraying her, yet hungry for more. The touch of his lips on
her throat caused the strangest sensations deep inside her.

He brought his lips to hers, and her mouth opened to receive his taste. There was about this man danger, and darkness, and the secrets of desire. And yet, for some reason that
eluded her, she had a desperate need to learn all that he
could teach. She could no more resist his lips than she could
refuse the air that she drew into her lungs.

The sound of a door opening penetrated the mists that
shrouded her mind.

With a low, savage oath, Morgan lifted his head. For a
moment Brenna felt bereft. Then she became aware of the
sound of footsteps across the floor of the sitting chamber.

"My lady."

Still holding her, Morgan turned his head. Dazed, Brenna
followed suit.

A serving girl glanced at them, then quickly looked down,
studying a spot on the floor. "Her majesty has sent a seamstress to begin your gown for the festivities, my lady."

Brenna noticed a stooped old woman standing just inside the doorway. She became aware of a chill breeze blow-
ing off the Thames. Why had she not noticed it before?

"Thank you."

The servant hurried away. The seamstress began setting out her bolts of fabric.

Embarrassed, Brenna tried to pull away, but Morgan continued to hold her. Lifting her chin, he stared down into her eyes and read her confusion. A smile touched the corner of his lips.

"I think, my lady, you do not find my touch so repulsive as you claim."

She felt her cheeks flame. What had he done to her? How had she become so lost in his caresses that she forgot who he was, what he was?

"Go now. Have your gown made. But remember, this thing between us is far from settled."

She pulled away, suddenly mortified by her lapse.

He leaned a hip against the balcony railing as she fled into the sitting chamber. Then he turned and watched as the small boat disappeared around a bend in the river. His hands, he noted, were not quite steady. Perhaps Brenna was right about him. If they had not been interrupted, he would surely have taken her here on the hard, cold floor of the balcony. Like the savage she thought him to be.

Chapter Eight

"Is it not good to be back in England?" Alden pulled a chair in front of the fire and settled himself comfortably.

"Aye." Morgan stood in front of the fireplace and lifted a goblet of ale to his lips.

From behind the closed door of Brenna's sleeping chamber could be heard the babble of women's voices and an occasional muffled exclamation. The servants, it would seem, were having a fine time preparing the Scotswoman for the queen's festivities.

"This time you will stay a while."

"So it would seem. Concern for the queen's safety has altered my plans. If the whispers prove to have substance, I will bring swift justice to any who would plot against Elizabeth." His hand clenched at his side. She was more than his beloved monarch; she was his dearest friend, his closest confidante. No one would threaten her life and live to boast of it.

When that matter was taken care of, he thought, swallowing another drink, he would put an end to this other trouble in his life. "See to the guards." His voice was low, conspiratorial. "They are to watch the lady at all times. But they must be discreet."

"How discreet, old friend?"

"They are not to parade around the palace with drawn swords. But they are not to let the lady out of their sight except when she is in these rooms."

"Is that necessary? Do you really think she can flee this fortress?"

Morgan's hand clenched around the stem of the goblet. "You were not with us in the Highlands. Nor on the journey home." He touched a hand to the dressing on his wound. He would not soon forget Brenna's skill with a knife. "The lady has a mind of her own."

"Aye. I have heard the men talk."

Alden flushed when Morgan arched an eyebrow.

"I will have their heads if I catch them spreading rumors about the Scotswoman while she is under my protection."

"I merely meant that the men speak of her with respect," Alden was quick to add. He stood. "I will alert the guards."

As Alden started for the door, Morgan added softly, "When this is over, we need to find another war to wage, somewhere far from here, old friend."

"I thought you had grown weary of the battle."

"That was before I was made nurse for the female."

"Aye." Alden shot him a quick grin before departing.

The sooner the queen found a partner for Brenna, Morgan thought with a trace of anger, the sooner he could get on with his life.

His life. His world. He had made a satisfying life for himself. Whatever mistakes had been made, he had risen above them. He had no wish for the disruption of this woman in his well-ordered life.

The tapers had all been lighted, casting a soft glow over the room. From the windows could be seen the dark curtain of night sky. Morgan walked to the balcony and stared down at the lights of villages in the distance. His gaze was drawn to the shimmering torches of boats far out on the river.

He had a sudden yearning to sail the Thames. To be one with the sky and the water, in a peaceful setting far from the political intrigue of the court.

He heard the door open, and listened to the soft rustle of skirts as the servants swept from the room. When there was only silence, he slowly turned.

Brenna stood just inside the doorway of the sitting chamber.

Once, when Morgan was a callow youth, he had challenged a soldier reputed to be the most skilled equestrian in all of England. During the jumping, the soldier's mount had taken the tall hedgerow easily, while Morgan's horse had pulled up short and refused to jump. Sailing through the air, Morgan had cleared the hedgerow, but landed on the far side on a boulder the size of a wagon seat. The blow would have killed a lesser man. He would never forget the feeling when all the air was knocked from his lungs, leaving him struggling for breath.

He felt the same way now.

Her gown was crimson satin, with a fashionably low neckline revealing high, firm breasts and a tiny waist. The skirt fell in soft gathers to the tips of her crimson slippers. The sleeves and skirt were inset with bands of delicate lace. A wide ruff of the same lace formed a stiff collar at the back of her neck.

Her dark hair had been pulled to one side and allowed to drift in soft curls over her breast.

Her pale column of throat was unadorned by jewelry. The effect was simple. And stunning.

The thought came unbidden to his mind. Every man at court would ask for her hand. The queen would have no trouble finding a suitable husband. Why did that thought bring such an unpleasant taste to his mouth?

The door to the sitting room opened and Alden entered. For a moment he glanced at his friend. Then his gaze was riveted on the beautiful young woman.

Alden cleared his throat. "You look lovely, my lady."

Morgan said nothing. Mere words could not convey what he saw when he looked at her. How could he describe skin as pale as alabaster, eyes the shade of the violets that grew deep in the forest glades?

"Thank you, my lord."

She gave Alden a shy smile, and Morgan realized that he would give anything to see her smile at him that way. If the Lady Brenna was beautiful when angry, she was breathtaking when happy.

Then the hint of a smile was gone, replaced by a shy look. "Your queen's seamstresses must have magic in their needles. Though I am skilled in sewing, I have never made anything as splendid as this."

Morgan crossed the room and picked up a goblet of wine from a silver tray. When he handed it to her, their fingers brushed and he felt the heat.

"The gown would be nothing without the woman who wears it."

Was that a blush he saw on her cheeks? It pleased him, though he couldn't say why.

Brenna took a sip of wine and felt a rush of warmth. It was the wine, she told herself. Not the nearness of this man. Though he had exchanged his soldier's garb for slim breeches and an elegantly tailored black silk tunic emblazoned with his family crest, he still had a look of danger about him. She must take great pains to keep her distance from him.

She turned to Alden. "I am unaware of your customs, my lord. Will anything be expected of me at your queen's feast?"

"Our customs are not so different from your own. We will merely eat and drink, and enjoy the company of good friends."

"Friends."

Alden blithely ignored the sarcasm in her tone. "These people will be your friends if you let them. Of course," he added with a gleam of humor in his eyes, "there will be many toasts to the queen's health. I would advise you to use caution, my lady. Enough toasts and the wine will go to your head.''

''Thank you. I shall remember.'' The frown was back. It was necessary to keep her wits about her. Alden and Morgan were her enemies. As were the people below stairs.

She set the goblet down.

Morgan drained his glass before reluctantly offering his arm. The mere touch of her caused a tension in him that was completely out of character. He steeled himself against feeling anything for the woman beside him.

As they left the room, Brenna noted the two soldiers positioned outside her sleeping chamber. They came to attention and followed a few paces behind. So. Even here in the queen's palace, her freedom was to be restricted.

As they descended the stairs, they could hear the hum of conversation, the occasional burst of laughter. But when they entered the withdrawing room, all conversation suddenly ceased. All heads turned to watch the handsome couple.

A ripple of excitement coursed through the crowd. Hands were discreetly lifted while whispered exclamations were exchanged. Those who had been at court earlier were surprised at the transformation in the Scotswoman. Gone was the travel-weary creature, and in her place a vision of perfection.

Many a man in the crowd felt a twinge of envy at the prize Morgan Grey had captured. Many a woman hated her on sight.

Morgan felt the slight trembling of Brenna's hand upon his sleeve. So, the lady was not immune to the stares of these strangers. Though he was not aware of any kindness in his gesture, he covered her hand with his, as if to lend her his strength.

He led her across the room toward their regal hostess. Brenna felt the curious stares of the guests. But she kept her head lifted at a proud angle, looking neither left nor right.

When they came to a stop before the queen, Brenna curtsied, while Morgan bowed slightly, then lifted Elizabeth's hand to his lips.

"Can this possibly be the same ragged waif you presented at court, Morgan?"

"Aye, Majesty. The Lady Brenna remarked that she thought your seamstresses had magic in their needles."

"There is indeed magic here." The queen studied the beautiful young woman with a thoughtful look. "Or perhaps witchcraft." With a laugh she turned to Morgan. "Beware, my friend, lest you be the one bewitched."

"You know me better, Majesty."

"Indeed."

Morgan led Brenna to one side as the queen continued to greet the guests who formed a long line behind them.

After each guest had been presented to the queen, they paused in front of Morgan for an introduction to the lady who had caused such speculation. After an hour he could read the fatigue in her eyes.

"So many names and titles," she whispered.

"Aye. But in no time you will know them as friends."

"They are your friends, my lord. To me they are English."

If her words angered him, he gave no indication.

Madeline d'Arbeville, Duchess of Eton, and her husband greeted Elizabeth with warmth. The affection was obviously returned, as the queen smiled and chatted before turning to include the others.

"Charles, your wife seems to have made a friend today. But you have not yet met the Scotswoman. Introduce the lady, Morgan."

"Charles Crowel, Duke of Eton, may I present Brenna MacAlpin, recently of the Scottish Borderland."

As the courtly gentleman bent to brush his lips over Brenna's hand, she studied the man who was married to the Frenchwoman. His green eyes were friendly, his smile genuine. His dark breeches and emerald satin tunic were perfectly tailored to his tall frame. His dark hair was gray at the temples, giving him a look of charm and elegance.

"Madeline has told me about you, my lady." He released Brenna's hand and continued to smile as he entwined his fingers with his wife's.

Charles and Madeline made a handsome couple. And a happy one. That thought caused an ache around Brenna's heart. Whatever match the queen made for her, she would never truly be happy.

"We look forward to having you visit our home when you are comfortably settled in England."

Morgan glanced at Brenna in time to see the look of consternation that suddenly crossed her face. Like the queen, these good people were taking for granted that she would settle and become a wife to an Englishman. The thought sickened her. And though she made a valiant effort, she could not hide it.

As he watched her, Morgan felt his respect for this Scotswoman growing. She was handling a difficult situation with great control.

As more people came forward to greet the queen, Charles and Madeline moved aside. Madeline touched Brenna's hand as she passed. "There will be little time to visit tonight. But soon, if Morgan will permit it, I will arrange a tea, *cherie*. There are many here who are eager to get to know you."

Morgan's permission indeed, Brenna wanted to cry out. But before she could comment, another couple was presented to her. And another, until the names and faces seemed to blend together into a jumbled blur.

A man strode forward alone and greeted the queen, then turned expectantly, awaiting an introduction to the beauty beside Morgan.

"Ah, Lord Windham." The queen became animated in the company of this man. "You have not yet met our Scotswoman. Morgan, will you handle the introductions?"

"Brenna MacAlpin, may I present Lord Windham, aide to the queen." Was it her imagination, Brenna wondered, or was there a trace of tension in Morgan's voice?

"Lord Windham." She looked up into gray opaque eyes the color of the sky before a storm. His clothes were perfectly tailored to his long legs and slender form. The scarlet of his tunic would have been suitable for royalty. He was the most splendidly dressed man in the room.

"My lady." His eyes raked her before he bent to brush a kiss to her hand. As his lips touched her skin she instinctively cringed.

When he straightened, he continued holding her hand until she pulled it free. "The queen tells me you are Morgan Grey's spoils of war."

Brenna itched to slap his arrogant face. Instead she lifted her head a fraction and straightened her spine. "I am no one's spoils of war, my lord."

"Are you not?" He smiled, and Brenna thought it the most evil smile she had ever seen. "You mean you came to England to seek a husband willingly?" His smile grew. "Are there so few satisfying men in your homeland that you would abandon them for one such as Morgan Grey?"

When Brenna remained silent he spoke loud enough for the entire assembly to hear. "I was told that the queen intended to make a match for you. But if, as you say, you are not here against your will, perhaps you will go to a man's bed most willingly?"

"Enough, Windham." Morgan's voice was low, intended for Lord Windham's ears alone. But though he spoke softly, there was a thread of steel in his tone. "The lady should expect better treatment at the hands of an English gentleman."

"And how would you know how a gentleman behaves? The entire realm knows about you and the men who serve under you, Morgan Grey. You are all savages who are only happy when you are spilling an enemy's blood on the field of battle."

"At least I am not a nobleman whose only task in life is despoiling helpless maidens."

The two men faced each other for long moments. It was the queen who broke the silence.

"Two stallions should never be allowed in the same pasture," she said dryly.

There was an extended silence.

The queen touched his arm. "Have you brought no lady with you, Lord Windham?"

"Nay, Majesty. There were so many beauties in the kingdom hoping to enjoy your hospitality. And I am but one mere man."

The queen threw back her head and laughed at his joke. "From the gossip at court, I would say you have the stamina of ten men, my lord."

He shared a smile with her. "One cannot believe all the court gossip, Majesty."

"If even half of it be true, Lord Windham, your social life leaves little time for other duties."

"One must take pleasure where one finds it." Lord Windham cast a speculative glance at the woman beside the queen. "And perhaps a man's duty can also become his pleasure."

Brenna saw the way Morgan tensed. But before he could speak, Alden smoothly interrupted.

"The line of subjects eager to bask in your beauty grows restless, Majesty."

Lord Windham shot him an icy look before stalking away.

"Beware, my friend," Alden commented as Morgan's adversary threaded his way among the guests. "One day Windham may grow weary of your barbs and lift his sword against you."

"Only if I show him my back. He is too cowardly to face me in a fair fight."

"Then be warned. A coward is the worst kind of enemy. He never does what is expected."

"Do not waste a moment's worry over me. It is the queen who needs our concern."

The queen's butler announced that the banquet was awaiting her majesty.

With a knowing smile the queen looked over the assembly, studying the beautifully dressed men and women who formed the inner circle of her court. These were the wealthy, titled nobles with whom she could be at ease. All of them looked up expectantly, eager to see who would be singled out as her escort for the meal.

Lord Windham watched her with a smug expression. If Elizabeth chose her favorite companion, the Scotswoman would be without an escort. He had every intention of offering his arm to the Lady Brenna. It would be great sport to flirt with, and perhaps seduce, the Scotswoman.

If, on the other hand, the queen allowed Morgan Grey to be with the lady he had captured, that would leave Lord Windham as the most eligible escort in the room. He would surely be the queen's choice. That was why he had not brought a lady with him. He would enjoy being at Elizabeth's right hand for the rest of the evening. He thrived on being the center of attention.

The queen knew that there was no love lost between Morgan and Lord Windham. And though Morgan was her dear friend, she enjoyed Windham's dry humor. Besides, he was a worldly, elegant man who could converse with ease. And he was a splendid dancer. If Morgan could not be beside her, Windham would.

"Lord Windham. You will accompany your queen to sup."

With a look of disdain in Morgan's direction, Windham offered the queen his arm and led her toward the banquet room. The rest of the assembly followed.

"Morgan," the queen called over her shoulder. "You and the Scotswoman will sup with us."

Inwardly Morgan groaned. It took all his willpower to be civil to Windham. Yet he gave no sign of his distress.

"Aye, Majesty. It will be our pleasure."

Morgan offered his arm to Brenna.

As the guests took their places at the large tables, Brenna and Morgan followed the queen and Windham to the head table, where all could see them.

Morgan held Brenna's chair. As she brushed past him she murmured, "It would appear that the queen and Lord Windham are exceedingly close friends."

"Aye. He is often invited to join the queen's company."

"And you, my lord?"

"I also enjoy a—close relationship with my queen."

"I noticed."

Was that a trace of jealousy he heard in Brenna's tone? Or was he merely imagining something that didn't exist?

Morgan took the seat beside her. Though he had chafed at the thought of spending a long evening with the queen's peacocks at court, Morgan suddenly found himself looking forward to the next few hours. The Scotswoman, it would seem, was not as indifferent to him as she pretended. And there was nothing he enjoyed more than a duel. Especially a duel with a bright and beautiful woman.

Chapter Nine

The banquet hall at Richmond was festive. Servants in colorful satin livery attended each table. There were platters of whole roasted pig, as well as trays laden with pheasant, partridge and dove. There were baskets of bread still warm from the ovens and bowls of steaming pudding. The goblets and tankards were filled and refilled with wine and ale. With each course there were endless toasts to the queen, to her health, to her country and her people.

A man in brilliant robes took a seat at the end of the queen's table. Each course was presented to the queen by a servant on bended knee. The queen inspected it, nodded with a slightly bored expression, then turned away as the tray was carried to the man at the end of the table.

"Who is that?" Brenna whispered.

"Lord Quigley, the queen's taster."

Brenna watched in amazement as the white-haired man tasted a morsel of each serving before giving his approval. Then the servant approached the queen again on bended knee and waited while a second liveried servant spooned a portion of each food onto the queen's plate.

Though this went on through course after course, neither the queen nor Lord Quigley acknowledged each other.

Brenna was seated at the queen's table between Morgan and Lord Windham. But though there was a whirlwind of activity around her, she found herself mesmerized by the man beside her. His voice was low and deep, in contrast to the shrill sounds of laughter around them. And his eyes pinned her, daring her to try to look away.

"How did you happen to become the MacAlpin?" Morgan asked as a serving wench filled his goblet with ale.

Her eyes lit with a passionate fire that fascinated him. "My father was murdered by a coward, and my older sister, Meredith, assumed the leadership of the clan."

He heard the venom in her voice and felt a wave of pity for the man who had dared to cross her family. "Was this coward an Englishman?"

"Nay. He was one of our own countrymen, who coveted our land."

"So." A smile touched the corner of his lips. "Not all the evil villains in the land are English."

She failed to see the humor of his statement. "We have had our fill of English."

He was in no mood for a debate while in the presence of the queen. He decided to steer the conversation to a safer course. "Why is your sister no longer the MacAlpin?"

Brenna's voice took on a softer note. It was obvious that she adored her elder sister. "Meredith married a Highland chieftain and went to live in his mountain fortress. As next eldest, the task of defending my clan fell to me."

"So, you think it was a love match between your sister and her husband?"

She glanced at him. "Why do you ask?"

"Because you seemed glad when you spoke of it. This Highland chieftain makes your sister happy?"

"Aye." Brenna actually smiled, and Morgan was reminded once more how truly soft and delicate she appeared. "The rogue stole her heart. 'Tis true love."

Lord Windham, hearing their discussion, made a derisive sound. "That will last a year or two at most, while they explore the pleasures of their bed. Then true love will show its true colors."

Brenna looked horror-stricken at his words. "I saw the undying love that shone between my father and mother. That same love shines between Meredith and Brice. It is there in their eyes, in their touch, in the gentle way they treat one another."

Resenting Windham's intrusion, Morgan steered the conversation once again. "What about the villain who murdered your father?"

Morgan Grey, she realized, was very good at changing the subject when it suited him. "He is buried with those of his clan who dared to cross the MacAlpins."

Morgan studied the young woman before him. Though there was no doubt that she was every inch a lady, he had witnessed another side to her. She had the respect of her people. People who had been besieged for generations. And she thought like a soldier. Twice she had nearly outwitted him. He lifted a goblet to his lips and smiled. Twice she had been foiled.

Aye. He would enjoy dueling with the lady. With both words and skill.

With each toast the crowd grew more raucous. With each sip of ale, the young noblemen at the banquet grew bolder, until at last Lord Windham stood to offer his own toast.

"To my gracious queen, Elizabeth, the most wonderful monarch God ever created." Windham pressed his hands to the table to steady himself. His voice rose with emotion. "To her hair, which shines like the sun's own radiance. To her eyes, like perfect sapphires. To her mouth, which emits only pearls of wisdom."

He paused, wiping a tear from his eye, too overcome by his own brilliance to continue.

"You neglected to mention my teeth," the queen said in an aside that only Morgan and Brenna could overhear. "They are my own."

Morgan threw back his head and roared. For a moment Brenna was so surprised at the queen's dry humor that she could only stare. Then a smile tugged at the corner of her lips.

"To her teeth," Windham began.

But Morgan lifted his glass, and the others in the room did the same, drowning out whatever the nobleman was about to say. He sat down flushed and happy at what he considered a monumental success.

"What think you of my feast?" The queen leaned across Lord Windham to direct her question at Brenna.

"It is quite wonderful," Brenna replied honestly. "I have never seen so many splendidly dressed gentlemen and ladies."

"I see you have not touched your wine." Elizabeth motioned toward Brenna's nearly full goblet.

"I was warned that there would be many toasts, Majesty. I did not wish to make a fool of myself."

"You would be in excellent company," the queen said. "The room is full of fools. Is that not so, Windham?"

"Aye, Majesty." His words were slightly slurred. "We are fools in love with your beauty."

"You see why I chose him to be my escort? I bask in his honeyed words."

Morgan set down his goblet. "A woman of your strength and intelligence needs no empty flattery to fill her head."

"That is where you and I disagree, my Lord Grey." Elizabeth gave a gay, girlish laugh. "Even a strong, intelligent woman desires pretty words. Is that not so, Brenna MacAlpin?"

Brenna was startled by the question. "I would prefer honesty to flattery."

The queen's eyes narrowed on her guest. "You are indeed a rare woman. But I think, if the right man were to flatter you, you would discover that you harbor a bit of the same weakness."

The queen turned from her guests to watch the musicians. Suddenly she stood and the entire assembly scrambled to their feet.

"I have had enough of feasting. I wish to dance." The queen took Lord Windham's proffered arm, then turned to Brenna. "Do you dance?"

Brenna shook her head. "John Knox considers dancing a tool of the devil. It is now forbidden in my country."

"Ah, yes. Knox." Elizabeth gave a short laugh. "How terrible for my fun-loving, romantic cousin, Mary, that such a dull man could hold sway over her people." She studied the lovely young woman for a moment, then glanced at the man beside her. "Morgan, bring our—guest along. While she is on English soil, we shall cast aside those prophets of gloom and teach her the joy of an open English society."

Once again Brenna was forced to take Morgan's arm and follow behind the queen.

While the crowd hastily assembled, the musicians began to play. Within minutes the queen and her escort formed a circle with several other couples and began a racy, naughty dance.

Morgan led Brenna to a chaise and handed her a goblet of wine before seating himself beside her. When he stretched out his long legs she found herself staring at his muscled thighs, until she suddenly blushed and looked away.

Watching the dancers was no better. Everywhere she looked, she saw hints of seduction. The women bowed low, baring their bosoms to their partners. The men in tight-fitting breeches, strutted in circles, then caught the women in shockingly close embraces before beginning the dance steps. Brenna was amazed to note that none of the women seemed to mind being held so intimately. In fact, from the giggles and whispers, they encouraged it.

When the dance ended, the men bent low and kissed the ladies' hands. A few of the women offered their cheeks to be kissed. And one woman actually lifted her lips for her partner's kiss. Seeing it, Brenna blushed and lifted the goblet to her mouth to hide her embarrassment.

Morgan was fascinated by her reaction. "Are you blushing, my lady?"

She felt her cheeks grow red and hotly denied it. "I am just a bit warm, my lord."

"Perhaps a walk in the night air." His voice was warm with unspoken laughter.

"Nay." She realized at once that she had rejected his offer too quickly. Now he would have even more to laugh at.

"I suppose you will not dance."

"I cannot."

"Then we will sit here and enjoy our wine."

He lifted his goblet and watched as she drained hers. A serving wench quickly refilled it.

"Morgan, you must dance," the queen called as she twirled by on the arm of a new partner.

Morgan turned to Brenna. She shook her head and stared at the floor.

"Is it John Knox you fear? Is that why you cannot dance?" Morgan smiled. "I do not think anyone from the queen's court will carry tales of this night back to your people."

"I do not fear John Knox."

"Is it the sin itself, then? Will you be damned if you dance?"

"I do not consider dancing sinful, my lord."

"Then why can you not dance?"

She sighed. "Except with my sisters, and a few of the youth at wedding feasts, I have never danced. I fear I would be—clumsy."

His smile gentled. "Clumsy? You, my lady? That would not be possible. Come." He stood and held out his hand.

She bit her lip. "I do not know what to do."

"I will teach you." Taking the goblet from her, he set it on a small table and took her hand.

While the musicians played a tender ballad, Morgan led Brenna through the intricate steps of the dance.

"Allow me to lead. In my arms, you need only follow."

"But I am moving right while you move left."

She was achingly aware of the hand at her back, pressing ever so lightly as he guided her. She could feel every one of his fingers touching her flesh.

"Do not watch your feet," he whispered, tipping up her chin.

Her gaze fastened on his as his fingertip stroked her cheek. Oh, why did he have to have such a gentle touch? Why was he so graceful in the dance?

She fit so perfectly into the circle of his embrace. It was as if she had been made for his arms alone. He drew her closer and moved to the music. And the woman in his arms began to move with him in perfect rhythm.

"I pray that John Knox does not choose this night to visit the Queen of England," Morgan murmured against her temple.

"I told you, I do not consider dancing a sin."

"Perhaps. But anyoné watching us can see what I am thinking. And what I am thinking is definitely a sin, my lady."

Her cheeks flamed. Only a crude Englishman would dare to make such a joke. She did not know how to deal with such a blunt manner.

"Forgive me, my lady." His deep voice whispered over her senses, causing a prickly feeling along her spine. "I can see that a sheltered woman would feel lost in such decadence."

He gave a chuckle that sent icy shivers along her spine. She tried to pull away but he gathered her even closer and continued to sway to the music.

She was caught in the gentlest of prisons. Through her satin skirts she could feel the brush of his thighs against hers. Her breasts were crushed against his chest. Each time he breathed, she felt the warmth of his breath ruffle the hair at her temple. Slowly, against her will, she closed her eyes and with a sigh gave in to the overpowering need to surrender to his touch. Her fingers played with the dark hair at his

nape. The hand engulfed in his relaxed until their finger
were gently laced.

"You are an excellent student, my lady." His words were
whispered against her temple.

She sighed. It was not the student who was excellent; i
was the teacher. But she was too content to speak.

"Is there anything else you would like to learn, my lady?"

Her lids snapped open. She found herself staring into his
dark, laughing eyes.

"I fear there is nothing else you could teach me."

"Would you care to bet a gold sovereign on that?"

She suddenly resented his mocking laughter.

"I no longer wish to dance with you, Morgan Grey."

An aging earl stepped forward and tapped Morgan on the
shoulder.

"It seems your every wish is my command, my lady."
With a smile Morgan took a step back, breaking contact.
Before she knew what was happening, Brenna was swept
away in the old man's arms. When she glanced over his
shoulder she saw Morgan dancing with the queen. Lord
Windham was standing in the center of the floor looking
over the dancing couples.

From her vantage point, Brenna watched as Morgan
swept the queen around the dance floor. It was obvious,
from the ease with which they moved, that they had danced
together many times. Elizabeth looked up into Morgan's
eyes and said something that made him laugh. He then
lowered his head to whisper in her ear. Brenna stared in
fascination, unable to turn away from such an intimate
scene.

What was this strange emotion she felt? Jealousy? She
instantly rejected such a notion. How could she feel any
jealousy toward a man she cared nothing about?

Within minutes Brenna was dancing with another partner. She looked up to find herself in the arms of Charles
Crowel, Duke of Eton.

"My wife, Madeline, is quite taken with you, my lady."

"And I with her. I shall never forget her kindness to me."

"Madeline is a tenderhearted woman. She has not forgotten what it feels like to be a stranger in a strange land. But my friends have gone to great lengths to make her feel welcome in England."

"Your wife is a truly good person. I feel that I have at least one friend in England."

"My dear, if you let us, we will all be your friends."

"Thank you, sir." She gave him a grateful smile. "You are most kind."

"And you are most beautiful, my dear. I fear Her Majesty will have twenty and five suitors vying for your hand before this night is over."

Brenna was still laughing when she was suddenly turned into another pair of arms.

"Lord Windham." The smile vanished from her lips.

"I have been waiting for this opportunity," he said.

His hand at her waist drew her firmly against him. His eyes had none of the warmth or humor of Morgan's. Instead, they burned with an intensity that alarmed her.

"You have dazzled all of the gentlemen in the queen's company," he muttered. "It seems you shall have your pick of titled Englishmen from which to choose."

"Perhaps," Brenna said, striving to keep the conversation light, "I shall be unable to choose just one."

"All the better. I like a woman who can please many lovers."

"I did not mean..." She bit her lip. There was no point in attempting to explain to this crude man.

He swept her gracefully through the crowd and continued dancing. Brenna was unaware that they were heading toward a deserted balcony until they stopped dancing. She looked around in surprise.

"Why have you brought me here?"

"Why does a gentleman usually take a lady away from the crowd?" He smiled and she felt a tiny tremor of fear along her spine. "I thought you might wish to escape from Morgan Grey."

"Escape? You offer me escape, my lord?"

He took a step closer and ran his finger suggestively along her arm. She gave an involuntary shudder and took a step back. But as she took another step, her back pressed against the cold stone of the balcony railing. At her look of fear Lord Windham's smile widened. "Are you playing the part of the coquette, my lady?"

"I..." She licked her lips and fought back the rush of fear that caused her throat to go dry. "I do not understand what you mean."

"Oh, I think you do." He stepped very close, until their bodies were touching. He felt the way she recoiled from him and gave a cold laugh as he brought his hand to her shoulder. "You are teasing me, my lady. Playing the part of the innocent. And it is most effective."

"Please, my lord. I wish to go back to the others now."

"All in good time." He caught her by the upper arms and pressed his thumbs into the softness of her flesh. "You are a beautiful, desirable woman, Brenna MacAlpin. It was most kind of Morgan Grey to fetch you here for my pleasure."

His breath reeked of ale. Brenna strained against the hands that clawed at her.

As he drew her close and lowered his head, he heard the sound of swords being drawn. Stunned, he turned to find two of Morgan Grey's soldiers facing him, their swords lifted in a threatening manner. Behind them was Morgan Grey himself.

Brenna was so elated to see them, she nearly threw herself into Morgan's arms. She took a step toward him, but the look on his face stopped her.

"Did you not think it rude to leave the festivities before your queen, Windham?"

Lord Windham's face was a cold mask of fury. "You have no right to intrude, Grey."

"I have every right. Have you forgotten that the lady is my prisoner?"

Brenna froze. For just a moment she had forgotten that the guards were not there to protect her, but to keep her from escaping. And Morgan Grey was not worried about her safety; merely about the way it would look if she disappeared while his soldiers were supposed to be guarding her.

"Could it be that you think the lady is your own personal property?" Windham saw the way Morgan's eyes darkened and realized that he had hit a nerve. He gave a shrill, nervous laugh. "So. That is it. You think you are the only one allowed to dally with the prisoner." His voice lifted in agitation. "Have you already decided how to spend the lady's dowry, and how to cut up her lands to your satisfaction?"

At his words Morgan felt a wave of fury. "That is not even worthy of a reply. I care not what you think, Windham." Morgan's voice was low; his words deliberate. "Be warned. The lady is off limits to all but the man who petitions the queen for her hand."

Windham's words were slurred. "Perhaps that is what the lady and I were discussing." He pushed past the guards and stormed away without another word.

Brenna was left alone to face the furious, accusing look on Morgan's face.

Chapter Ten

"You will take my arm, my lady."

"You do not care to hear what happened?" Her heart-beat was still racing. Her voice trembled. Despite his cold demeanor, she had experienced waves of relief at her rescue from this frightful scene. Though she had always dealt with her own problems in her own way, she had an unreasonable yearning to cling to him and weep over her embarrassing ordeal.

"Nay. It is finished."

Finished? She studied his shuttered expression, his stiff stance. "Can it be that you believe that I came here willingly with that evil man?"

"You made it abundantly clear that you would do anything to escape me. But if you saw Windham as an ally, you made a poor choice. Now we will speak of it no more, my lady. But be warned that I will not tolerate such foolishness again."

Brenna glanced at the guards. They stared straight ahead, awaiting orders from their leader.

With a sigh of resignation, she placed her hand on Morgan's sleeve and walked by his side. There was no point in attempting to defend herself. This man was having none of it.

On the dance floor the queen was going through a series of intricate dance steps in the arms of the Duke of Eton. A crowd ringed the room, clapping their hands. As Morgan and Brenna approached, Madeline turned to greet them.

She took one look at Brenna's flushed cheeks and Morgan's unreadable expression and gave a little laugh. "*Mon dieu.* You two have been naughty, slipping away like that. Could you not at least wait until the evening is over?"

Morgan's eyes narrowed.

Madeline turned toward the dancers. "Is Charles not the best dancer in England?"

For a moment her question was met with only silence. Then, to cover the awkward moment, Brenna cleared her throat. "Aye. He cuts a fine figure with the queen."

Madeline heard the slight tremor in her voice and touched a hand to her cheek. "You are overwrought, *cherie*. It is this rogue, Morgan Grey, is it not?"

Feeling the prickle of tears, Brenna shook her head and blinked quickly.

Madeline's concerned look quickly turned to one of understanding. "Ah. I see. You are weary then, *cherie*."

Brenna nodded, afraid to trust her voice. She had a desperate need to flee this room, these people.

"A pity. For no one can leave until the queen does."

Brenna groaned inwardly and tightened her grip on Morgan's sleeve. If he noticed her discomfort, he gave no indication. He continued to stare at the dancers as though she didn't exist.

In his mind's eye he could still see Brenna locked in Windham's embrace. The little fool. Did she not sense the danger in playing with a man like Windham? He was no better than an animal, deflowering maidens for his selfish pleasure, then leaving them to deal with bruised hearts and sometimes, if the rumors be true, battered bodies.

If she was so desperate to escape that she would even choose Windham for her champion, Morgan would have to save her from her own folly.

The music ended. The queen and the Duke of Eton acknowledged the applause. The duke returned Elizabeth to the arm of her escort. Then the crowd parted as the queen and Lord Windham bid good-night to their guests and headed for the door. There, the queen made a great show of bidding good-night to Lord Windham. When he had dutifully kissed her hand, she clapped for her servants. Immediately a flock of serving girls and the queen's ladies circled Elizabeth. With a flurry of women's high-pitched voices, the queen and her retinue headed for the royal quarters.

Windham, drunk not only from the amount of ale he'd consumed, but from the attention paid him by the queen, strutted around the room accepting the congratulations of his friends.

The musicians began to play. Many in the crowded room returned to the dance floor, while others followed the queen's example and bid good-night.

"Now you can rest, *cherie*." Madeline turned from Brenna and linked hands with her husband as soon as he approached.

He drew her close. "Will we stay with the revelers, my dear, or would you prefer to return to our quarters?"

"I think I could dance until the morning light."

The duke gave a fleeting glance toward the door as if regretting the sleep he would be forced to miss. Then he touched her cheek in an affectionate gesture. "You shall have your wish, my love." He turned to Morgan. "Will you linger awhile?"

"Nay. We will see you on the morrow." Morgan's words were clipped.

Brenna bid good-night, then placed her hand on Morgan's arm, moving stiffly at his side as they took their leave.

They spoke not a word as they ascended the stairs to their suite of rooms. Morgan held the door for Brenna, then paused to speak to his men before following her inside.

The rooms had been prepared for the night. In the sitting room, a fire crackled in the fireplace. A chaise had been positioned in front of it. To one side a table held a decanter of wine and two goblets. On a tray were fruit and pastries.

A perfect room for lovers, Brenna thought. But she and Morgan Grey were far from lovers; they were enemies. And each day her dislike for this man grew.

A servant looked up as they entered. Seeing Morgan's scowling face, she filled a goblet with wine and placed it in his outstretched hand.

Brenna pushed open the door to her sleeping chamber. A cozy fire burned within. The bed linens had been turned down. Across the bed was draped a gauzy ivory night shift of hand-worked lace and finest linen. The Queen's seamstresses must have worked throughout the entire evening to turn out something so fine.

A second serving girl looked up from the fire she had been attending. She hurried to Brenna's side and began to assist her in removing her gown and petticoats. When Brenna was dressed in her night shift, the maid brushed her long hair until it fell in soft waves to her waist.

Brenna thought about old Morna, her nurse since childhood. Those old, awkward fingers would have fumbled with the buttons of this fine gown. And the hairbrush would have snagged and pulled at her long hair. But oh, how desperately she missed that dear, wrinkled face.

"Would you like anything, my lady?"

"Nothing. Thank you."

Brenna watched as the serving girl scooped up her clothes. On the morrow they would be clean and pressed and hung neatly, awaiting the next time their mistress needed them.

"Good night, my lady."

"Good night."

Before the door closed, Brenna's smile faded. The shadow of a guard could be seen just beyond the open doorway, reminding her again that all this finery did not hide the fact that she was a prisoner. Morgan Grey took no chance that she might attempt to escape into the night.

She felt a wave of loathing for the man who had brought her to this place of horrors. It was because of him that she had been taken from her home. And because of him she would be forced into marriage with one of his countrymen. She would rather face death at the hands of her guards than endure such a fate.

She buried her face in her hands, to blot out the terrible thought of a lifetime spent in such decadence.

Morgan dismissed the servants. He needed to be alone. To think. To brood.

He drained his goblet and stared into the flames of the fire. He was still seething with fury at the scene he had witnessed on the balcony.

What fine irony that he should feel anything at all for the Scotswoman. She was not his responsibility. He had merely been following Elizabeth's orders. He'd no choice but to bring her here. But that decision had cost him. Cost him dearly.

He was a man who lived alone by choice. He liked his life the way it was. And he resented having this woman thrust upon him like a stray pup. His eyes narrowed. Especially now that he had discovered the sort of woman she was.

Lord Windham. His hand curled into a fist. He reached for the decanter and filled his goblet. If she had gone off with anyone but Windham, he might have been able to overlook it.

He drank again and shook his head slightly. Nay. That was a lie. Even if it had been one of the others, he still would have been angry. But the thought of her with Windham sickened him.

He drained his goblet, then suddenly hurled it against the hearth where it shattered into a thousand pieces. With a savage oath he turned and stormed toward Brenna's sleeping chamber.

At the sound of shattering glass and the door opening, Brenna turned. The commanding figure of Morgan Grey filled the doorway.

For a moment she could not speak. Then she swallowed back her fear and stiffened her spine.

"You have no right to come into my sleeping chamber."

His voice was controlled and tight with fury. "You will not speak to me of rights."

"I order you to leave here at once."

"You order, my lady?" There was the thread of steel in his tone. "Have you forgotten that you are no longer in Scotland? You can issue no orders here, Brenna MacAlpin. You heard the queen. Until she decides what to do with you, you are my prisoner—" he spoke each word very carefully "—to do with as I please."

Her throat went dry. "Why have you come here?"

There was something new in her tone. Fear? That thought pleased him. She should be afraid of him. His temper was something to be feared and it was time she had a taste of it.

He studied the way she looked in the glow of firelight. Her hair, black as midnight, fell in a luxurious cloud around her face and shoulders. The pristine night shift gave her a look of innocence. But this was no innocent child before him. She was a woman. A beautiful, enticing creature. Every line and curve of her lush body could be seen through the opaque fabric. Her little scene with Windham on the balcony had shown him that she knew very well how to use her body, her beauty, to her advantage.

He'd had the impression, when they were in her country, that the lass was an innocent. But now he knew better. He felt his temper slip another notch, until he could no longer control it. She was no better than the women at court.

A warning sounded in his mind, but before he took the time to think, his hand snaked out, catching her by the wrist.

"I came here to teach you a lesson."

"No." She tried to pull back but she was no match for him.

He dragged her roughly against him and pulled her hands behind her in a painful grip. "You have strained my patience to the breaking point." His breath was hot against her cheek. "And I am not a patient man."

"Damn you, Morgan Grey." She felt a welling of tears and blinked them away. "Damn you to hell."

He shot her a dangerous smile. "Oh, I already know my eternal destination, my lady." He plunged a hand into the tangles of her hair and drew her head back until he was staring deeply into her eyes.

He had not come in here for this. In fact, he'd had no plan in mind. It was merely his intention to vent some of his anger. But now that he was holding her, there seemed to be no turning back.

Slowly, ever so slowly, he lowered his head.

She knew what he intended to do, but she was helpless to stop him. Her heart began a painful hammering in her chest. She could not cry out; could not even speak. Her eyes remained open, watching, watching until his lips closed over hers.

As his mouth met hers she felt the first wild rush of sensation and struggled to resist it. This was, after all, not a kiss, but a punishment. She had to resist feeling anything at all for this monster. But the fire in him engulfed her, like a flame set to dry leaves.

The kiss was raw and savage like the man. There was so much passion in him.

Again it seemed there was no time for soft, seductive kisses, or sweet, honeyed words. There was only this need building inside with the force of a raging tide. And as his mouth plundered hers, she gave up all attempts at a struggle and endured rigidly in his arms.

His hands moved along her back, drawing her firmly against him.

The first stirrings of pleasure curled along her spine. Where had all these strange new feelings come from? How was it possible that this cruel tyrant should be the one to open the floodgate to a passion that had slumbered for so long?

Slowly, against her will, her arms found their way around his waist. Her lithe young body strained against his.

He felt her gradual surrender and thrilled to it. For a moment he lifted his head and touched a finger to her swollen lips. Lips that seemed to have been made for him alone.

What was there about this damnable female that brought out a tenderness in him that he was determined to deny? His hand stroked her cheek, then slid around to cup the back of her head. He avoided looking into her eyes, and concentrated instead on lips still swollen from his kiss.

He was not, he thought savagely, a tender man. Whatever tenderness he had once known had been brutally cut away years ago.

His lips covered hers once more in a hot, hungry kiss that left her breathless.

His big hands slid along her body to her hips and dragged her against him, alerting her to his complete arousal. Though she thought of pushing away, the thought was gone in an instant.

Kisses were no longer enough. He longed to fill himself with the taste, the smell, the feel of her. He needed to fill himself with this woman.

She felt herself slipping beyond reason into a world of mindless pleasure, where the only thing that mattered was this man and the feelings he aroused in her.

His lips left hers to follow the line of her jaw to her neck. He ran kisses along the sensitive column of her throat, and thrilled to her trembling response.

She sighed and arched in his arms, giving him easier access. But when his strong fingers tore at the lace bodice of her gown, a moment of sanity rose through the layers of mist that clouded her mind.

"This is madness."

"Aye. Madness." For an instant he lifted his head and seemed to remember who they were, where they were. He studied her lips, swollen from his kisses. Though he knew that he had no right, he could not stop himself. He brought his lips to hers, tasting, nibbling, seducing.

No woman had ever tasted as sweetly innocent. Was she truly what she appeared, or was she just a clever actress? At the moment it didn't matter. At this moment nothing mattered except the pleasure of her lips.

Brenna felt everything, experienced everything, with unbelievable clarity: the musky, masculine scent of him; the warmth of his breath as it mingled with hers; the way his hands felt, strong and firm; the fragrance of candle wax and wood smoke as it filled the room; the sound of their heartbeats thundering in perfect rhythm.

Morgan hadn't wanted this; hadn't planned it. If anything, he had wanted her to taste his temper, not his need.

Need. Never had he needed anyone with such desperation. What had this woman done to him? How had he let it go this far? She was taking over his senses, filling his mind, crowding out all other thought. And yet she was wrong for him.

He was a soldier, who had probably met her father, her uncles, her clansmen, on the battlefield. She was a foreigner, who hated his beloved land.

She was too innocent, too inexperienced, for a rake like him. Aye, his first instincts about her were correct, he knew, as his lips moved over hers. She was a virgin who would expect the man who took her innocence to wed her.

Marriage. The thought seemed to come from nowhere. Marriage to Brenna MacAlpin would be an adventure like no other. She was the kind of woman who made a man think about marriage, and children, and forever.

He came to his senses, abruptly cutting off such thoughts. What foolishness was this?

He knew he had taken her too far, too fast. Or had she taken him? Still he lingered, unwilling to break contact. One more kiss. One more taste of her. One more touch.

Morgan tasted her honey sweetness one last time and dragged himself away.

They were both shaken by what they had just experienced. And both too proud to admit it.

Brenna was shocked by the strange new feelings that surged through her. Hundreds of tiny pulses seemed to throb within her. Her body hummed. Her knees were weak, and to hide it, she stood very still, lifting her head at a haughty angle.

Morgan tensed, watching her. He held his hands stiffly at his sides. He had come in here to shake her, to throttle her. Instead, he had just lost something of himself to this woman. Something he'd sworn no woman would ever again take.

His voice was rough. "I have decided that we leave on the morrow for Greystone Abbey."

"Greystone Abbey?" Her eyes widened.

"My manor house in Richmond. Where you can be removed from anyone who might be persuaded to help you escape England. Once there you will do nothing without my permission. And where you go, my soldiers go with you. Is that clear?"

"And . . ." She hadn't known it would be so difficult to speak. She swallowed and tried again. "If I wish to bathe, my lord?" Her voice dripped sarcasm. "Will you at least have the decency to leave me to my privacy?"

His eyes flashed. "Unless I say otherwise, even that privilege will not be granted." His lips curved into a thin, tight line. He lifted her chin, forcing her to meet his eyes. "I may, of course, enjoy keeping you under my watchful eye while you bathe."

She slapped his hand away.

His eyes narrowed. "You will not be alone, do you understand?"

"I understand that you are a cold, unfeeling animal."

His hand snaked out so fast she had no time to move. He caught her by the arm and dragged her close, until his lips were mere inches from hers. Once again she felt drawn to him.

"I am neither cold nor unfeeling, my lady, as we both well know. But I am not about to become a fool for you. I suspect that you will use anything, or anyone—'' his thoughts flew to the scene with Windham and his fury returned ''—to help you evade your fate and return to Scotland.''

''Scotland.'' Her voice broke and he saw the way her lower lip suddenly trembled as tears filled her eyes. ''Aye. I will never rest until I am allowed to return to my home.''

''England is your home now.'' He turned, unwilling to be moved by her pain. ''The queen has decreed it. And I intend to see to it that you do not attempt another escape with the likes of Windham.''

He strode quickly from the room, suddenly eager to escape from her. As he moved to his own sleeping chambers, he heard the scrape of something heavy being moved in Brenna's room.

His eyes narrowed. Damn the woman. She was barring him from entering her room. Were he not so weary, he would tear down the door and send the barricade crashing across the room.

He entered his room and peeled his clothes away. He would deal with her even more harshly on the morrow.

Chapter Eleven

Brenna stood on the balcony and watched as the first light began to color the hills to the east. Her eyes were red-rimmed from lack of sleep. All night she had tossed and turned, running from demons that had relentlessly pursued her in her troubled dreams.

Her gaze followed the guards who patrolled in the courtyard below. Were all of them there to protect the queen? Or had Morgan ordered them to see that his captive did not escape?

Beyond the door she heard the sounds of morning activity. Fresh tapers were being placed in the sconces. Logs were being added to the hot coals in the fireplaces. Servants scurried along the hallways, carrying fresh linen and basins of water. A few personal maids were already assisting their ladies with their morning toilet. From the refectory came the mouth-watering fragrance of bread and roasting meat.

Brenna tensed when she heard the sound of footsteps in the sitting chamber. Her glance flew to the heavy chaise she had pushed against her door. But before she could hurry across the room and move it, there was a tremendous crashing sound and the chaise was rolled end over end as the door was kicked in.

Morgan stood in the doorway, his feet apart, hands on his hips. He wore tight-fitting breeches tucked into his tall boots. He was shirtless, and his dark hair was slightly mussed. A stubble of beard darkened his cheeks and chin.

His first thought upon awakening had been to teach this damnable woman a lesson.

"If you ever attempt to bar me from this room again, I will force you to sleep in my room, where I can watch you night and day. Is that understood?"

She thrust her chin out defiantly. "If you had but given me a moment's notice, my lord, I would have removed the barrier."

"There was no reason to place a barrier at your door in the first place."

"I believed there was."

She forced herself to meet his dark look. She had never before seen a man who had just awakened. And though Morgan's arrogant stance and scowling face caused her heartbeat to race, she couldn't help thinking that there was something oddly appealing about his rumpled appearance. What foolish thoughts, she reminded herself. Only an arrogant lout would appear before a lady in such an indecent manner.

His gaze swept her, noting the throw she had snatched from the bed and draped over her shoulders for modesty. He nearly laughed at her prudishness. Did she think that little bit of cover could hide her beauty? In his mind's eye he could still recall the way she had looked last night. Beneath the opaque night shift he could still see every lush curve of her body. His fingers could remember the flare of her hips, the waist so tiny his hands were able to easily span it.

Such thoughts had caused him a long, sleepless night.

Her hair was a mass of dark tangles that begged for his touch. He clenched a fist. His gaze roamed her body, then came to rest at her bare feet. Such small feet.

He forced himself to look away, and noticed the up-ended chaise. He seemed relieved to have something to do. Bending, he righted it as effortlessly as if it were a child's toy.

Brenna found herself staring in fascination at the powerful muscles of his back and arms. As he turned she studied the mat of dark hair that covered his chest and dipped below the waistband of his breeches.

Her cheeks were hot. She blamed it on anger. "If you will be so good as to leave, my lord, I will begin my morning ablutions."

"And if I choose not to leave?"

She glared at him a moment, then turned her back, making an attempt to completely ignore him. "If you insist upon playing the part of my jailer..." She poured water into a basin. "So be it."

As she began to wash her hands and face, Morgan leaned a hip against the door and watched. He had never seen a woman move with such grace. She lifted a linen square to her face to blot the water, and he had a sudden desire to lick each tiny droplet from her cheeks and lips. The mere thought left him reeling.

The first rays of sunlight streamed through the balcony window, bathing her in liquid gold. She picked up a gilt-handled brush and brought her hair forward over one breast. As she ran the brush through the tangles, Morgan had an almost overpowering urge to take the brush from her hand and complete the task himself.

He curled his hand into a fist and held it firmly by his side.

There was a knock on the door and a serving girl entered. Over her arm was a morning gown of soft ivory wool and several petticoats. She looked from Brenna, still clad in her night shift, to the man who stood, half-naked, watching her. It was a most intimate scene.

"Forgive me, my lord," she sputtered, as she began to back from the room. "I shall return when the lady summons me."

"Nay." Morgan saw the look on Brenna's face and nearly laughed aloud. She well knew that before the end of the day, everyone in the palace would hear of this. "Stay and assist the lady. It is time I dressed."

He had a sudden devilish thought. Under the serving girl's watchful eye, he crossed the room and caught Brenna's chin in his hand. Lifting it, he brushed his lips lightly over hers.

He had not expected the rush of feelings that could be caused by such a simple touch. He felt the jolt, sudden, shocking, and forced himself not to react as he turned away with a negligent shrug.

"Do not dally. We leave for Greystone Abbey within the hour."

Brenna was too stunned to respond. That was the first time he had ever kissed her with any tenderness. And though she knew it meant nothing to him, her body was still tingling.

She knew why he had played that little charade. He enjoyed humiliating her in front of others. He wanted her, and all the others, to know that she was powerless.

As he strolled across the room her hand tightened on the handle of the brush. How she itched to toss it at his imperious head.

"Come. The horses are ready."

Morgan wore his familiar black. Breeches, doublet, tunic, all were black. But the effect was softened by a crimson cape thrown rakishly over one shoulder.

Brenna tossed a heavy wool traveling cloak over her shoulders and lifted the hood. Morgan offered his arm and Brenna touched her hand lightly to his sleeve. She felt the ripple of muscle beneath her touch and saw in her mind the way he'd looked earlier, without his shirt. It was an image she could not easily dispel. She felt her cheeks redden slightly.

When they left the room the guards fell into step behind them.

In the courtyard were a dozen horses being held by grooms.

"Greystone Abbey is more than an hour's ride, my lady." Morgan motioned to a gleaming carriage and six white horses. "The queen has offered her carriage. Or, if you prefer, you may ride one of her spirited mounts."

"I would ride, my lord. The carriage is too confining."

He was oddly pleased by her choice. "I, too, much prefer the freedom of a mount to the confinement of a carriage. But do not think," he added crisply, "that you will ride to your freedom. My men and I will be vigilant."

Morgan helped her into the saddle, then mounted his own steed. To the doorman he called, "My Lord Clive. Convey to the queen our gratitude at her hospitality. And tell her that I shall return on the morrow."

"You may tell her yourself."

Morgan chuckled at the sight of the queen surrounded by her ladies and a dozen or more nobles from the court.

"I had thought you to be preparing to break your fast, Majesty. I did not wish to disturb you."

"What disturbs me more is seeing you go, Morgan. I had hoped to persuade you to stay on at Richmond."

"I have been away from home too long, Majesty. There is much to see to."

"When you have your affairs in order, I hope you and the Scotswoman will return to the palace."

"Perhaps I can persuade Your Majesty to come to Greystone Abbey for a day of hunting," he called.

The queen's eyes lit with fire. "Ah. You know my weakness, you rogue. I would like nothing better than the thrill of the hunt. You will arrange it?"

"Consider it done."

The queen gazed at the woman whose horse was flanked by two mounted guards. "Godspeed, Brenna MacAlpin. May your fate soon be decided."

Brenna bowed her head. "Thank you, Majesty."

Lord Windham pushed his way through the crowd and paused beside Brenna's horse, catching the reins. "A pity that you must leave just when we were becoming acquainted. Of course,'' he added loudly enough for Morgan to hear, "I could always arrange to attend the hunt with the queen. That way—'' a mocking smile touched his lips "—we could continue what was so rudely interrupted on the balcony last night.''

Snatching the reins from his hand Brenna nudged her horse into a trot. As she did, she saw the black look on Morgan's face.

The queen and her followers called and waved as Morgan and his company moved out smartly.

Before Brenna's departure Madeline d'Arbeville had stopped by her chambers to relay what little she knew about Morgan Grey's home. Greystone Abbey, it would seem, was an isolated manor house where Morgan went to be alone. No one had ever been invited there. He did all his entertaining in his London house. But rumors persisted that the queen was often entertained at Greystone Abbey. Entertained alone, without servants or the others who always accompanied her on her brief sojourns in the country.

What shocking secrets did he hide in that remote place?

Though Brenna inwardly trembled at the thought of being alone with Morgan Grey, she was relieved to be doing more than sitting in a room awaiting her fate. Perhaps there was something to occupy her time at Greystone Abbey. Or perhaps, she thought with a sudden lifting of her spirits, there would be a chance for escape.

Seeing her thoughtful expression, Morgan brought his horse close to hers. "If you are plotting your escape from my manor house, my lady, I would suggest that you reconsider. I have no intention of allowing you the freedom to move about as you please.''

Brenna shot him a look full of hate. "Perhaps you can chain me to my bed. Would that please you, my lord?''

The thought was not an altogether unpleasant one. Especially if he shared the bed with her.

His eyes crinkled with laughter. "Perhaps. Though if I were going to chain you, 'twould more likely be in my scullery, where you could at least earn your keep."

"Some day, when I am free of your tyranny, I will show you how I would deal with a scoundrel like you in Scotland. I will find a special way to thank you for every injustice."

He glanced down at her, enjoying the way her eyes darkened with anger. It was most interesting to see how the cool, haughty woman from Scotland could lose her composure. "You are most welcome, my lady."

She looked up to see the laughter touching the corner of his mouth, lurking in his eyes. Her temper grew. "You are enjoying my helplessness."

"You, my lady?" He threw back his head and laughed aloud, then touched a hand to the wound that, though healing nicely, still caused him enough pain to curse her name at times. "I do not believe, in your whole life, that you have ever been helpless. And I bear the scars to prove it."

She felt the flush creep along her throat and color her cheeks. There were many men who would have relished holding captive one who had so viciously attacked them. To his credit, Morgan Grey had shown restraint toward her. She had to admit that he had treated her far better than she would treat him under similar circumstances.

Brenna bit back the retort that sprang to her lips. He was trying to goad her into a fight. She would not give him the satisfaction.

Instead she let down her hood and savored the breeze in her hair. It was a perfect summer day. The sky was a clear, cloudless blue. She lifted her face to the sun.

Morgan turned to study her. Under the dazzling sunlight she was as breathtaking as she had been by candlelight.

"Tell me about your home, my lord."

"It has been in my family for generations. Elizabeth's father, King Henry, built his palace nearby so that the two could meet whenever Henry desired my father's council."

Morgan was unaware of the sparkle that came into his eyes while he spoke of his home.

"And now Elizabeth has you nearby, in the event she desires your council or—comfort."

"Aye." His voice held a note of amusement. "Does that bother you, my lady?"

Brenna's brows arched in question. "Bother me? Why should I care whom the Queen of England chooses as her council? Or her lover?"

Oh, he enjoyed sparring with her. "Why indeed, my lady?"

They crested a hill and Morgan reined in his horse and pointed. "There, my lady. On that distant rise is my home. Greystone Abbey."

Brenna stared at the green rolling hills and heavily wooded forests that surrounded a graceful castle built of smoky gray stone.

As they drew closer, they approached a sleepy village. The word was quickly passed that the lord of the manor was returning home. By the time their horses entered the main road of the village, most of the residents had flocked for a glimpse of Morgan Grey.

The women smiled shyly. Many of them held their children aloft for his admiration. A woodsman stepped into the path of the lead horses and removed his hat.

"So, William," Morgan called. "Has the game been plentiful?"

"Aye, my lord. Thanks to you, we have all had our fill."

"The queen desires a hunt. Come to Greystone Abbey on the morrow. We will make arrangements."

"Aye, my lord." The man's face was wreathed in smiles. "I would be honored."

Brenna studied the faces in the crowd and felt more than a little surprised. She had heard that the English queen wasted food while her people went hungry. Yet these people looked happy and well fed.

In no time they had traversed the lane and were headed along a wide road that led to the manor house.

As they entered the courtyard, several servants spilled from the door and hurried forward to assist Morgan and his men from their mounts.

Morgan reached up and lifted Brenna from the saddle. She steeled herself against his touch.

"Welcome, my lord. 'Tis good to have you home again."

"Thank you, Mistress Leems." He turned to a plump woman who stood in the doorway wiping her hands on her apron. "Does Richard know we are arrived?"

"Aye, my lord. He has been most anxious since your messenger told of your plans. He has been at the window since sunrise."

Morgan placed his hand beneath Brenna's elbow, propelling her toward the doorway. "Mistress Leems, this is Brenna MacAlpin. She is to be our—guest."

Brenna was so shocked by Morgan's unexpected kindness, she could have wept.

The housekeeper bowed. "Welcome, my lady."

"Thank you, Mistress Leems."

Before she could exchange pleasantries, Morgan hurried her inside. His impatience was evident.

They crossed a long hallway and paused before huge double doors. As Morgan pulled open the doors to the great room a man, seated in a chair by the window, turned.

Sunlight gleamed on his gray-streaked hair, and his dark eyes crinkled with laughter. "Morgan." His voice boomed out. "You've been gone too long this time."

"Aye." In quick strides Morgan was across the room and clasping the man in a great bear hug.

"Did those Scots bastards engage you in battle? Or did you find their wenches too tempting? I can think of no other reason for you to be gone this long."

"Guard your tongue. There's a lady present."

The man turned to study the slender figure who paused in the doorway. "By all the gods. Don't tell me you've brought home a bride."

"You know better, Richard. She's the Scotswoman whose marriage will be arranged by Elizabeth."

"Why is she here?"

"The queen has decided that since I brought her to England, she is my responsibility until she is wed."

"Your responsibility?" The man roared with laughter. "You mean the wench is your prisoner?" He turned to her. "Come closer, lass, into the light where I can better see you."

She tossed her head in annoyance. She cared not for this rude man who did not even bother to rise in her presence.

"Brenna MacAlpin," Morgan said softly, "I would have you meet my brother, Lord Richard Grey."

Brother? Aye. She could see the similarity in their eyes, and in the way their mouths were touched with the same roguish smile.

The man extended his hand and she offered hers. As he lifted her hand to his lips, her glance slid to the fur throw that covered his lap. The blanket had slipped, revealing his withered limbs.

She felt a twist of remorse at the unkind thoughts she had entertained. This handsome man, Morgan's brother, did not rise to greet her because he was confined to the chair.

Chapter Twelve

"Lord Grey."

"Richard," he corrected in his booming voice. "Else we'll never know which Lord Grey you're addressing." He studied her. "You're a pretty thing. So you've come to England to be wed."

"To be bartered," she said quickly. "For the cause of peace."

"Ah." His eyes crinkled. "Life is unfair, isn't it, lass? Some men give their lives on the battlefield for peace. You must give up your freedom. And I..." He patted the robe on his lap. "All I had to offer were my legs."

She prayed that her shock was not visible in her eyes. "How, my lord?"

"A cart crushed them as I lay wounded on a Norwich battlefield. Now they wither from lack of use. But it is a small price to pay to put down a rebellion."

"Small price? You are not bitter?"

"Aye. At times I burn with the unfairness of it all. But I've learned that bitterness is a painful boil on the soul, lass. If allowed to fester it will sap all the joy from life. Better to lance it, no matter how painful, and allow the healing to begin. A bit of wisdom I've tried to pass on to my brother," he added with a wry laugh, "to no avail."

His eyes crinkled as he looked up at Morgan. "Mistress Leems has had the servants running about like sheep preparing a feast for your return. She knows how you like to eat."

"Good. We have had little to eat this day. I was impatient to be home."

"How does Greystone Abbey look to you?"

Morgan met his brother's smile. "As always, I am glad to be back in this peaceful place. I miss it when I am gone too long."

"Aye. I recall the feeling."

For a moment both men grew silent. Then Morgan pressed a hand to his brother's shoulder. "We will talk soon." He walked to the door. "If you will follow me, my lady, I will show you to your rooms."

As Brenna followed him from the room, she was aware of Richard's dark gaze following her.

"Hurry back, lass. It's been a long time since Greystone Abbey was graced with such beauty."

She shot him a quick smile before following his brother.

"How much older is Richard than you, my lord?" she asked as she climbed the stairs beside Morgan.

"He is younger by a year."

"Younger. But his hair is streaked with gray."

"He lived hard and fast. Thank the Lord," he added. "For now his whole world consists of that chair and that window."

She thought of the man beside her, and his reputation as a warrior and a scoundrel. Was that what drove him? The fear that at any moment it could all be taken from him in a single battle?

"I hope you will be comfortable here," he said, showing Brenna to a suite of rooms on the second floor.

She glanced around at the dark stone walls hung with rich tapestries. The floors were thickly carpeted. The furniture was ornate and comfortable.

Outside the balcony window, the green hills were dotted with flocks of sheep and cattle.

Everywhere there were signs of Morgan's great wealth. Yet the man did not seem affected by it. The people in his village had greeted him like a friend rather than the lord of the manor.

Brenna crossed to the sleeping chamber. A servant looked up from the wardrobe, where she was hanging Brenna's traveling cloak.

"I am certain I will be most comfortable, my lord."

She continued to the balcony and glanced down. He saw the flash of disappointment in her eyes as she spotted the guards below her window.

"In case you have any thought of leaving, my lady," he said, crossing to another door, "be warned." He threw open the door and she could see his crimson cape on the bed. "My rooms are beside yours. And I will permit no lock between them."

A serving girl, bearing a pitcher of water, paused outside the door.

"Refresh yourself," Morgan said abruptly. "Mistress Leems will summon you for a midday meal soon."

Brenna sat in front of the looking glass while the serving girl arranged her coal-black hair in a cascade of soft curls entwined with ivory ribbons. The shirred bodice of the morning gown enhanced her high, firm breasts. The long sleeves, inset with beaded silk roses, were tight from wrist to elbow, then billowed to the shoulder. The voluminous skirt fell from a narrow waist. Beneath the hem could be seen pale kid slippers. The effect was stunning.

"You look lovely, my lady." The servant stood back to examine her handiwork.

"Thank you, Rosamunde. How long have you served Lord Grey?"

"Since I was a babe, my lady." She smiled shyly. "My mother began as a scullery maid in the queen's own palace when she was but nine years."

"Is it not rare for the child of a scullery maid to become a personal maid in a fine home such as this?"

"Aye. When my mother was ten and five she showed a kindness to the young Princess Elizabeth, who was being held in the Tower."

"The Tower? The queen was a prisoner in her own land?" When the girl nodded, Brenna realized that her knowledge of the woman who sat upon England's throne was vague. "Why was the princess in the Tower?"

"Her half-sister, Mary, suspected that Elizabeth plotted against her. The young princess spent two months in the Tower until the queen was persuaded that the charges were false."

"How did your mother help Elizabeth?"

"She managed to bring her hot food and a warm blanket, which my Lord Grey supplied to her," the girl said proudly. "'Twas cold and damp in the Tower. And the prisoner, though of royal blood, was treated badly. My Lord Grey warned my mother that if she were caught, she would be put to death. But she risked her life rather than see the princess suffer. When she became queen, Her Majesty rewarded my mother by making her one of her personal maids. I also worked in the palace until I was old enough to come here to Greystone Abbey. My life is much changed because of my mother's kindness those many years ago."

Brenna tried to imagine the proud Elizabeth, haughty queen of England, as a humble prisoner in the Tower of London. The thought caused her to shiver. A sudden thought intruded. The queen would be able to recall those terrible feelings of helplessness, and perhaps sympathize with one who suffered such a fate. Brenna felt her hopes rise. Could it be that in the queen, Brenna had found an ally?

Seeing her thoughtful expression, the young servant looked concerned. "Is there something I have forgotten to do for you, my lady?"

Brenna shook her head. "Nay. But I am grateful. It would seem that you have inherited your mother's kind and generous spirit."

"Thank you, my lady. My Lord Grey wanted you to know that he would be below stairs with his brother."

"Thank you, Rosamunde." She stood, then hesitated. "Are you happy working for Lord Grey?"

"Oh, aye, my lady. He is a kind and generous man. The people of our village have always been treated fairly by Lord Grey."

With a thoughtful look Brenna lifted her skirts and made her way down the stairs. Though they made no sound, she knew that the guards followed her, as they followed her every move.

She followed the sound of masculine voices and paused in the doorway of a room whose shelves were lined with books. A cheery fire blazed in the fireplace. A desk, piled with ledgers, dominated the center of the room. The two men, seated on either side of the fireplace, were engaged in quiet conversation.

"Norfolk covets the throne. As does the Scots queen, Mary. But of the two, I would suspect Norfolk, the queen's cousin. He has friends in high places."

"Then you truly believe there is a plot?"

Morgan let out a long sigh. "I know not. But I do not believe in coincidences."

Both men looked up when they noticed Brenna in the doorway.

"Come in, my lady," Richard called.

"I do not wish to disturb you."

"Nonsense. Come in. Will you have a glass of ale with us?"

Brenna could not help but smile at his friendliness and compare it with the wall that seemed to exist between herself and his brother. "Aye, my lord."

Morgan filled a goblet and handed it to her. When their fingers brushed, she looked down quickly, avoiding his eyes.

"Has the queen set a date for your betrothal?" Richard asked.

"Nay. She said only that she wished me wed as soon as a nobleman speaks for me. She wants me off her hands. As does your brother."

"He does, does he?" Richard glanced at his brother's closed look, then turned back to Brenna. "Seeing you, I believe there will be many men seeking your hand, my lady."

"I pray you are wrong, my lord."

"Richard," he corrected.

"Aye. Richard. For I am in no hurry to be an Englishman's bride."

He grinned at her. "Would it be that bad?"

"Aye."

At her vehement response he laughed all the louder.

The housekeeper peered around the corner. "Your midday meal is ready, my lords."

"Thank you, Mistress Leems." Morgan set down his tankard and pushed his brother's chair. It began to roll across the floor.

Brenna was amazed at the cleverness of it. "A chair on wheels!"

"Aye. Morgan devised it. A carriage maker assisted him. Without it, I would be forced to stay in one room. I fear I am too heavy to carry like a baby, even for one as strong as Morgan."

"Then I'd bounce you on your head a time or two, just to keep your wits about you."

The two men enjoyed the joke. Brenna found herself relishing the sound of their laughter as she followed them to the refectory, where the housekeeper oversaw the meal.

This room, like the other rooms in the castle, had walls of dark stone. A log smoked on the hearth, emitting a cloud that filled the room. Servants milled about in disorderly confusion.

There were trays of mutton and partridge, and a thick gruel, as well as ale and mead.

Morgan's soldiers trooped into the room and immediately began eating. As soon as Brenna was seated, Morgan and Richard tore into their food. The brothers, Brenna realized, had matching appetites. They took no time for conversation as they ate lustily, then washed each mouthful down with ale. By the time they were finished, there was no food left on the trays. And the housekeeper was beaming with pride.

"Will you have more, my lord?"

"Nay, Mistress Leems. That was sufficient." Morgan rewarded her with a warm smile. "I have missed your cooking, Mistress Leems. Now I am truly home."

The plump woman beamed at his compliment, then nodded to the servants, who began gathering up the platters and refilling goblets with ale and mead.

Brenna toyed with the food on her plate.

"Is there something wrong, my lady?" Richard asked.

"The lady has little appetite." Morgan drained his tankard.

"Anyone who cannot eat Mistress Leems's gruel must be unwell. Are you unwell, my lady?"

"Nay. It is as your brother says, my lor—Richard. I have little appetite for English food." Or English manners, she thought, if the truth be told.

"I would have more ale." Richard held his tankard.

Before a servant could reach for the decanter, Brenna lifted it and poured.

From across the table, Morgan watched with interest. He was touched by Brenna's attention to his brother.

Richard gave her a warm smile and leaned back. Now that he had eaten his fill, he desired pleasant conversation. For too long he'd been starved for company. Now he had not only his brother, but this lovely lady as well.

"Morgan tells me you are leader of a warrior clan, my lady."

"We are a peace-loving people. But when pushed to fight, we show skill with our weapons."

"I have had occasion to taste the Scotswoman's skill," Morgan muttered.

Richard grinned at Brenna. "My brother showed me his wound. Though not mortal, it was most ably inflicted. Well done, my lady." He turned to Morgan. "I imagine you do not display your battle scars with much pride."

Seeing the flush on Brenna's cheeks, Morgan grinned, enjoying his brother's teasing humor. "Aye. 'Twould not sit well if my men thought I could be bested by this mere slip of a female."

Brenna's eyes flashed. But with great effort, she managed to hold her silence.

"It would be most distressing to face a woman in battle," Richard mused.

"Aye. You would not know whether to disarm her or charm her."

Brenna flushed, thinking of her scuffles with the man who sat smiling at his brother. Finding her voice she asked the question that had long perplexed her. "How is it that you and Morgan chose to be soldiers, Richard? Men of wealth do not usually seek such a life."

"Our father, Lord Matthew Grey, was King Henry's chief council. We grew up at court, a part of the wealthy, privileged few who were fortunate enough to live among royalty."

That would explain why Morgan was so comfortable with the queen. And why he was unaffected by the pomp and ceremony that surrounded the throne.

"But why the harsh life of a soldier?"

"Morgan and I formed a pact when we were young." Richard idly watched as Morgan's men began parading from the refectory. A part of him yearned to be with them, to seek their latest adventure. But he had made his peace with his life. Another part of him enjoyed the luxury of unhurried conversation with this lovely lady. She was not like so many of them he had come to know at court. She seemed truly interested in those around her. She showed a shrewd mind.

And she seemed completely unaware that she was a beautiful, desirable woman. A beguiling combination. Brains and beauty.

"When Elizabeth ascended the throne, Morgan and I agreed to be in service to our queen. She was more than our monarch—she was friend and sister to us. But do not think us too noble." His eyes twinkled with merriment. "Both Morgan and I have enjoyed our lives of adventure. We would have withered at court, with nothing more challenging than an occasional wager on who would be the latest to seek the queen's hand in marriage."

"Are there many?"

"Who seek to wed Elizabeth?" He laughed. "Aye. Philip of Spain, the Archduke Charles, the Earl of Arran. Arran has a claim to the Scottish throne, I believe." When Brenna nodded, he added, "Erick of Sweden, Sir William Pickering, the Earl of Arundel, Lord Robert Dudley. He is the leading contender at the moment. And, of course, Morgan."

So. It was as Brenna had suspected. She drew in a long breath and glanced at Morgan. "So many suitors."

"Elizabeth is ruler of the most powerful kingdom in the world."

"And still she has not wed."

"She is a lady after your own heart, Brenna MacAlpin. Elizabeth would choose her own destiny."

"Aye. I can understand that."

The door opened and the young servant, Rosamunde, entered. Behind her were two serving girls carrying an assortment of gowns and accessories.

"My lady," Rosamunde said gently. "My Lord Grey ordered Mistress Leems to find you some clothes. She hopes you will approve of these until something better can be made by the seamstress."

"Thank you for such kindness, my lord." Brenna shot Richard a look of gratitude and was surprised when he said dryly, "You thank the wrong Lord Grey. 'Twas my brother, Morgan, who thought of your wardrobe."

She blushed clear to her toes. "Thank you, my lord."

Morgan's lips twitched, but he held the smile at bay. "You are most welcome, my lady."

Brenna stood on the balcony and studied the hills in the distance. How far to the Scottish border? If she were to slip away under cover of darkness, could she evade the soldiers who would most certainly come after her? Would she perhaps find a peasant who would take pity on her and offer her a safe haven? Or would the queen put a price on her head, making her capture all the more challenging?

She turned to find Morgan standing in the doorway between their rooms, watching her intently.

"Plotting again, my lady?"

She flushed. Could the man read her mind?

"No matter." He strapped on his sword and scabbard, and Brenna realized he was dressed for travel. "My men have their orders. If you attempt to flee, they will subdue you in any manner necessary."

As he walked from the room she followed. "Do you think I fear death at the hands of your soldiers?"

He paused on the stair, then began his descent. With her hands on her hips she gave him a contemptuous look as she flounced by his side. "It is far more tempting to face an English sword than marriage to an English dog."

He turned on her, catching her by the upper arm and dragging her against his chest. He forced her back against the cold stone of the deserted hallway. His breath was hot against her cheek.

"You will hold your tongue, woman. I am sick to death of the sound of your voice."

His sudden temper caught them both by surprise. This irritating female had a way of bringing out the worst in him.

Brenna tossed her head, unwilling to let him see any show of weakness. "And I am sick to death of the sight of you, my Lord Grey." Her eyes flashed. "The obvious solution to both our problems is to release me and send me back to my people."

"I see there is only one way to still your voice."

Without warning he lowered his head and kissed her, hard and quick.

White-hot liquid poured through him. And though it burned him, he could not step back. He realized he hadn't thought it through, or he'd have never touched her. But now it was too late for that.

Brenna went very still, absorbing the shock that collided low and deep in the pit of her stomach.

The hands at her shoulders softened their grip, until his thumbs made lazy circles across her flesh. The kiss, too, gentled until it was the softest touch of mouth to mouth.

Even in this dim hallway, or in the inky blackness of midnight, she would know his lips, his touch, his taste. From that first time he had touched her, they had become imprinted firmly on her mind. With her eyes closed she could trace the outline of his lips, the shape of his fierce brow, the texture of his skin.

There was such strength in the hands that moved along her shoulders. They could snap her bones like the wings of a hummingbird. And yet they held her as gently as if she were a fragile flower.

Morgan realized it would be so easy to forget how small and delicate she was when her mouth was so eager and agile. Despite her innocence he could sense the simmering passion in her. And though the first ripples of desire stirred, he knew that she exerted great effort to keep them under control.

What would it be like to lie with her and coax that desire from her until it was stoked into full-blown passion? The urge rose in him. How he longed to watch that cool control slip until she moaned and writhed beneath him in helpless surrender.

He wanted her. Dear God. Each time he touched her he wanted her. All the denials in the world would not alter that simple fact. He wanted her as he had never wanted another woman.

He dropped his hand and took a step back.

Brenna took in a long, deep breath. Had he felt it? When they kissed, did he experience all these wild, tumultuous feelings that were so new and frightening to her? Or was she the only one who was so confused, so terrified by all that was happening between them?

She could read nothing in his dark, narrowed gaze.

At the strange sound of Richard's wheeled chair being rolled along the wooden floor, they both looked up.

"I am informed that your mount is ready," Richard said. "Will you return before dark?"

"Aye. In time to sup with you. Mayhaps you would see to the woman."

"'Twould be my pleasure."

Morgan turned to Brenna. "The guards have their orders. See that you do not push the limits of my brother's patience. Or you will answer to me."

As he strode away, Brenna stood beside Richard's chair and felt her heartbeat slowly begin to return to its natural rhythm. She was grateful for the dim candlelight in the hallway. In sunlight, she feared, her conflicting emotions would be there in her eyes for him to read.

Chapter Thirteen

"I must leave Richmond soon, Morgan, or go mad. The palace smells like a barnyard."

"It is not safe for you to travel, Majesty. There have been too many accidents."

"I will have you by my side." The queen gave Morgan her most persuasive smile. "What can go wrong when you are with me?"

"I cannot be two places at once. You want me to guard the Scotswoman, and you want me to keep you safe."

Elizabeth's temper flashed. "I wish to relieve this boredom. I must get away from Richmond."

He strode to the balcony and stared at the gentle, rolling countryside. Who could believe that an evil plot could be brewing in this tranquil setting?

He turned as a sudden thought struck. "Would you be willing to spend some time at Greystone Abbey now?"

The queen clapped her hands and got to her feet. "Oh, yes, Morgan. I've been hoping you would invite me. We could hunt. And have a splendid tea in your gardens. And a great feast..."

He held up his hand to stop her. "I had thought you would come alone."

"But I must have my servants. And a cook. You know I cannot abide Mistress Leems's cooking. And Madeline and Charles. And..."

She saw the look on his face and hesitated. "I will bring only those who are absolutely necessary to my comfort and happiness, Morgan. I promise you."

He gave an exasperated sigh. "As you wish, Majesty. I will make the necessary arrangements."

"I was just heading for the garden, my lady." Richard took pity on the young woman who spent most of her time locked away in her chambers while his brother rode each day to Richmond Palace. He had been quick to note the tension between these two. There was something between Brenna and Morgan. Something more than captor and captive. "Would you care to accompany me?"

"Aye." She moved along by his side while a servant pushed his chair.

The garden consisted of rows of hedges interspersed with formal plantings of roses. Stones had been set in the ground to form a walkway. Here and there in the garden were benches set beneath gnarled old trees. Like the house, the garden had a look of loving neglect, still clinging to a faded beauty of another time.

"Would you prefer the sun or the shade?" Brenna asked.

"The sun. It shines all too seldom to suit me."

"Aye." Brenna paused to inhale the fragrance of a drooping pink blossom. "Your roses need tending, my lord."

"Aye. As does everything at Greystone Abbey." Richard signaled for the servant to leave them. He idly plucked a rose and lifted it to his face. "How I used to love tending the roses. This garden was our mother's favorite. When she was alive, it rivaled even the queen's own. But since her death, there is no one to love it and care for it."

"A pity. 'Tis such a lovely, peaceful place."

"Aye. I suppose I could resume tending the flowers." He lifted his head to study the flight of a songbird. "If I but had wings."

Brenna studied him while he spoke. For a moment she saw in his eyes a fire. Then he blinked and it was gone.

He turned to look back at the house. "Greystone Abbey, too, has grown shabby from neglect. It lacks a woman's touch." He grew pensive for a moment. "Perhaps we all do."

"Tell me about your mother."

"She was the daughter of a Scottish nobleman."

"A Scot? Your mother was not English?"

"Nay." He chuckled at the look in her eyes. "Are you scandalized, lass?"

"Aye." She leaned forward, her eyes aglow, her features suddenly animated. "How was it that your father did not marry one of his own?"

"The Greys have ne'er held with tradition. While on a mission to Scotland for King Henry, my father beheld a lass who took his breath away. He inquired about her, and asked the king to arrange a meeting with her family. When they refused permission for my father to marry their daughter, he vowed he'd win her anyway. In the dark of the night he climbed to her balcony and spent the night persuading her to love him. By morning they had lain together. And her father, knowing that his daughter had been sullied by the English savage and was thus no longer desirable to the Scottish lairds, reluctantly permitted their marriage."

Brenna's eyes were wide. "Did your mother live to regret her hasty decision?"

"Regret? Nay, lass. I have never known two happier people than my father and mother. Until the day death separated them, they were deeply in love."

"How did your father's English family accept his bride?"

"As I told you, the Greys do not follow tradition. My father's mother was from Wales. And my father's brother married an Irishwoman." Richard saw the look on Brenna's face and said softly, "As my grandfather used to say with a twinkle in his eye, 'The Grey family speaks in many dialects, but the heart understands them all.'"

Brenna bowed her head and studied her clasped hands, digesting all that he had told her. Was it not true of her own family as well? She had been horrified to learn that her beloved sister, Meredith, had given her heart to a Highland barbarian. But there was no denying the love between them.

"Come, lass. Let me show you the rest of the garden."

With Brenna pushing his chair, Richard pointed out the trees he and Morgan had planted as lads, and the fountain, now broken, where they had splashed away many a summer's day.

"Morgan was always like a young bull, storming into every fray with his fists raised, his blood hot for battle. And as often as not he'd end up with his nose bloodied and his eyes blackened. But he never learned. The next day he'd be back, ready to do battle again."

She couldn't help but laugh at Richard's amusing stories, and found it oddly appealing to think of Morgan Grey as a young boy. Appealing and quite touching.

"Greystone Abbey must hold many happy memories for you," she said as they moved toward the courtyard.

"Aye. It was here that I came after my—" he studied the robe that covered his legs "—accident. London was too busy. I felt lost there. There was no place for a cripple who could no longer fight in battle."

Brenna saw the pain in his eyes and without thinking dropped to her knees and clasped his hand in hers. "Please my lord—Richard—do not speak so cruelly of your affliction."

"Cripple? Does the word offend you?" He touched a hand to her hair and with a gentle smile lifted her palm to his lips. "It no longer matters, lass. I know what I am. I accept the fact that I cannot do the things I once did. Here I have found peace. Greystone Abbey has always been a soothing balm for my family."

For some of his family, perhaps. As Brenna smoothed down her skirts and directed Richard's chair through the entrance, she thought of the other Lord Grey, tense, angry, concerned for the queen's safety. He had spent the past week traveling constantly between his home and the queen's palace at Richmond.

Though she told herself that she dreaded their next confrontation, she found herself listening for the sound of his horse's hooves. When at last he returned, she felt her heart begin to race.

Could it be that she was actually beginning to enjoy her verbal duels with this Englishman? There could be no other logical reason she would look forward to the return each day of Morgan Grey.

"I will wear this gown to sup, Rosamunde." Brenna pointed to a delicate lavender gown of satin, with bodice and sleeves encrusted with pearls.

"It is beautiful, my lady." With a minimum of words Rosamunde set about ordering one serving girl to prepare a bath while the other set out the gown and layers of petticoats. There were stockings, matching kid slippers and even pearl-encrusted ribbons for her hair.

"How do you magically come up with these beautiful clothes, Rosamunde? In the weeks I have been here, you have surprised me with a new gown each day."

The girl put a hand to her mouth and gave a shy laugh. "There is no magic. My lord Grey has instructed the seamstresses to provide whatever you request."

"Which Lord Grey? Richard or Morgan?"

"Lord Morgan Grey, my lady."

Again Brenna felt the familiar ripple of pleasure at the maid's words and wondered about it. Why should a simple kindness from Morgan cause her such joy?

"And since you are too much of a lady to ask for anything," Rosamunde continued, "I do it for you."

Brenna laughed. "I have no need of all these clothes. A simple morning gown is enough."

"My lady, you spend far too much time lately overseeing the scullery and kitchen, and not nearly enough time worrying about your wardrobe. A fine lady should not bother with such mundane things as the household supplies. Soon you will be the wife of a wealthy nobleman, and you will no longer need to concern yourself with Greystone Abbey."

Her words caused a surprising ache in Brenna. She forced herself to hide the pain. Why should she care about this faded old manor and the people who dwelled here? Were they not, after all, hated English?

"I have seen the fine work Mistress Leems does. But she is overburdened in the refectory and seems glad of my assistance."

"Aye, Mistress Leems has told everyone of your gracious help."

Brenna brushed aside her compliment. "I welcome the opportunity to have something to do. It passes the time."

Rosamunde tied the last ribbon in Brenna's hair, then gave a nod of satisfaction. Shooing the other servants from the room, she scooped up Brenna's discarded clothing and prepared to take her leave.

Touching her arm, Brenna stopped her. "Since leaving Scotland I have thought often about my old nurse, Morna, who has been with me for a lifetime. Despite failing eyesight and gnarled old hands, she is truly a treasure. As, it seems, are you."

For a moment the servant seemed overcome. In all the years that she had been in service, she had never before been thanked for her work. The wealthy were accustomed to pampering. They took it for granted that it was their due.

"I would be your friend as well, my lady," she murmured.

"I am most grateful. I can use a friend."

Both women looked up at the sound of footsteps. Rosamunde opened the door, then bowed her way from the room. Morgan stood in the doorway, his gaze fastened on the vision before him in lavender satin.

"It would seem that the seamstresses from the village have earned their pay."

She felt the warmth rush to her cheeks at his compliment. "You are too generous." Brenna crossed the room and accepted his outstretched hand. She steeled herself for the jolt that always came at his touch. "I have no need of such fine gowns."

"Since it is my fault that you have no wardrobe, it is my responsibility to provide one that befits my guest."

He placed a hand over hers and led her down the stairs. "Mistress Leems has been crowing about your skill with the household. She says it is at your direction that the heavy draperies at the windows have been taken down, thus allowing the sunlight to touch even the darkest corners of this old house."

"I hope you do not mind. I thought perhaps Richard could see more clearly with the windows free of clutter. He spends so much time there looking at the world outside these walls."

"I am most grateful, my lady."

Morgan studied the gleaming hallway floors as they made their way to the refectory. Inside, the darkened walls had been scrubbed until they shone. The scarred wooden tables were freshly polished. The dark draperies had been removed, allowing sunlight to play over the spotless marble floors. The chimneys had been swept, allowing the smoke to escape instead of filling the room. Everywhere he looked, it was as if Greystone Abbey had awakened from a deep slumber. The servants whispered about the lady who worked alongside them, polishing everything until it gleamed. She would be considered a harsh taskmaster, except for the fact that she did not order anything done that she would not do herself.

"Did you oversee your home in Scotland with such care, my lady?"

"Aye." She felt a fleeting pang at the thought of her home. "My sisters, alas, detested woman's work, preferring to practice the use of weapons with our father's men."

"I seem to recall that you showed no lack of skill with a knife, my lady." He touched a hand to the scar at his chest, causing Brenna to blush.

"Aye. And given a sword I could best many of your soldiers, my lord. 'Twas as much a part of our training as baking bread or sewing a fine seam."

"Beware, brother. A potent combination." Richard, seated in his chair at the table, looked up at their arrival. "A woman who can cook, sew and wield a sword. Your chances for betrothal grow more numerous with each passing day, my lady."

Brenna felt the heat on her cheeks and ducked her head, missing the scowl on Morgan's face. But it was not lost on his brother. So. Morgan was not as eager for the lady to be taken off his hands as he claimed. Richard decided to pay a little more attention to Morgan and Brenna while they supped. He enjoyed nothing as much as a chance to tweak his obstinate brother's nose.

When Morgan's men were seated the servants entered the dining hall bearing steaming trays of venison, pheasant and partridge, as well as baskets of bread warm from the ovens.

Richard and Morgan filled their plates, then began to eat in their usual lusty manner. Brenna picked at her food and watched as the men devoured everything and signaled to the servants for more.

"What have you done to this venison?" Morgan asked the housekeeper.

"I prepared it a new way, my lord. Do you disapprove?"

"Nay. It is the best you've ever made, Mistress Leems."

The housekeeper cast a shy glance at Brenna. "The Lady Brenna told me how her family prepared venison in Scotland. I thought I would try it."

Morgan glanced at the woman beside him, then continued eating.

"Even the bread tastes different. Better," Richard added, taking a mouthful.

"The Lady Brenna showed the cooks how to make scones and clotted cream."

Richard reached for several more before dismissing the servant.

"What is this?" Richard asked.

"Brandied pudding." Mistress Leems watched as he savored the new treat. "Do you like it, my lord?"

"Very tasty." When he had eaten every bite, he called the servant over for more. "Why have you never made this before, Mistress Leems?"

The housekeeper stifled a smile. "I had not the recipe, my lord, until the Lady Brenna told me about it."

"You had a hand in this as well, lass?" Richard turned to Brenna.

"Aye. 'Twas my father's favorite."

"I can see why." Richard filled his plate, then watched as Morgan helped himself to more.

"Lass," Richard said between bites, "is there anything you cannot do well?"

She could not contain the smile that split her lips and touched her eyes. "I am pleased that you enjoyed your meal, Richard."

"What about you, Morgan?" Richard stared across the table at his brother. "You seem to have put away an inordinate amount of food."

"Aye." Morgan turned to the woman beside him. "I do not remember when I have enjoyed a meal more."

A warm glow enveloped Brenna as she left the refectory. Beside her Morgan pushed his brother's chair. She could not fathom why she had begun to care what this Englishman thought. But if she would be honest with herself, she had to admit that she'd been holding her breath throughout the meal in hopes that he would not be angry at the changes she had suggested.

Morgan paused outside the door to the library. "Do you wish to retire to your room?"

"I am not at all weary, my lord."

"Then perhaps you will stay with us a while."

"Thank you." She followed them inside the cheery, book-filled room.

A servant entered bearing a tray containing a decanter and goblets.

Brenna paused beside a chess set and ran her fingers along the ornately carved pieces.

"Do you play, my lady?"

"My father was an avid player. It was a rare treat when one of my sisters or I managed to beat his strategy."

"Then I challenge you," Richard said.

With a laugh Brenna took a seat across from him and made the first move. Within minutes they were caught up in the game.

Across the room Morgan poured himself a goblet of wine and studied the woman whose dark hair glowed in the light of the fire. She frowned over the chess piece in her hand, then made her move. Richard burst into gales of laughter at her mistake and snatched up her piece. After a moment's hesitation, she joined him in laughter until the two of them were wiping tears of laughter from their eyes.

"You take advantage of the fact that I have not played this game in many years."

"It is like holding a sword, lass. You never forget."

"Aye. It will come back to me. And when it does, I will best you."

"Of that I have no doubt. Your move, lass."

Brenna bent over the board and studied the pieces, then made another move. This time Richard's brow arched as he shot her a look of admiration.

"I see that it is all coming back to you, lass."

"Aye." She watched as he made his move, then countered.

After only four more moves, Richard realized that they were hopelessly deadlocked. With a little bow he grinned. "Are you certain you have not played this game in years, lass?"

"Well, I may have played a few times with my sisters."

"Ah. And you simply forgot to mention that fact."

She shrugged, avoiding his eyes. "I may have forgotten."

Richard threw back his head and roared. "You are devious, lass. Like a soldier on a battlefield. You deliberately caused me to relax my guard so you could learn my strategy."

She smiled at him across the table. "Aye, but no matter. 'Tis only a game."

"Nay. For a soldier who can no longer go to battle, it is more than a game. It is a challenge of skill. To beat me, you must think like a soldier."

"Aye." She studied the man across the chessboard. "When next I challenge you, Richard, I will beat you."

"I look forward to our duel, lass." He looked up at his brother, who stood beside the fireplace, his hand resting on the mantel. "Bring me a goblet, Morgan, and let me celebrate the fact that I have finally found someone who will force me to work at this game. Unlike," he added with a wink to Brenna, "most of those who challenge me in this place."

With a smile Morgan filled two goblets and handed them to Richard and Brenna. It pleased him to see his brother so animated. How ironic that it should be this reluctant Scotswoman who should bring such changes to Greystone Abbey and its inhabitants.

As Morgan handed his brother a goblet he grinned. "You only beat me because I allow it."

"You have not beaten me at chess in over a year. I only challenge you to keep my hand in the game."

As Morgan filled his goblet, Brenna studied the flames of the fire. Except for the hiss and snap of the logs, there was no sound to break the stillness.

"There is such peace here," Brenna said to Richard. "I can understand why you wanted to be here."

"It was not peace I sought. 'Twas sanctuary from the cruel stares, the helplessness I felt."

She heard the pain in his words and grew silent. But with effort, Richard pulled himself out of his dark thoughts. "Is there such a place in your land, lass?"

She shook her head. "If only there could be such peace for my people. It is my most fervent wish for them. Alas, my poor land has been besieged for generations. There is no safe refuge for my clan."

"If you accede to Elizabeth's wishes, there can be peace between our people." Morgan's tone was abrupt. "Is marriage to an Englishman such a terrible price to pay?"

Brenna went very still. Hadn't the same question been troubling her for days now? Yet, if the thought of sacrificing herself was repugnant, the thought of sacrificing her sister was too painful to contemplate.

"I believe I could endure anything for the sake of my people. If your queen would agree that my marriage would seal a bond of peace, I would accede to her wishes. But I will not allow Megan to be part of the grand design."

"Megan?" Richard was suddenly alert.

"My younger sister. She escaped into the Highlands before I was captured."

Richard looked impressed. "She eluded your men, Morgan?"

"Aye. At her sister's coaching she made it to the safety of the forest, where she was swallowed up. But there was no need to go after her. The Lady Brenna was our prize."

Prize indeed. Richard stared at the woman who sipped her wine, then glanced at his brother, who watched her through narrowed eyes. He finished his wine and stifled a yawn.

"I would retire now, Morgan."

"So soon?"

"The Lady Brenna had me in the garden for hours today, supervising the planting of trees."

Morgan was suddenly alert. "You planted trees, my lady?"

Brenna flushed, knowing that she had overstepped her bounds. "Forgive me, my lord. But several of the trees were beyond saving. And I thought..." Her cheeks grew several shades darker. "I had no right."

"If Richard approved of them, you had every right." He turned to his brother. "Where are the trees planted?"

"Near our old fountain. They shade our mother's old rose garden."

Morgan felt both a flush of pleasure and a trace of annoyance. "I will see these trees on the morrow."

Stepping behind his brother's chair, he began to push it toward the doorway. A waiting servant took the chair when they had bid good-night.

"Come, my lady," Morgan said abruptly. "I will see you to your room."

As they climbed the stairs Morgan said casually, "I have invited the queen to Greystone Abbey for a hunt. She will be bringing Madeline and Charles along. I thought you might like to see them."

Brenna's smile was quick. "Aye, my lord."

"Then I shall invite them to stay on for several days if you would like."

"Thank you." At the door to her room Brenna paused. "When will they be here?"

"As quickly as it can be arranged."

Brenna felt her spirits soar. She would not feel nearly so alone with Madeline here.

"Thank you, my lord."

He startled her by touching a hand to her cheek. "If I had but known that Madeline's visit would bring such a bloom to your cheeks, I would have invited her here days ago."

The rush of heat was so swift she felt suddenly light-headed. For long minutes he stared down into her eyes, and she sensed that he was going to kiss her.

For a moment her heart forgot to beat. She waited, anticipating the touch of his mouth to hers.

Morgan paused, toying with the idea of brushing her lips with his. A warning bell sounded in his mind. It was extremely dangerous to kiss this woman. Each time, he'd had to walk through fire to resist taking her.

He studied the soft, seductive lips, the invitation in her eyes, and stepped back, breaking contact. It was difficult enough to sleep, knowing the woman slept but a room away. If he were to kiss her, sleep would elude him for the entire night.

"Sleep well, my lady."

He dropped his hand and strode quickly away.

Chapter Fourteen

"Why is the deed not yet done?"

In the distance the misty turrets of Richmond Palace could be seen. Two shadowy figures stood in the woods just before sunrise, speaking with muted voices.

"I have tried."

"Aye. And failed."

"The queen is never alone. Since Morgan Grey's return to England, he is with her every day. She refuses to go anywhere without that savage at her side."

"Then eliminate him." The tone was tense, angry. "I do not pay you for excuses. The deed must be done soon, else I will lose favor with those who would obtain the throne. If you cannot see to it, I will find someone else willing to take the risk."

"You know it is not the risk I fear. I have already risked much. But we must be cautious and choose a time and place where there will be no witnesses to the deed."

"Do you have a plan?"

"Aye." The man gave a chilling smile. "The queen plans to leave for Greystone Abbey, Morgan Grey's manor house near Richmond. It is very secluded."

The other man rubbed his hands together. "The perfect time and place for an—accident. But," he asked with a sudden frown, "how do you know you will be included in the queen's plans?"

"Leave that to me."

"Beware. Our future, and the future of all England, depends upon this. You must be willing to kill anyone who gets in the way of our plan."

"I am aware of the urgency, old friend. Do not fear. And as for the killing . . ." The man's laugh sent a ripple of terror along his companion's spine. "I look forward to it."

The two men clasped hands before going their separate ways. Within minutes the mists had swallowed them up, leaving no trace of their meeting.

As the first rays of sunlight slanted through the windows, Brenna bounded from her bed, eager for the day.

How sweet the anticipation. Madeline d'Arbeville would accompany the queen this day. Her first friend in England. How she needed a friend to keep her from the homesickness that gnawed at her soul.

As Rosamunde helped her dress, she chided her mistress. "I have never seen you so animated, my lady."

"Aye. I am eager to see the Duchess of Eton once more. She was most kind to me at Richmond."

Rosamunde finished the last button on Brenna's gown, then lifted the brush to her hair. When she was finished she stepped back to survey the results.

"You look lovely, my lady."

"Thanks to you." Brenna lifted her skirts and turned, nearly colliding with Morgan, who was just entering her room.

Her startled eyes looked up into his as he brought his hands to her shoulders to steady her.

"I did not hear you, my lord." Why did her heart thunder so at his touch?

"Where are you off to in such a wild rush?"

"I must see to the guest rooms before Madeline arrives."

There was a note of amusement in his voice. "That is why we have servants, my lady."

"But I want everything to be perfect for our guests."

Our guests. Though Brenna seemed unaware of what she had said, Morgan felt oddly pleased by the term.

"Do you have time to break your fast, my lady? Or must you begin your work immediately?"

She flushed, realizing that she was the object of his teasing laughter. "I suppose I can spare a few minutes to eat, my lord."

"Mistress Leems promised me a fine meal." He offered his arm and felt the slight pressure of her hand. It was a most pleasant feeling that radiated from her touch. Pleasant but dangerous. Her skirts whispered as she moved along beside him. Soft. Seductive. He must remember that beneath the softness was a woman who would stop at nothing to return to her home. "Is this to be another of your recipes?"

Brenna glanced at him from beneath lowered lashes. "Would that please you?"

He shrugged, unwilling to admit his feelings. "A soldier learns to eat anything, so long as it fills his stomach."

She couldn't hold back the laughter that bubbled up within her. "Then I will ask Mistress Leems to cook you some of her gruel, my lord. That should fill your stomach and remind you of the battles you are missing."

A hint of laughter warmed his voice. "Bite your tongue before she hears you."

"Hears what?" Richard looked up from his place at the table as they entered.

"Your brother cares not for my fancy food. He cares only to satisfy his hunger."

"Then it is as I thought," Richard said with a frown. "Too many battles have left you daft." He watched as Morgan sat down beside Brenna. It was obvious that his brother was taking great pains not to touch her as he took his seat. But why? Could it be that Morgan was afraid to touch this little creature? Afraid of the feelings she stirred in him? The very thought made Richard stifle a laugh.

"A good meal is like a beautiful woman," he said with a satisfied smile. "Both are meant to be savored, to satisfy not only the hunger of the body, but of the soul as well."

Morgan felt a tremor as Richard's words touched a chord deep inside him. There had been many women in his life. And yet none had ever satisfied the hunger in his soul.

Choosing to ignore the knowing look on Richard's face, Morgan bellowed, "You may begin serving, Mistress Leems."

"Aye, my lord." The housekeeper directed the servants, who carried in trays of warm biscuits and steaming meats, as well as breads dripping with honey and fruit conserves.

The men at the tables fell silent as they relished their meal. When the others had finished, Morgan and Richard continued to eat until at last, replete, they sat back.

"My compliments, Mistress Leems." Richard lifted a bite of roll, dripping with fruit conserve, to his lips.

The housekeeper flushed with pleasure.

Morgan took a taste of the conserve. "Another of the Lady Brenna's suggestions?"

"Aye, my lord."

Richard studied the woman who sat quietly beside his brother. "I, for one, am grateful, my lady. I look forward to your next surprise."

Morgan glanced at her in time to see the smile that touched her lips. And though he said nothing, he could not deny the fact that he, too, was enjoying the subtle changes Brenna's presence had wrought at Greystone Abbey. Each day she seemed to reveal another surprise.

As they left the refectory Brenna said, "If you will excuse me, my lord, there is much to see to before Madeline arrives."

As she scurried off, with Mistress Leems and several servants in tow, Morgan stared after her until he became aware of Richard's scrutiny beside him.

"The lady seems in high spirits."

"Aye." Morgan frowned. "It is good that Madeline is coming for a visit. Brenna has been isolated for too long."

"Is that not precisely what the queen intended for your prisoner?"

Prisoner. Morgan was taken aback. He had begun to think of Brenna not as a prisoner but a guest. A most delightful guest, if the truth be told.

He warned himself not to be lulled into a false sense of security. The guards must continue to maintain their vigil. Else the lady would snatch the first opportunity to escape.

Morgan stood by his desk and watched as Brenna moved slowly through the rose garden, snipping a bouquet of flowers. Two guards, their swords at the ready, trailed discreetly behind her.

The ledgers he had been working on were forgotten as he leaned a hip against the sill and studied her. Sunlight filtered through the branches of the trees, dappling her with light and shadow. The breeze caught her hair, and it streamed out behind her like a silken veil. She lifted her head to watch the path of a hawk and he studied her in profile. Her brow was smooth, unwrinkled. Her nose was small and upturned. Her mouth was curved into a smile of pure delight.

Without a thought to what he was doing he tossed the papers on the desk and strode from the room. Moments later he was on the path leading to the garden.

She rounded a bend, her arms filled with colorful blossoms. He felt his throat go dry at the sight of her. God in heaven, she was so lovely, she took his breath away.

She hesitated in midstride. "Did you want something, my lord?"

Now that he was here, he had no idea what to say. He wanted nothing more than the opportunity to look at her, to be with her.

"I thought you might need help carrying those."

"Thank you, my lord." If she was surprised at his sudden act of kindness, she hid it well. When he held out his arms she filled them with flowers. In the process his hands encountered the softness of her breasts. She pulled back quickly, but not before he saw the sudden flush on her cheeks.

"What will you do with the flowers?" He watched as she bent to cut a perfect rose. His fingers still tingled from that brief encounter with her soft flesh.

"I will fill the guest chambers with them." She buried her face in a mass of blooms, then cut them and added them to the bouquet in his arms. "Their fragrance will perfume the air."

He breathed in the sweet, rich aroma and was reminded of her. "But within a few days they will fade and die."

"Then," she murmured, pausing to snip another bloom, "I will dry the petals and use them to line chests and wardrobes, my lord. And their fragrance will live on as a reminder of this lovely summer day."

He watched her as she moved through the garden like a beautiful butterfly. He would need no reminder of this day. He needed only to close his eyes. Though he told himself that she was nothing more than a pawn in a political game, he could not deny the fact that her image was already becoming indelibly imprinted on his heart.

"Carriages arrive, my lady."

Brenna finished arranging the last of the flowers, then hurried down to the courtyard where Morgan was already waiting.

As the carriages halted there was a flurry of activity. Trunks were unlashed from the backs of the rigs. Cloaks were handed down to the servants who had accompanied the queen and her party.

"Ah, Morgan," the queen said as she stepped from her carriage. "Always, coming to Greystone Abbey is like coming home."

He caught her hand and led her past the servants who had lined up to greet their queen. She smiled and offered a few words to each one.

Brenna noted the affection between these people and their monarch. They were deeply moved by her simple act of kindness.

Nearly a dozen ladies emerged from carriages, as well as the titled gentlemen who were at court in Richmond.

"Cherie." Madeline stepped from the carriage and flew into Brenna's arms. After a quick hug she held Brenna a little away from her and studied her with a critical eye. "I have long wanted to visit this private retreat, which Morgan so jealously guards. How are you bearing the loneliness of this place?"

"I am fine, as you can see."

It was true that there was a bloom on Brenna's cheeks that had not been there at the queen's palace in Richmond.

Madeline arched an eyebrow, then turned to Morgan. "And you, *mon cher.*" She kissed his cheek. "Have the two of you declared a truce?"

"At least while you are here."

"Beware, old friend," Charles said with a laugh, "or my wife may extend her visit for weeks just to assure peace between her two friends."

Morgan joined in the laughter.

As a second carriage opened, a handsome young man stepped down. He turned to assist a young woman. Madeline caught their hands and led them toward her host. "I have had a most pleasant surprise. My brother and sister have journeyed from Paris to be with me. The queen insisted that I bring them along."

"I am glad you brought them," Morgan assured her. "You would have broken Brenna's heart if you had canceled your visit."

Madeline wondered at his words. Could it be that Morgan Grey cared about the condition of his prisoner's heart?

Motioning them closer, Madeline smoothly handled the introductions. "Brenna MacAlpin. Morgan Grey. I would have you meet my brother, Cordell, and my little sister, Adrianna."

Cordell was a suave, self-assured young man with the same angular face and large almond eyes as Madeline. Sandy hair curled over the collar of his beautifully tailored tunic. In the brilliant sunlight his hair was touched with gold. He seemed aware that he cut a handsome figure. It was obvious that he enjoyed charming the ladies.

"My lady." He stared at Brenna a long moment, as if captivated by her beauty.

His admiration of the lady was not lost on Morgan, who stood to one side and watched the exchange. Jealousy was an alien feeling for Morgan. And yet he found himself battling just such an emotion now. Was it possible that he was experiencing jealousy of this callow youth? He cursed himself for such childish behavior and brushed aside his feelings.

Yet he remembered how Hamish MacPherson had fawned over Brenna at her home in Scotland. And how she had returned his interest.

Cordell bowed low over Brenna's hand and brushed his lips over her knuckles. When he lifted his head there was the slightest flush to his cheeks.

He turned to Morgan. "I suggested to my sister that our visit was inconvenient. We are, after all, foreigners in your land. But Madeline insisted that we accompany her. And now that I have met the Lady Brenna, I am most grateful for your hospitality."

"My home is open to my queen and all her company," Morgan said. But his voice lacked its usual warmth.

"Adrianna." Brenna took the younger woman's hand, sensing her unease at being among so many strangers. "How wonderful that you can visit with your sister. It will ease her loneliness in this land."

"Your speech is not English," Adrianna said softly.

"I am from Scotland."

Adrianna smiled shyly. "It greatly relieves my mind that I will not be the only foreign guest in this fine home."

"If you are Madeline's sister," Morgan said, bending gallantly over her hand, "you are more than a guest in my home. You are with friends."

"You are most kind." When she lifted her gaze to her stern host's face her cheeks had turned a becoming shade of pink.

Adrianna was small and slender, with hair more red than brown. It fell in long ringlets to her waist. She wore a gown of green satin that caught the green glints in her amber eyes. There was a sweetness about her that added to her artless beauty. "I am most grateful for your hospitality, my lord."

From the corner of his eye Morgan saw another figure emerge from one of the queen's carriages. Though he felt the anger surge through him, the only sign he gave was a slight narrowing of his eyes.

Lord Windham made a great ceremony of greeting Brenna. Lifting her hand to his lips, he grazed her flesh and pressed her fingers between his.

"You look lovely, my lady." His gaze raked her and Brenna felt a shiver of revulsion at his intimate look.

From the earliest days of his manhood, Windham had known how to play the parlor games that enticed the women at Court. This one, he told himself, was no different; merely more clever at masking her feelings.

"What a delight," Lord Windham said, turning to include the others. "Traveling with so many beautiful women has my blood eager for the hunt."

"Ah, but we will be hunting four-legged creatures," the queen said with a laugh.

"Perhaps so, Majesty. But I see no harm in adding a few other lovely creatures to the hunt. Do you, Grey?"

Morgan turned a cool look on Windham, then said to the queen, "If you will allow me, Majesty, I will escort you into my home."

Stung by Morgan's snub, Windham offered his arm to Brenna, who pretended not to notice. Instead she caught Madeline's hand and the two women followed Morgan and the queen through the open portal.

Brenna tried to shake off the trembles that went through her at the thought of Windham. Why had the queen brought him along?

"What a treat this will be, Brenna," Madeline whispered. "I have so longed for a visit to Morgan's home."

Madeline's sister and brother joined the ladies and the others who trailed the queen into the house. Charles strolled leisurely behind them, joined by a scowling Lord Windham, while Mistress Leems stayed behind, issuing orders to the servants to deal with the baggage.

When they entered the house, Lord Windham glanced about admiringly at the tapestries that adorned the walls. Beneath their feet a fine rug cushioned their steps.

"So this is Greystone Abbey. I wonder, since it is so beautiful, why Grey has refused to entertain guests in his manor house?"

A voice from across the room startled him. "Perhaps my brother did it to protect my privacy."

"Brother?" After the bright sunlight, the guests had to strain to see the figure seated before the fire.

"Aye." At a curt command a servant pushed the wheeled chair closer. The figure in the chair bowed his head to the queen. "Welcome, Majesty."

Elizabeth greeted her old friend, then turned to the others. "This is Lord Richard Grey, Morgan's brother."

Many in the crowd shifted uncomfortably. Several of the ladies turned their heads away, unwilling to be caught staring at the man who could not stand and bow before the queen.

A fierce sense of protection welled up inside Brenna. She hurried forward to stand beside Richard, placing her hand upon his shoulder in a proprietary manner.

Her reaction was not lost on Morgan, who stood in the doorway watching.

"Ah. I have often heard about Morgan's handsome brother," Madeline said quickly, to fill the sudden silence. "But I did not know you resided at Greystone Abbey. A pity to hide such good looks away from the world."

Richard gave her a warm smile, easily dismissing her compliment as an act of kindness by a gentle woman. "You are too kind, my lady."

As she offered her hand, Richard brought it to his lips.

Madeline lifted an arm to indicate the two who moved to stand beside her. "This is my brother, Cordell, and my sister, Adrianna."

Cordell and Richard exchanged greetings. When Richard took Adrianna's hand, he felt the jolt, sudden, unexpected. It had been a long time since he had felt that rush of sexual excitement. Taken by surprise, he studied the young woman for long moments.

There was about this French girl such youth, such innocence, he felt as if a stray sunbeam had suddenly found its way into the room.

As Richard held her hand he thought about the ease with which he had once charmed all women. There had been a time when women young and old had flocked around him, eager to be a part of his teasing manner, his roguish laughter. But that had been a lifetime ago, when he was whole and his future had been as bright as the morning star.

He reminded himself that that part of his life was over. Any chance he had with women was as dead as the lifeless limbs that could no longer support his weight. He would not be the object of a lady's pitying glances.

With studied casualness he lifted Adrianna's hand to his lips. "Welcome to Greystone Abbey, my lady." Summoning all his willpower he forced himself not to react to the flare of heat.

"Merci." From beneath a fringe of lashes the Frenchwoman watched him. At the mere brush of his lips over her hand she felt a little pulse flutter in the pit of her stomach. She chided herself for her foolishness. It was obvious that he had not felt anything.

Adrianna's cheeks, Brenna noted, were flushed when Richard released her hand. She studied the way the two looked at each other when they thought no one was looking. "You will wish to refresh yourselves after your journey," Morgan said. "We will show you to your chambers."

He offered his arm and the queen placed her hand upon it, moving by his side.

Madeline linked her arm through Brenna's. Together they climbed the stairs to the guest chambers. The others followed, while Richard stayed behind, staring after them.

An entire wing of the house on the second and third floors had been prepared for the guests. The finest rugs had been aired and positioned on the floor of the sitting chamber. Several chaises, covered in softest velvet, flanked the fireplace. A fire crackled on the grate. Masses of flowers stood in vases on the mantel as well as on several tables around the room. Their fragrance perfumed the air.

"Mon cher." Madeline turned a smiling face toward Morgan. "Your home is so beautiful. And your hospitality overwhelms me."

"Greystone Abbey is lovely," the queen murmured. "But never have I seen the rooms so fresh, or so tastefully arranged."

"Brenna is the one who drove the servants unmercifully until Greystone Abbey was suitable for royalty."

Brenna flushed with pleasure. To cover her embarrassment she said, "Perhaps you would like to see your sleeping chambers, Majesty."

A fire crackled invitingly in the sleeping chambers on either side of the sitting chamber. The massive beds were swathed in delicate linen draperies that offered warmth as well as privacy. Thick, ornate rugs covered every inch of floor. Tall vases of roses stood on either side of the fireplace. The air was sweet with their perfume.

"There is ample room for all of your servants," Brenna said, indicating several doors that led to smaller servants' chambers.

The queen gazed around, then fixed Brenna with a look. "I am impressed."

Brenna flushed with pleasure. It would take much to impress a queen who was accustomed to only the best.

Lord Windham remarked dryly, "Perhaps we should all petition you, Majesty, for a prisoner such as this one. My home could use the lady's touch, as well."

Feeling all the attention focused on her, Brenna's cheeks burned. It was Morgan who came to her rescue.

"When you have refreshed yourselves," he said, "we will await you in the great room below."

As he and Brenna walked down the hall he noted the flush on her cheeks. His tone was tender. "Your work was not in vain, my lady. Everyone was overwhelmed by your care."

He offered his arm as they descended the stairs. When she placed her hand on his sleeve, he steeled himself for the jolt that always came at her simplest touch.

"I am glad, for Madeline's sake. I wanted her first visit to be perfect."

He savored the breathless quality of her voice. It was rare when they could speak to each other without rancor. "Did you always take such pains with your guests in your home in Scotland?"

Home. She felt the pain, swift, sharp. Would it always be so? "Aye. There were so many visitors. Our doors were open to all. I remember our home always filled with the sound of voices raised in laughter."

He opened the door to the great room and felt the press of her body as she moved past him. The fragrance of wild-flowers still clung to her hair and clothes. "I would like you to treat Greystone Abbey as your own home, my lady. For the next few days I pray that you can relax with Madeline and the others and enjoy this happy time."

"Shall I think of it as a reprieve, my lord?" She turned and he saw the way her eyes suddenly darkened, as she remembered who and what she was. "Before the queen sentences me to a lifetime of slavery?"

"Damn you, woman." Without thinking he caught her roughly by the arm. The moment he touched her, he realized his mistake. The heat that flowed between them was a shocking reminder that it was impossible to touch her and feel nothing.

His voice lowered to a hiss of anger. "Must everything with you be a contest of wills?" His grip tightened. "Can you not forget for a little while that you are Scots and I am English? Can we not simply be two people who enjoy the company of good friends?"

At her gasp of pain he realized that he was hurting her. Immediately his touch gentled, and he unwittingly ran his thumbs in circles over the bruised flesh of her upper arms.

She struggled to ignore the little fist that tightened deep inside her. Why did this man's touch have the power to affect her so? Why, even now, in the full heat of anger, did she react so violently to the nearness of him?

"Would you have me forget that I am your prisoner, my lord?"

Prisoner. Aye. One of them was a prisoner. But he was no longer certain which one. He stared down into her eyes and saw himself reflected there. The urge to kiss her was so strong he had to call on all of his willpower to resist.

"I will summon Mistress Leems. Our guests will need sustenance." As he turned away he was aware that his hand was none too steady. And the sweat on his brow had nothing to do with the heat of the fire. It was was caused by the damnably cool woman beside him.

Chapter Fifteen

Mistress Leems fluttered around the great room, seeing to the placement of the silver tea service and trays of cakes and scones and clotted cream, as well as little pots of fruit conserve.

A fire crackled invitingly in the fireplace. Though it was still early afternoon, candles burned in sconces along the walls, adding a soft glow to the room.

When they had removed the dust of their journey, the guests began descending the staircase in clusters of twos and threes. Soon the tinkle of fine crystal and the hum of conversation filled the great room.

All conversation ceased when the queen entered. Elizabeth was resplendent in a gown of scarlet satin shot with gold thread. Gold and silver had been worked into scrolls on the sleeves and bodice. A cap of gold and silver filigree set with precious stones nestled in her red hair. She wore a necklace made of dozens of rubies surrounded by diamonds, and matching diamond and ruby earrings.

Everyone in the room curtsied. A servant positioned an elegant, ermine-covered chair in front of the fireplace, beside Richard's. The queen sank down gratefully. Mistress Leems handed Lord Quigley a cup of tea and a plate of freshly baked scones. After he had tasted, he handed them to a servant, who offered them to the queen. With one taste, she arched an eyebrow in surprise.

"Your scones are the finest I have ever tasted, Mistress Leems. Please teach my cook how to make these fine biscuits."

The housekeeper beamed with pleasure.

"Ah." Elizabeth sighed in contentment, then turned to Richard. "I have yearned for the peace, the solitude of Greystone Abbey."

"Aye, Majesty. I know the feeling."

She glanced at him. "There are times I envy you, Richard."

Envy. He stifled a laugh.

"There are so many people tugging at me, wishing my ear. I am never alone, with time to collect my thoughts. Solitude is a luxury a monarch cannot afford."

"Perhaps, when your consort is chosen," Madeline said innocently, "your husband will lift some of the burden from your shoulders."

The queen's eyes flashed. "Husband. It does not seem fair that I should have no choice in the matter." Her gaze fastened on Brenna. "But then, as you have learned, life has never been fair to those of our sex, has it?"

Brenna's lips curved into a smile. "As a child I used to wonder what it would be like to be born queen of the land. Now I realize that life is life. Whether in a palace or a hovel, there is birth and death, love and hate, and obligations, no matter how distasteful, to be met."

"Then you are indeed wise for your age, Brenna Mac-Alpin." The queen gave her an odd little smile. "But I have always enjoyed a challenge." Elizabeth turned to Madeline. "It is good to have your sister and brother with you, is it not?"

Brenna glanced at Adrianna, who sat primly beside her brother, her eyes downcast. Every so often she glanced at the man in the wheeled chair. But each time he looked at her, she flushed and stared at the floor.

"Aye, Majesty. I miss them so much when we are apart. Ours is a large, happy family."

"Family." The queen spoke the word softly. "I have no family left. 'Twas my fondest wish that Edward could have lived."

Brenna detected the note of pain in Elizabeth's tone as she spoke the name of the young prince who had died of tuberculosis at the tender age of sixteen.

"I adored my half-brother. As you and Richard did, Morgan."

"Aye, Majesty." Morgan placed a hand over the queen's in a gesture of comfort and affection. "Richard and I taught him to ride. As we did you."

She chuckled. "You were very impatient teachers. You allowed me to fall on my royal—" She seemed to catch herself, remembering that there were strangers in the room. "I threatened to have you both whipped. Do you remember?"

Morgan and Richard burst into laughter. "Aye. We hid in the wine cellar for hours to escape your punishment. And by the time we finally crawled out, we were both too drunk to remember anything."

"You drank the royal wine?" The queen lifted an eyebrow in a haughty gesture, then dissolved into peals of laughter.

"What else could we do in the wine cellar? We had to wait until your royal temper cooled."

"Sometimes," the queen said, wiping tears of laughter from her eyes, "I am amazed that the two of you lived to manhood."

"Aye, Majesty. Sometimes we are amazed as well."

"Do you recall how I begged the two of you to become my ministers?"

"And we argued that we yearned for a life of adventure, away from the stifling rules of court."

"Aye." The queen looked fondly at her two friends.

Across the room Lord Windham watched with a look of fury. How he envied Morgan and Richard Grey their close friendship with the queen.

Brenna sipped her tea and nibbled a morsel of cake, and lost herself in thought. It was strange to picture Morgan as a lad. Even living among royalty, it would seem, he managed to be himself, a teasing, fun-loving rogue, and to discover adventure. She smiled. Aye, it was strange to imagine Morgan playing pranks with Richard and a very young Elizabeth.

She glanced at Richard. What must it be like to lose the ability to walk, run, fight? To a strong, virile man like Richard, it must be a nightmare from which he never woke. And yet, he seemed less affected by it than his brother.

She saw the way Richard's gaze followed the young French woman. And she noted the lingering looks the girl gave Richard when she thought he was not looking. There was no pity in Adrianna's eyes; only admiration for the handsome rogue who sat beside the queen.

Brenna realized for the first time since her arrival in England, she felt completely relaxed. Was it, she asked herself, because the queen had gone out of her way to be kind? Or was it because she was seeing Morgan Grey as a person, and not as her jailer? Usually, whenever he was around, there was a tension in her that she could not explain.

"And what of your childhood in Scotland, Brenna? Was it so different?" Elizabeth asked.

"I think not. I learned to ride as soon as I could walk. My earliest memories are of being astride my father's shaggy red stallion while he stood beside me, speaking words of encouragement in that deep, wonderful voice of his."

Morgan listened with interest. It was rare to hear Brenna speak of her childhood.

"And what of women's work?" Madeline asked.

"My mother often despaired of her daughters ever learning a skill with needle and thread, or in the kitchen. We adored our father and wanted to share his life." Brenna smiled. "But after my mother's death, the many duties of running a household were thrust upon me. Though I must admit that even now the adventure of the hunt is a great love of mine."

"So the man who weds you will have the best of both teachers, the warrior and the wife." Cordell was gazing at Brenna with a look of pure adoration.

Across the room Morgan felt a wave of annoyance and an instant dislike for the handsome youth who was devouring Brenna with his eyes. The elegantly attired Frenchman would look more at home at the queen's court than on a battlefield. It would seem that apple-cheeked boys whose hands were not as yet callused from holding a sword or earning their bread were always attracted to the beautiful Brenna.

Seeing his scowl, Madeline asked, "What is wrong, *mon cher?* Are the cakes not sweet enough for your taste?"

He shoved the plate aside. "I have had my fill of tea and cakes."

"Ale, my lord?" Mistress Leems signaled a servant to fill his goblet.

He gave her a grateful smile.

"I have begun to think," Lord Windham said to the queen, "that the Scotswoman would indeed be a prize for a titled Englishman. She is easy to look at. She is quite charming. And she can manage a household."

He stared pointedly at Brenna, and she felt the heat rise to her cheeks. Her eyes darkened with anger. The man was studying her, speaking about her, as if she were a prize sow.

"Have you forgotten her temper, Windham?" The queen leaned back, enjoying herself.

"Nay, Majesty. But I have found that a woman can be controlled much the same as a spirited mare—a firm hand, a tight rein, and," he added with a cruel smile, "a whip, when all else fails."

Glancing at him, Brenna felt an icy chill at the smile that split his lips. In his eyes there was neither warmth nor humor. She had no doubt that the man was a tyrant who would derive pleasure from inflicting pain.

Morgan's hand curled into a fist at his side. A whip, indeed! He had spotted the fear in Brenna's eyes before she blinked it away. He had an almost overpowering urge to go to her and offer his strength and comfort. Though he would derive more pleasure at the moment if he could hold a whip over Windham's head until he begged for mercy.

Richard glanced from his brother to the woman who held his gaze. Clearing his throat he said, "I pray the tea and cakes have soothed you after your journey, Majesty. Mistress Leems has planned a special dinner. But first, I am certain you will wish to rest."

"Aye. In a moment." Elizabeth pursed her lips in thought, then said, "I have been informed that a legion of Highland warriors is seeking an audience with me in London."

Brenna's heart soared. Megan had reached the Highlands. Brice would take her from this place.

Elizabeth went on, "It seems that they seek to deliver a petition from my cousin, Mary of Scotland, on behalf of Brice Campbell, to free his wife's sister."

Everyone in the room glanced at Brenna, whose eyes were touched with sudden light.

"I sent word with a messenger that I am unable to meet with them at this time. I urged them to return to Scotland secure in the knowledge that the woman they seek is in good hands." The queen stood, and the others followed suit. "I would sleep an hour or two before we sup."

Morgan filled the awkward silence. "Then I bid you good rest, Majesty."

Richard kissed her hand and Morgan did the same. When the queen and her company left the room, Brenna fled to the privacy of her chambers. But while the others slept, she paced the floor, struggling to calm the storm that raged within. She had allowed herself to be lulled by this peaceful retreat. But she was not safe anywhere in England. The queen had no intention of freeing her. And her last hope, her countrymen, had abandoned her.

At any moment, Brenna knew, the queen could decide her fate. A fate that could make her the wife of any Englishman who asked for her. Even a madman.

Lord Windham's words had struck terror in her heart.

"I tell you he intends to ask for the Lady Brenna."

Richard's words were an urgent whisper.

"What would you have me do?" Morgan stood by the window, staring bleakly at the sky.

"God in heaven, man. I have seen the way you look at her. You are not immune to her charms."

Morgan turned. "I cannot marry her."

Richard's hands balled into fists. "If I had legs to carry me, I would wrestle you to the floor and fight you like I did when we were lads until you came to your senses."

"It would do you no more good now than it did then."

"Aye. You were always the most stubborn, obstinate lout in all of England."

Usually such words would bring a wry smile to Morgan's lips. But his mood was so foul, not even a hint of laughter touched his eyes. Richard watched as Morgan squared his shoulders and began to walk toward the door.

In his fury Richard grabbed a crystal goblet from the table beside him and hurled it. It shattered against the wall just above Morgan's shoulder, spraying him with shards of broken glass.

"Of the two of us, you are the cripple," Richard shouted. "Even after all these years you have never allowed yourself to heal."

Without emotion, Morgan brushed the glass from his tunic and opened the door. When it closed behind him, Richard looked at it for long, silent minutes before turning to stare broodingly into the fire.

Dinner was to be a formal affair. All the guests were assembled when a servant announced the arrival of the queen. When the doors were opened, Elizabeth stood beside Morgan. She was arrayed in a scarlet gown; he in a scarlet tunic. Both of them looked very grave, their heads bent in intimate conversation. Everyone curtsied. Elizabeth acknowledged their greeting, then accepted a goblet from one of the serving wenches.

"Dinner is served," Mistress Leems intoned.

"I am ravenous," the queen said. "After your excellent confections earlier, Mistress Leems, I am anxious to see what other surprises you have for me."

"The Lady Brenna has been most helpful in choosing the menu, Majesty."

Elizabeth shot a glance at the young woman who stood beside Madeline. "Then we shall all have a chance to judge your skill in the kitchen, Brenna.

Out of the corner of her eye, Brenna saw Lord Windham cross the room toward her. Just then Cordell offered her his arm.

"May I accompany you in to sup, my lady?"

"Thank you." She placed her hand on the young Frenchman's arm and together they swept past Windham, who stood scowling after them.

Quickly recovering, he offered his arm to Madeline, who cheerfully accepted. The others fell into line behind them. A servant pushed Richard's chair. Seeing him, Adrianna slowed her steps until she was moving along beside him.

Richard glanced at the lovely young French woman, then away. It galled him that he could not stride gallantly along beside her. Each time he thought he had made his peace with his infirmity, something came along to challenge him. Something or—someone.

"You have a most lovely home, my lord," Adrianna said softly.

He loved the accent that softened all her words. "Thank you. In truth, it is my brother's, since Morgan is the eldest."

"But you live here."

"Aye. I find life in London too fast for my taste."

"I have visited my sister in London."

"Do you like it?"

She shrugged. "It is like Paris. As you said, very fast. But here . . ." She glanced around as they entered the large, airy refectory. "Here there is time to think, to feel, to breathe."

"Aye. To breathe. The air is sweeter here than anywhere on earth."

She smiled shyly. "I noticed. From my chambers I can smell the roses from the garden. They are so lovely."

"Do you like roses?"

"*Oui*. They are my favorite, I think."

His smile grew. "Then I shall have to show you my mother's rose garden."

"I would like that."

"Tomorrow," he whispered as they took their places at table. "After we break our fast."

She nodded, then looked up as Morgan offered a toast to the queen.

Beside her, Richard found himself almost trembling with anticipation. He felt as he had when he was a young apprentice, about to enter his first joust.

"A finer meal I have never eaten, Mistress Leems." The queen sat back, content, replete. She was a woman accustomed to the best. But this time, Morgan's housekeeper had outdone herself.

"I took the liberty," the queen said to Morgan, "of inviting my musicians to accompany me."

"You are too kind."

"If I need not be at court, I intend to enjoy myself. I wish to dance, to laugh, to forget the troubles of the Crown for a little while."

"Then we shall dance, Majesty."

Morgan offered his arm and the queen stood. Around the table the others stood and followed Elizabeth and her escort to the great room, where the musicians were assembled.

At the queen's signal, they began to play. The men and women who had accompanied the queen from Richmond Palace took up their positions for the dance.

Brenna stood to one side and drank in the view. With their long, stiff skirts billowing around their feet, the women in their colorful gowns seemed to float across the floor in the arms of their partners.

The queen accepted Morgan's outstretched hand. Madeline's husband kissed her fondly before offering her his arm. Cordell bowed before his sister and was surprised when she demurred.

"You will not dance?"

"Not now," she said softly. "I would prefer to stay here and watch." She took a seat beside Richard, all the while keeping her shy gaze averted.

Richard's smile grew until it was dazzling.

Cordell approached Brenna. "Will you dance, my lady?"

She hesitated for only a moment before placing her hand in his. With a laugh he twirled her around. And then they were caught up in the crush of laughing, dancing couples.

When the dance ended, Cordell returned Brenna to the side of the room, where servants had set up tables and chairs.

Before she could catch her breath Morgan was standing before her. She placed her hand in his and he led her to the dance floor. Without a word he drew her into his arms and began to move. And as if in a trance she moved with him, following his lead as easily as if they had always danced together.

"You have not forgotten." His breath was warm against her temple.

"I have forgotten nothing, my lord." Neither the way his strong arms held her as gently as if she were made of crystal, nor the way her heart raced each time they came together. If only he were not English. If only they had met at some other time, some other place. She could have so easily loved him, she thought.

Love.

Her eyes widened and she glanced up at him as if fearful that he could somehow read her mind.

"What is it, my lady?"

Her throat was so dry she could not speak.

"Is something amiss, Brenna?"

"Aye." Something was terribly amiss. She felt tears very close to the surface and blinked them away. What had come over her? What in the world was happening to her?

"Tell me." His voice was rough. "What has caused you such discomfort?"

You, she thought. You have been the cause of all my pain, all my fears, all my disquieting dreams. And you do not even know the power you wield over me.

Without realizing it, her look softened. Her eyes had the look of a woman in love. Her lips parted in invitation.

"I do not know, my lord. There are times when I feel— lost, confused."

"You are not lost, Ice Maiden." He drew her close. His hand tightened over hers. If he had it in his power, he would keep her safe with him forever.

Forever. What a strange thought when he knew that there was no such thing. Forever was a foolish dream, a silly child's concept that had no place in his world. Still, though he knew better, he yearned for that which was unattainable. Forever.

The music ended all too soon. Both Brenna and Morgan were reluctant to step apart. When Brenna walked from the dance floor, her cheeks were flushed, and on her face was a glow that had not been there earlier. But before she could accept a goblet of wine from Morgan's hand, Lord Windham caught her in a firm grasp.

"Would you do me the honor, my lady?"

"I fear I must take a few moments to catch my breath, my lord." She tried to pull her hand away, but he held her fast.

"There will be ample time for that." He placed a hand at her shoulder and propelled her into the circle of dancers.

Brenna felt his hand at her waist and forced herself to show no emotion. It was, she reminded herself, merely a dance. But she could not forget his cruel words, his evil threats.

"You are turning many heads," he muttered as he swept her in a graceful arc.

"You flatter me, my lord."

"I desire you, my lady. As I know you desire me."

The color on her cheeks deepened. Her eyes rounded in surprise at his boldness.

He stared down at her, his gaze piercing. "There are many rooms here in Grey's home where a man and woman can hide from prying eyes."

At his sinister tone she felt her blood go cold. Never again would she permit this man to force her into a compromising situation as he had at the queen's banquet. With an unexpected shove, she managed to dislodge herself from his arms. As he reached out she evaded his touch and took another step back.

"You must excuse me, Lord Windham. I fear I must rest a moment from the rigors of dancing."

Lifting her skirts, she nearly ran in her haste to escape him. As she reached Morgan's side, Windham caught up with her.

Morgan glanced from Brenna's flushed cheeks to Lord Windham's dark scowl and reacted instinctively by taking a menacing step closer.

Windham studied the protective way Morgan stood beside Brenna. A hint of a cruel smile touched his lips. So, Morgan Grey had become the lady's protector. Nothing would give him more satisfaction than putting Grey in his place. He turned to the queen.

"Majesty." His sharp tone commanded the attention of everyone in the room.

"I should like to ask your blessing on a most—delicate subject."

Elizabeth's interest piqued. "Is this not something that can be decided upon at court?"

"Nay, Majesty. You have expressed a desire to have this matter settled as quickly as possible."

"What is it, Lord Windham?"

"I request permission to wed the Lady Brenna Mac-Alpin." At his words, there was a collective gasp from those around him. And then a sudden, shocked silence.

Brenna stood rooted to the spot. Shock rippled through her. She stood, head bowed, hands gripped tightly together, trying desperately to hold to some thread of control.

This could not be happening. Please God. Not marriage to this man. Though she had once thought all Englishmen were kin to the devil, she now knew that to be untrue. A few of the men here were kind and generous souls. And one here had a special place in her heart, though she was loath to admit it. But there was about Lord Windham a hint of evil that set her teeth on edge. It was not love that drove him to seek her hand. Nay, it was something dark and chilling. Something she could not name that sent terror churning in her veins.

Except for a slight narrowing of his dark eyes, Morgan showed absolutely no emotion. He studied Windham, noting the look of triumph on his features. Aye, it would please Windham to wear Brenna on his arm like a trophy won in the games. From the time they were young, Windham had always wanted the finest mount, the biggest estate, the most beautiful woman at his side. Most of his possessions had been gained by less than honorable means. And always, when his interest waned, he would cast them aside for something even more exotic.

When the queen did not respond to Windham's request, he drew himself up to his full height and lifted his head in an arrogant pose. "As you have said, Majesty, the lady's temper would be a problem for most men. But I am certain

I can control her. I am willing to do the noble thing and take her as wife.''

Brenna was trembling so violently, she was forced to grip her hands together until her knuckles were white with the effort. When the queen opened her mouth to speak, Brenna stared at her with a pleading look in her eyes. She swallowed the lump that threatened to choke her and heard the queen's imperious tones.

''How kind of you, Lord Windham, to offer to take on the challenge of marriage to the Scotswoman.'' Elizabeth's voice purred, with just a hint of sarcasm. ''Would that all loyal subjects were so noble.''

Brenna closed her eyes and prayed that she would not embarrass herself by fainting again. If it killed her she would hold her head high, her spine rigid, and face her punishment like a true Scots.

''Unfortunately,'' the queen continued, enjoying the drama of the moment, ''you are too late.''

Someone gasped. Brenna wasn't certain if it had been her or someone else.

The queen's words sent another shock through the guests. ''Morgan Grey has already asked for the lady's hand.''

Chapter Sixteen

"**I** will choose a day for their official betrothal," the queen stated.

The crowd erupted into a great clamor of exclamations and congratulations.

Brenna heard but a single word. Betrothal. Not to Lord Windham, but to Morgan Grey. She was besieged by conflicting emotions. Relief, that she had been spared the ordeal of marriage to the cruel Windham. Outrage, that her fate had been so callously sealed without regard to her feelings. But deep inside, despite her denials to herself, she felt a thread of excitement that this man, whose very touch thrilled her, would seek to wed her. English or no, he made her burn as no other man ever had.

Morgan stood very still and regarded her reaction.

"A wedding. *Cherie,* how wonderful." While the others surged around them, Madeline drew Brenna into her arms and hugged her, then turned to Morgan with a laugh. "How could you have kept such a thing from us during tea? You rogue. How soon will you wed?"

"As soon as I have—" he turned toward the queen with a grave look "—completed a favor for Her Majesty."

Richard pulled Morgan down in a fierce hug. "Secrets, brother? I thought we told each other everything."

"I would have told you. If there'd been time."

"But you gave not a whisper."

"Aye. Some things are decided quickly."

"I am happy for you." Richard glanced at Morgan's grim features. He threw back his head and laughed before muttering, "Smile, Morgan, else they will think it is a funeral you are planning."

Morgan forced a grim smile to his lips.

His reaction was not lost on Brenna.

Cordell's face fell, but only for a moment. Covering his dismay, he kissed Brenna's hand. "My lady, I am fortunate to be here at such a time in your life. I wish you all happiness."

"Thank you." Brenna felt her lips quivering and prayed she would not give in to the tears that threatened.

From the time she had been a young girl, she had dreamed of a romantic courtship and a fine wedding, with her sisters attending her and all the people of their clan surrounding her.

What a foolish child she had been. A lump formed in her throat. What silly, romantic dreams she had spun.

The Frenchman turned to Morgan and offered his hand. "You are most fortunate, Lord Grey. Never have I met a lovelier lady than yours."

Morgan could read the sincerity in the young man's eyes. And though he still considered the callow youth to be offensive, he accepted his handshake.

On Lord Windham's face was a look of unveiled hatred. For long moments he studied the Scotswoman, then turned toward the man who had won her hand. How many times had he been bested by Grey in the past? He felt a wave of fury. Too many times to count. His need for vengeance was a living, palpable thing. And yet, he cautioned himself, the duel was not yet won.

He carefully composed his features and bowed over Brenna's hand. "A pity, my lady, that you must be saddled with frayed baggage like Morgan Grey."

"Frayed baggage?" She seemed puzzled.

"You did not know?" His lips curled into a cruel smile. "Your intended has been wed before."

Wed before? Morgan had a wife? Brenna felt herself reeling from his statement. But as she turned to Morgan for reassurance, Lord Windham continued, "Arrangements like this are common enough. As he did the last time, Grey now acquires another piece of land, and you acquire an English title. And in a few short months the two of you will feel free to move on to other conquests." His smile grew. "Other lovers."

Brenna shuddered at his suggestion.

He turned to Morgan, whose only show of anger was the little muscle that worked in his jaw.

"Congratulations, Grey. I pray this lady remains loyal at least until after the wedding."

The crowd had grown uncomfortably silent.

"Enough, Windham." The queen clapped her hands and ordered her musicians to play a tender ballad. "This shall be the lovers' dance. Morgan, dance with your intended."

Morgan turned to Brenna, whose face had gone pale.

"I fear I am overcome with—emotion, my lord."

He drew her firmly into his arms. She stiffened at his touch. The queen's command merely added to her misery. How could she be expected to dance in front of all these people when her whole life had just been forever altered?

"Please, my lord. I feel faint."

His mouth hardened into a grim, tight line. Damn Windham for leaving him no room for explanation. And damn the fates that had forced this awkward situation.

Against her temple he whispered, "You will dance with me. And you will observe protocol. You may not leave until the queen has excused herself from our company. Then, and only then, will we speak of this. When we are alone in our rooms."

Alone. Her heart nearly stopped. Through gritted teeth she muttered, "Aye. I will play your game, Morgan Grey. Until we are alone."

He pressed his lips to her temple. Instantly she felt the flame.

"And then what, my lady?"

The hand at her waist tightened perceptibly. Her breasts were flattened against his chest. Even in her anger she felt her body react to him. How was it that this man's touch could move her?

All eyes in the crowd were upon them. And though she cursed the desire that surfaced, she could not deny it. With each movement she was achingly aware of the thighs that brushed hers, of the strong, sure hand that guided her.

"When we are finally alone, I will show you how a Scot fights."

He smiled down at her, a rogue's smile that could melt any woman's heart, including hers. "And I, my lady, will show you how an Englishman loves."

When the queen had taken her leave, the women fluttered about, their voices a chorus of chattering birds.

"Did you see how Morgan devoured the Scotswoman with his eyes?"

"Aye. And did you see the way they whispered while they danced?"

"Is it a love match?" someone asked Madeline.

"How can it be otherwise, *cherie?* Are they not a handsome couple?"

"Is she very wealthy?"

"I have heard she commands an entire Scots army."

"What titles will she acquire upon marrying Morgan Grey?"

"He has received many honors from a grateful queen. His wife will be a titled English lady."

"There are fabulous jewels in the Grey estate. Will he lavish them upon his wife? Or will he save them for future mistresses?"

"What of his London house? Will the lady see it before the marriage?"

As Brenna stood beside Morgan and bid good-night to their guests, she heard comments. Her head was buzzing with words of congratulations and whispered innuendos.

Wealth. Jewels. Mistresses. Did no one care that all this had been forced upon her against her will?

Richard saw the look on her face and caught her hands, drawing her down for his kiss. "I have always wanted a sister," he murmured, hoping to ease some of her pain. "I cannot think of a better addition to our family than a wife for Morgan who can cook like an angel and wield a knife like Satan himself."

His words caused her to smile in spite of herself.

"Rest now, lass. And when you wish to talk, I will be here to listen."

"Thank you, Richard."

As a servant wheeled his chair through the doorway, Adrianna's gaze followed them.

When all their guests had taken their leave, Brenna placed her hand on Morgan's arm and walked stiffly beside him up the stairs. By the time they reached the sitting chamber, Brenna's heart was thundering in her chest. So many questions. So many things about this man that she did not know. And yet they were to be wed. Wed. God in heaven. How had her mother felt when she had been betrothed at ten and five? And Meredith. When had she known, truly known, that she loved Brice, her Highland barbarian? Oh, if only she could seek their council. If only she had spent more time learning the ways of men and women.

In the sitting chamber a fire had been started on the grate. Candles added a soft glow. A decanter of wine and two crystal goblets rested on a silver tray on a low table.

Brenna's room was in darkness. No fire had been laid on the hearth. From the open doorway she stared around her sleeping chamber. The bed linens had been removed, as had her clothing.

"I do not understand." She turned.

Morgan pointed to his sleeping chamber. "The servants have placed your things in my room, my lady."

Moving toward the fire, Brenna clutched her arms around herself and shivered. Seeing it, Morgan filled the two goblets and crossed the room to her.

"This will warm you."

She accepted the goblet and drank, grateful for anything that would ease the chill that seemed to have seeped through to her soul.

"I regret," Morgan said, staring at the flames, "that you were forced to endure that—public display, my lady. If I could have, I would have prepared you for the ordeal. But there was no time."

When she said nothing he continued. "As for the shocking news of my previous marriage, it is common knowledge among the London gossips. Of course, you are not privy to such things, and so you did not know."

Brenna turned to look at him. His gaze was locked on the flames that danced in the fireplace. His mouth was a thin, tight line of anger. "I was but a score when we were wed. In less than a year she was in the grave."

The look in his eyes was so bleak, Brenna longed to reach out to him, to offer him a measure of comfort. But she did not know how.

"I am sorry, my lord. Even now, your grief is such that it pains you to speak of it."

"Grief?" He turned to her then and she saw the pain etched on his handsome features. "You mistake bitterness for grief. I cannot grieve over what was never mine."

She blinked. "What are you saying?"

"The lady loved another. She only used me to make her lover jealous. And to give his child a name."

"Child! You have a child, my lord?"

"Nay." He drained the goblet and refilled it. "The child died in her womb."

Without thinking she touched a hand to his sleeve. "I am sorry, my lord."

He pulled away from her touch, but not before he felt the first stirrings of desire. "I do not want your pity."

She watched as he emptied the goblet a second time. There were no words that she could speak. And yet she had to ask the question that burned in her mind.

"Why..." She swallowed and tried again. "Why, when you are so bitter, would you ask for my hand? It is obvious that you do not wish to be wed again."

Why, indeed? Had he not asked himself this very question? His face became an unreadable mask. "I am, after all, responsible for bringing you to England. When I surmised that Windham would speak for you, I knew that I could not allow you to be placed under his cruel domination." He shrugged. "I accepted my responsibility."

"Your responsibility?" In her fury, Brenna's hand tightened on the stem of the goblet. "Your responsibility?" The temper she had kept under such careful control exploded. She turned on him with all the fury of a wounded tigress. "I will not be wed to a man out of some misguided sense of duty."

"Would you have me turn you over to Windham?"

"Nay. There is a much simpler solution to the problem. Let me return to my home in Scotland."

As patiently as if he were explaining to a child he said, "The queen has decreed..."

"Damn the queen! And damn you, Morgan Grey!" With uncharacteristic vengeance she hurled the goblet against the fireplace.

Before she could turn away his hand snaked out, catching her roughly by the shoulder. In his eyes was the barest hint of a smile.

"So. It is as I suspected. Beneath the cool facade the lady does have a temper."

"I told you I would show you how a Scot fights." She tried to push away, but the hands holding her were too strong.

He dragged her firmly against him. "And I told you I would show you how an Englishman loves."

"No. You cannot . . ."

He cut off her protest, crushing her mouth with his.

She felt the rush of heat that always seemed to swamp her at his touch. And then she felt the tremors begin as his mouth plundered hers. Wave after wave of feeling poured through her as his mouth moved over hers.

She pounded her fists on his shoulders until she was exhausted from the effort, but he continued to pin her as effortlessly as if she were a small child.

"Has any Scotsman ever kissed you like this?" he muttered against her lips.

He traced the outline of her lips with his tongue, and she gave an involuntary shudder.

He parted her lips and invaded the sweetness of her mouth. She gasped and tried to pull away, but he was too strong. For long moments he stared down at her, seeing the angry flare that darkened her eyes to midnight blue.

With his hands on either side of her face he kissed her slowly, thoroughly, lingering over her lips until the heat flickered, then flared, then burst into an inferno, threatening to sear them.

"Has any Scotsman ever made you burn like this?" His breath was hot against her cheek.

"Damn you."

"Aye. I am damned," he rasped, plunging his hands into her tangles of silken hair. She tried to pull away but his hands tightened, holding her head still.

He bent his head and kissed her again and again until she was forced to take in long, shuddering breaths to fill her lungs.

With a knowing smile he brought his hands around her, moving them slowly along her sides until his thumbs encountered the soft swell of her breasts. Instantly her nipples hardened and his excitement grew. "Damned to want what I should never have."

He felt her trembling response and thrilled to it. "Has any Scotsman ever touched you like this?"

"Stop. You must stop."

"Aye. I'll stop." He bent his lips to hers. This time she did not pull away or try to avoid his touch. "When you tell me you hate the sight of me, the touch of me." He muttered the words against her lips and took the kiss deeper.

Without realizing it, her hands fell limply at her sides. Her tongue met his, hesitantly at first, then bolder, until she opened her mouth to him and kissed him as he was kissing her.

Her hands rose to his arms, gripping him for support.

Morgan had intended to prove to her that she would respond to him, no matter how angry. Instead, he had just foolishly fallen under her spell. The very things he had so proudly managed to avoid for all these years had just ensnared him. The touch of her, the taste of her, were his undoing. He wanted her. God in heaven. He wanted her.

"Tell me, Brenna. Has any Scotsman ever made your blood run hot?" He kissed her until she was gasping for breath, and still he could not tear his mouth from hers. Against her lips he muttered, "Has any Scotsman ever made your heart thunder like this?" His hand covered her breast and he felt the wild pounding of her heartbeat. Its rhythm matched his own.

He plunged his tongue into her ear again and again, then once more covered her mouth with his. With one arm firmly around her, he lifted his other hand to the dark tangles of her hair and drew her head back. Before she could catch her breath he ran openmouthed kisses along the column of her throat, then lower, to the swell of her breast. Through her gown he felt her nipple harden at his touch. His excitement grew as he felt her trembling response.

She brought her arms around his neck and clung to him, hating him for being so worldly and knowing just how to make her burn with desire. She hated herself for giving in to this need that pulsed through her, robbing her of her will. And she hated this weakness that had taken over her control.

They dropped to their knees on the floor, entangled in each other's arms.

"Tell me you do not want this," he taunted, "and I will walk away."

He knew it was a lie. At this moment he could not turn away from her even if she pleaded with him. The need for this damnable little woman was stronger than anything he'd ever known.

Brenna lifted her tear-filled eyes to him. The feelings that churned inside her were so new, so frightening, they filled her with terror. She wanted this man. More than anything in the world. Never before had she felt so wild and free. But she feared the feelings that rippled through her, driving her to such wanton behavior.

"Tell me," he commanded.

"I . . ." Her throat was so dry she could not speak. She swallowed and tried again. But no words would come out. Instead she merely clung to him and offered him her lips.

The thought of her surrender added to his arousal. Desire clawed at him, stripping him of his pride. He would beg, he would crawl, to have her. The need for her drove him to be ruthless.

"You may deny all you want, my lady. But your body tells me the truth."

Her breath shuddered from between parted lips. His own breathing was ragged and painful.

Her tears spilled over, running in little rivers down her cheeks. Her words tumbled out, frightened, breathless, causing his heart to stop.

"I am so afraid. I have never been with a man before."

A virgin. God in heaven. Hadn't he always known? She was as sweet, as untouched, as a rosebud that had not yet come to flower.

Morgan felt a wave of disgust at what he had almost done. He had driven her mad with his own lust. He had nearly taken her here, on the cold, hard floor. Like some tavern slut.

He dropped his hands to his sides.

Brenna felt a sudden chill and wished that he would hold her. But when she looked up she saw that his eyes no longer smoldered. The hint of a smile was wiped from his lips.

In his arms she had come alive for the first time in her life. Though the feelings he aroused in her were terrifying, they were also exciting. And now that he no longer held her, she felt cold and lifeless. Why had no other man ever aroused these emotions? Had they always been there, waiting for this man? For a few minutes it had no longer mattered that he was English and she was Scots. They were a man and a woman who had come together in naked hunger. Without Morgan Grey, she sensed, she would never again be lifted to such heights.

He misunderstood her silence.

"Forgive me, Brenna." He lifted a hand to her cheek and wiped away her tears. "With you I am like a man possessed. I have never before tried to force my way with a woman. I had no right."

Though she yearned to tell him that she shared his needs, she could not find the words. These feelings were still too new, her emotions still too raw.

With great effort he stood and helped her to her feet.

"The goblet." For the first time she noticed the shattered glass that littered the hearth.

"Leave it. A servant will clean it on the morrow."

But who would pick up the pieces of her shattered heart?

She chanced another glance at him. His hands were clenched at his sides. His face was grim. "Good night, my lady. You will sleep in my chambers. I will remain here in the sitting chamber.''

''Good night.'' She walked to his sleeping chamber. When she closed the door, he was still standing where she had left him. Staring morosely into the flickering flames of the fire.

Chapter Seventeen

The only light that burned in Morgan's sleeping chamber was the light from the fireplace and from a single candle set in an ornate silver candlestick on a small table. Beside it were a basin and pitcher of water perfumed with rose petals.

The bed hangings had been let down to assure privacy. The coverlets had been turned down for the night. More rose petals had been scattered among the bed linens. Across the foot of the bed an elegant gossamer and lace night shift had been carefully laid out.

What was all this? Brenna frowned. So. The servants had already heard. That was why her room had been emptied of all her things, and why Morgan's room had been so thoughtfully prepared for lovers.

Lovers. She felt the sting of tears and quickly wiped them away. She would not cry over Morgan Grey. He was not worthy of her tears. He did not love her. He had admitted as much. In fact, she thought, struggling with the buttons of her gown, he was probably incapable of loving anyone except himself. He'd been steeped in hatred and bitterness for so long, there was most likely no room left in his heart for love.

Where was Rosamunde? she thought, feeling her temper grow. Had the servants conspired to leave her alone with only Morgan Grey to assist her in undressing? She felt a flush touch her cheeks. Aye. That was exactly what they'd had in mind. They had all retired to their beds early, convinced that the two lovers would prefer to be alone.

Alone. She felt more alone now than she ever had. Her heart tripped over itself each time she was near Morgan. But he was a man who was only capable of hatred and bitterness. She paused. What must it be like to be wed to one who loves another? What pain he must have suffered at the hand of such a callous woman. Quickly she berated herself. Had not her sisters always told her she was too tenderhearted? Soon she would find herself pitying Morgan instead of resenting him.

She undressed quickly and slipped on the night shift. She padded across the room and hung her gown on a peg, then crossed to the bed and snuffed out the candle. Climbing beneath the warm covers, she stared at the flickering flames and was reminded once again of the heat that had flared between her and Morgan. How had she allowed that Englishman to arouse her in such wanton fashion? She had always believed herself strong enough to resist anything. But this man needed only to touch her and some sort of weakness pervaded not only her body but her soul, as well.

He would use her, she cautioned herself. Use her shamelessly, then discard her. The man was incapable of loving anyone.

She stared at the flames until her eyelids fluttered, then closed. Exhausted beyond belief, she slept.

Brenna woke with a start. The fire had burned down to ashes. The room was immersed in darkness. Had she heard a sound? Or had she only dreamed it?

She lay very still, listening. Beyond the balcony she could hear the flutter and chirp of night insects, the rustle of leaves in the trees, the sighing of the wind.

She stiffened. There was the sound again. A door being opened, perhaps? She strained, peering into the blackness. Had it been her door?

She sat up, feeling a chill of apprehension. "Morgan. Is that you?"

For a long moment there was only silence, then the slightest movement, as though someone had stiffened at her words.

"Morgan." Her words were strained, angry. "I know you are there."

"Were you hoping for your lover?" There was the stench of ale as the whispered words hung between them.

"Who...?"

"Since you are alone, I would be your lover, too, my lady."

For a moment she was paralyzed with fear. Then she tried to twist away, but a strong hand caught and held her. Before she could cry out a hand closed over her mouth, cutting off her scream.

She felt the blade of a knife against her throat. "You will do exactly as I say. Do you understand?"

She nodded, unable even to swallow, lest the blade pierce her flesh.

"Good. That is very good, my lady."

She heard a muted laugh that sent fresh terror through her veins. This was a madman, who would not flinch at the thought of killing her.

Oh, for a dirk at her waist or a sword at her bedside. If she were not a prisoner in this place, she would have a weapon with which to defend herself. But she was rendered helpless.

"Take off your night shift."

"Please..."

"You have forgotten my first order. I shall have to teach you."

She felt a sharp pain, then a warmth along her arm. It took her a moment to realize that her attacker had cut her. With a snarl of rage she sank her teeth into his arm and bit down until he howled with pain.

With a savage oath he slapped her once, then again, snapping her head from one side to the other. While she still reeled from the blow, the blade ripped through the delicate fabric of her night shift, slashing it from hem to bodice.

"Now," he said with a laugh that seemed to grow more shrill with each new act of terror, "I shall teach you my second lesson."

Shirtless, Morgan sprawled in a chaise pulled up before the fire. The decanter of ale stood on a table beside him. It was his intention to drink the entire contents, if possible. At least then he would be assured of sleep.

The anger he had allowed to fester inside himself for so long seemed nothing compared with the disgust he felt for himself at the moment.

From the first minute he'd seen that cool, haughty Scotswoman, he'd been behaving like a fool. If he were going to be brutally honest with himself, he would have to admit that he dragged her here to England, not to do the queen's bidding, but because he had not wanted her to spend any more time with the apple-cheeked Hamish MacPherson. He had experienced in those days at her castle his first pangs of jealousy. And he had been too proud to admit it.

In fact, he thought, taking another long swallow of ale, it had been his pride that had been wounded from the first. He had wanted her to fall victim to his charms as most women did. If she had, he realized, he would have used her and discarded her like all the rest. But that damnably regal ice maiden would not behave like all the others. Aye, that was the thorn. She was like no other woman he'd ever met. She fought him when he least expected it. And fought like a soldier, if he would be honest. He loved her strength of will, loved dueling with her, seeing the way her eyes darkened like a summer's night before a storm. He loved the way she looked, all soft and feminine. Loved the way she constantly surprised him, saying or doing the unexpected. He loved the color of her hair, black as midnight, and her skin, pale as alabaster.

He poured another goblet, then paused, his hand in mid-air as the thought exploded through him. He loved her. God in heaven. That was the truth. He loved her. It was that simple. His heart contracted. It was that complicated.

But what to do about it? His first marriage had been a mockery of everything holy. It had left him badly scarred. What had Richard said? Aye, Morgan thought with a frown. That he was more a cripple than Richard. 'Twas the truth. And after so long a time, he was no longer certain if he dared to trust again. And after that scene with Brenna in the sitting chamber, he might not get another chance. She was a delicate lady whose sensibilities were no doubt offended by his unbridled passion. He felt another wave of disgust.

He looked up at a sound. A night bird perhaps?

He lifted the goblet to his lips, then paused. There was a sound coming from his sleeping chamber. Was Brenna crying? Dear God. Had she been crying all this time?

He set the goblet on the table and got to his feet. He would not invade her privacy. He had done a thorough job of that earlier. He would merely listen outside the door.

Brenna felt the mattress sag as her attacker leaned over her. In desperation she clutched at the candlestick and brought it crashing against his temple. He swore and snatched it from her hand, sending it rolling across the floor.

One of his hands caught at her hair, pulling her head viciously when she tried to turn away from his lips. Terror rose in her throat as she twisted away, determined to evade his cruel hands.

"No," she shouted. "You will have to kill me first."

"So be it."

She saw the dark shadow of the man loom up in the darkness, the knife poised above his head. With one quick movement she rolled to one side and the knife plunged harmlessly into the pillow where, just moments before, her head had been.

With quick, jerking movements she slid off the bed and raced toward the door. Before she could pull it open an arm closed around her neck. She was hauled backward against the man's body while the arm continued to press against her throat, cutting off her air. Though she fought with a strength born of desperation, she could not breathe.

With both hands she clawed at the arm, struggling to break free. But her attacker was too strong for her. She could feel her strength ebbing. Strange lights seemed to dance before her eyes. There was a loud buzzing in her ears. And then, just as she was beginning to lose consciousness, her attacker was suddenly pulled backward. The offending arm loosened its hold on her throat. She fell to the floor, gasping for air.

"God in heaven. Brenna."

As Morgan's voice washed over her, light spilled in from the sitting chamber, illuminating her where she lay choking. Blood streamed from the cut on her arm and ran in little rivers, staining the rug beneath her.

In quick strides Morgan was across the room, cradling Brenna in his arms. She clung fiercely to him, fighting the sobs that were wrenched from her bruised, aching throat.

They heard the sound of the outer door slam as the attacker made his escape. As a soldier, Morgan's first thought was revenge for this brutal attack. But one look at Brenna's helpless form and all thought of vengeance faded. She needed him. Nothing else mattered.

Seeing the blood Morgan swore savagely, then lifted her tenderly in his arms and carried her to his bed.

"You are wounded." His face was ravaged as he looked at her. "Oh, what has he done to you, love?"

Love. At his tender endearment she began to cry. And the more she cried, the more concerned Morgan became.

"God in heaven, he hurt you."

She wiped at her tears, but they would not stop. "It is not deep," she whispered, touching a hand to the cut on her arm.

"Are there other, deeper wounds? I speak not of cuts and bruises, but of more hateful ways to harm you. Did he—force you, love?"

"Nay. He tried. But you stopped him in time."

He felt a rush of relief. Burying his face in her hair, he held her close against him and rocked her as tenderly as any infant.

"Thank God. If he had harmed you . . ."

She felt the shudders that passed through him. Wonder of wonders, could it be that Morgan Grey was as frightened as she had been?

When he had composed himself he drew the coverings over her nakedness and crossed to the fireplace, where he added kindling and a log to the hot coals. Within minutes a crackling fire blazed on the hearth.

He held a taper to the candle beside the bed, then bent to examine her wound. "Though the blood still oozes, it should not cause you any great pain."

"I have the satisfaction that my attacker also suffers pain," she hissed.

"You wounded him? But how, love?"

Her eyes blazed. "Aye. With my teeth, which I sank into his arm. With my fingernails, that raked his chest until he bled. With a candlestick against the side of his head. I have left my mark upon him. He will not escape detection."

Morgan lifted his head and studied her for a moment, then threw back his head and roared. "Forgive me, my regal ice maiden. I believe you. We shall find him. Even if we have to examine the arms, chest and head of every man in England."

"If I had been allowed to have a weapon," she said through gritted teeth, "he would now be lying in a pool of his own blood."

He regarded her a moment. "From this night on you shall have your weapon."

Her eyes widened. "Do you mean it?"

"Aye." He lifted her hand to his lips. In his eyes was a look she had never seen before. "I will never again leave you helpless, Brenna."

He left the room for a moment and Brenna felt the tremors begin again. When he stepped through the doorway he saw the fear in her eyes.

"Forgive me. I should not have left you alone." He rushed to her and drew her into his arms, holding her until the tremors subsided. "But I wanted you to have this."

He handed her a knife. The hilt was dull gold, set with precious rubies and diamonds that winked in the firelight. Brenna ran her hand along the blade. It had been honed to a razor's edge.

"It was my father's. I have carried it since I was a lad."

"How do you know I will not use it on you, my lord?"

"There may be times when I deserve it. But I pray that you will give me another chance to earn your respect." He pressed the knife into her hands. "Keep it on your person always."

At the solemn look in his eyes she nodded. "Aye, my lord. Always. You can be assured of that."

He dipped a linen square in the basin of water and began to wash away the blood. As he did he found himself marveling at the perfection of her body. Though Brenna had recoiled from her attacker, she lay very still, secure in the knowledge that Morgan would never take advantage of her vulnerability.

The gentle touch of his hand upon her was nearly her undoing. She lay very still, her eyes closed, allowing his tender ministrations to soothe away her pain and fear.

When the blood was removed, he tied a clean linen strip around the cut on her arm. Then he drew the coverings over her and started to stand. Instantly she reached out and caught his hands.

"Do not leave me."

He saw the way she struggled with her fears. "Do not worry, Brenna. I will not leave you. I will be in the sitting chamber."

"No. Please. Stay here beside me."

God in heaven. He wondered if she knew what she was asking of him. To be so close to her and not touch her would be the most terrible of torments for him.

Still, he could see the need in her eyes, in the way her fingers clutched at him.

"Aye. If that is what you need."

"I could not bear to be alone tonight. As long as you are with me, I will be safe."

A few short hours ago she would not have said as much.

He pried off his boots and stretched out on the bed beside her. Being careful to keep the coverings between them, he took her hand in his.

"Hold me, Morgan."

He groaned inwardly. With all the tenderness he could manage he drew her into the circle of his arms. This was the sweetest of tortures. It would take all the willpower he possessed to lie beside her until morning and merely hold her.

She sighed softly. Despite the bed linens he could feel the way her breasts pressed against his chest. He was achingly aware of her thighs, just beneath the thin covering, pressed firmly to his.

"Sleep, little one," he murmured against her temple.

"You will not leave me?"

"I give you my word."

She closed her eyes. He felt the wild fluttering of her heart and drew her closer, as if to share his strength.

After what seemed hours her breathing became soft and easy. Her fingers loosened their death grip on his arms. She escaped into blessed sleep.

Morgan shifted and drew the covers over Brenna as gently as possible so as not to disturb her rest. He watched her as she fought the demons that pursued her even in sleep.

He had demons of his own to fight.

The woman who lay nestled against his chest was so soft, so inviting. A shaft of moonlight poured through the balcony window, bathing her in a soft golden glow. Her dark hair spilled across his arm, a stark contrast to the snowy bed linens. He bent his face to her and breathed in the fragrance of roses. The perfume of roses was everywhere—on the fresh breeze that wafted from the rose garden; in the water that he'd used to bathe her wounds; even mingled with the linens on which they lay.

He felt her suddenly stiffen in his arms and knew that the bad dream was upon her again. He watched as her fingers tightened on his arm. Her eyelids fluttered. Her lips moved in a soundless protest.

He pressed his lips to her temple and felt himself overflowing with love for her. If only he could, he would absorb all her pain, all her fears. How bravely she had fought her attacker. He thought of the first time he had seen her, facing down hundreds of English swordsmen with that cool, haughty demeanor. By the gods, she was magnificent. She could wilt her enemy with a single look. Yet she was the most tenderhearted woman he had ever met.

He watched as her breathing grew softer once more. Her fingers entwined with his. She slept as peacefully as a baby. But even then he did not relax his silent, watchful vigil.

Brenna lay very still, feeling disoriented. A man's arm was around her, pinning her to him. For a fraction of a second she was gripped by fear. The attacker. Had he come back to finish what he had started? Then she remembered Morgan's promise. He would stay with her and keep her safe.

Her lids flickered, then opened quickly. Morgan's dark eyes stared into hers. She wondered how long he had been watching her. It was a strange sensation to be lying so close to him.

She let out a long, deep sigh. "I knew you would be here."

He loved the way her voice sounded, breathless and still touched with sleep. "Did you?"

"Aye."

She smiled at him and he felt his heart leap to his throat.

She moved slightly until she lay facing him. The bed linens shifted, revealing the shadowed cleft between her breasts. It was impossible for Morgan to forget that she was naked beneath the covers.

He was wearing neither shirt nor tunic. She had probably noticed that after the attack of the intruder, but in the panic of the moment it had not registered. Now she could not take her gaze from him. How wide his shoulders. How massive his hair-roughened chest.

"Have you slept at all?"

He shook his head.

"But I did not mean to rob you of your sleep, my lord."

"I would rather watch you. Besides, it is enough to know that you are resting."

"How long have I slept?"

"An hour or more."

"I feel as rested as though I have slept the night away."

"There are many hours until dawn, my lady. You need have no fear. I will not leave you while you sleep."

Her voice lowered seductively. "I have no need of sleep now."

He heard the new inflection in her voice and felt himself tense. "Would you have me leave?"

Her hand closed over his. "Nay, my lord."

Morgan's eyes narrowed. Never before had the lady behaved in such a teasing manner. Could it be that he misread her meaning?

"If you do not plan to sleep, I must not stay."

"I want you to stay with me." Her hand slid along his arm. How different was a man's arm, with silken hair and corded muscles that rippled beneath her touch.

His tone roughened. "You ask too much of me, Brenna. I am a man, not a saint. How long do you think I can lie here beside you and not touch you?"

Her throat went dry. She touched her tongue to her lips. He watched the movement and had to fight the desire to bend his lips to hers.

"Then touch me, my lord."

For a moment he could not believe what he'd heard. His eyes flashed. "I do not jest, my lady."

"Nor do I."

He caught her chin in his hand and forced her to meet his direct gaze. "You have only just awakened. Perhaps you are confused."

"I am not confused."

"Then you are grateful that I saved you from your attacker. Do not mistake gratitude for some other, deeper emotion, Brenna."

"It is not gratitude I feel." She held herself very still, as if terrified of her sudden boldness.

He kept his tone deliberately stern, in order to ruffle her composure. "If I touch you, it will not end as it did before. I have not the strength to walk away again. I intend to make love with you, Brenna, the way a man loves a woman. And I will want you to make love with me, as well."

"That—is what I want, my lord."

Her gaze never left his. He expected to see fear, or at least hesitation. But what he saw was a look of cool determination. And the first soft stirrings of desire.

Chapter Eighteen

The fire had burned to embers, leaving the room bathed in a rosy glow. Pale moonlight filtered through the balcony window, touching the figures in the bed with a luminous light.

The silence of the room surrounded them. It was as if the night creatures had conspired to still their voices. There was no sound except the soft whisper of their breathing. And the wild thundering of their heartbeats.

"Are you afraid, love?" With his finger Morgan traced the curve of her brow, the slope of her cheek, the outline of her lips.

Love. His endearment filled her with sudden yearning. "Aye. I am terrified."

He touched his lips to hers and murmured, "There is no reason to be. I promise I will not hurt you. I will never hurt you, Brenna."

"That is not what I fear." She drew back. "I am afraid I will not please you."

With his hand at her back he drew her firmly against the length of him. "You already please me, Brenna." Brenna. Brenna. Her name sang like a litany in his mind. Never would he grow weary of saying her name. "You are the loveliest creature I have ever known. All the beauty, all the goodness of this world, are in your eyes."

She gave him a timid smile.

He sensed her uneasiness. With a gentle smile he said, "Trust me. It is true we are about to go to a new place. And the unknown is always frightening. But we go there together, love."

He buried his lips in the hair at her temple and felt the wild beating of her pulse. Forcing himself to go slowly, he moved his lips along her cheek to the tip of her nose.

"Such a haughty little turned-up nose," he murmured.

She chuckled and he felt her relax in his arms.

"You do not like my nose?"

"It is a fine nose. And your lips." He nuzzled the corner of her mouth until she sighed with impatience and turned her head until his lips were covering hers. "Such perfect lips." His words mingled with her breath and were swallowed up in the kiss. He lingered over her lips, loving the way they felt beneath his. Soft. Seductive. Inviting.

His hands moved along the warm, naked flesh of her back, igniting little fires wherever they touched.

"You are so small, Brenna. So delicate." He lifted himself on one elbow to allow his gaze to study her. Her skin was washed by moonlight. With a kind of reverence he trailed his hand along the soft curve of her hip to her narrow waist, then upward to the swell of her breast. "So beautiful."

She closed her eyes and he pressed his lips to her closed lids. As he explored her face with his lips, she relaxed, allowing herself to drift on a hazy cloud of contentment.

His lips traced her eyebrow, her cheek, her ear. With his tongue he traced the outline of her lips, then lingered, savoring all her sweetness.

The kiss was a promise of more. So much more.

He lifted her hand to his lips, then pressed a kiss to her palm and closed her hand around it. She trembled as he kissed her wrist, her elbow, her shoulder. She laughed softly as he nuzzled her neck.

Before she realized what he was doing, he bent his head. With the merest brush of his lips he pressed a kiss to her hipbone. She flinched and tried to draw away, but he held her firmly while his lips trailed the flare of her hips to her waist. She lay steeped in pleasure as he ran kisses across the soft flesh of her stomach, then upward across her rib cage.

Never had she dreamed that a man's lips could bring such pleasure.

He heard her quick intake of breath as his lips encountered the swell of her breast. As his mouth found her erect nipple, he heard her moan.

She felt the jolt, then the slow flame begin to build deep within her until she felt herself burning with need. Wild, pulsing need that drove her to clutch at the bed linens and arch herself tensely.

As he brought his lips from one breast to the other she sobbed and clutched his head, dragging his lips to hers. With a moan he dragged her against him and covered her lips in a hot, hungry kiss. She clung to him, loving the strength she could feel in him. Yet, despite his strength, she could sense the supreme effort he made to hold his needs at bay. He was exerting careful control, she realized, in order to give her the time she needed.

She was afraid to touch him. And yet the urge to run her hands over his naked torso was too tempting to ignore. She reached a tentative finger to his chest, then drew back, embarrassed by her boldness.

"Touch me again, Brenna."

At his urging she touched a hand to his chest and rubbed her open palm across the mat of hair. A bubble of laughter escaped her lips. "It tickles."

He smiled up at her. She was such a wonder. Such a delight.

Her fingertips brushed his nipples and she felt them harden. Instantly she drew her hand away, but he reached out and pulled it to him. "Nay. Do not stop, little one."

She ran a hand along his shoulder and thrilled to the ripple of muscle beneath her palm. Suddenly she encountered the raised scar made by her dirk when she had fought him in the Highlands. The laughter faded from her eyes. "I cannot bear that I inflicted this pain on you."

"It no longer hurts, Brenna."

"But it was made by my hand." Without thinking she brought her lips to the spot.

Instantly the heat flared, until he was engulfed by fire. He gave a moan low in his throat.

His reaction to her touch gave her new courage. Growing bolder she brought her hands to the flat planes of his stomach and felt him flinch.

Could it be that her mere touch had the power to weaken this mighty soldier? "Afraid, my lord?" Laughter warmed her tone.

"Nay, witch." His dark eyes were full upon her, daring her. "Afraid only that you will stop."

Accepting his challenge she moved her hand lower still, until her hand encountered the waistband of his breeches. When her fingers fumbled with the fasteners, he helped her, until this last barrier between them was discarded.

She studied him in the glow of moonlight and found herself marveling at the beauty of his body. How perfectly the angles and planes of his muscled body complemented the softness of hers.

"Touch me, Brenna. Touch me before the madness overtakes me."

She felt drunk with her newly discovered power. Moving her hand lower, she heard his moan of pleasure, saw his eyes narrow fractionally. Then, with his hand beneath her chin, he lifted her face to his and covered her mouth in a kiss so hungry, so impatient, she felt as if she were being devoured. When at last he came up for air she clutched blindly at his waist and brought her lips to his throat. The fire spread, heating their bodies, searing their blood.

When his lips lingered at her throat she arched, giving him free access, her head back, her eyes half closed in pleasure. But when they moved lower, to close around her breast, his name came out in a broken sob.

"Morgan. Please."

He nibbled and suckled until she writhed beneath him.

His lips, his fingertips moved over her, seeking out all the hidden pleasures until her body hummed with need. His fingers found her, moist and ready.

"Tell me, love. Tell me you want me."

She felt herself beginning to climb, high, then higher still, until she reached the first peak. But he gave her no time to pause before he took her even higher.

Needs pulsed and shuddered within her until she thought she would explode. "I do want you. Oh, Morgan, I love you."

Love. He savored the word as it washed over him. She loved him. It was more than he had ever hoped for. That this woman could love him, as he loved her. If he never had another blessing in his lifetime, this one would be enough.

Need ripped through him, shattering the last thread of his control. If he did not take her now he would go mad with the need for her.

Mad. Aye, it was madness that had driven him from the first moment he saw her. And there was no cure for it. Except this woman.

As he levered himself above her he looked down into her eyes and could read all the love, all the desire, in their blue-violet depths.

As he gently lowered himself into her and began to move, he was amazed to find that her strength, her needs, matched his. She moved with him, taking him higher, then higher still, until there was no longer any time for gentleness.

The fragrance of roses clung to her hair and skin. He breathed it in, filling his lungs. He was reminded of the field of heather, when he had wanted her with this same kind of desperation. From this moment on, whenever he smelled roses, he would think of her. And want her with this same terrible hunger.

He murmured words and phrases of love, or thought he did, as together they passed through a sky filled with shooting stars until they soared beyond the moon and felt themselves shattering into a million glittering fragments.

They lay, still locked in a fierce embrace, neither of them willing to break the fragile bond that held them.

Brenna's face was covered with a fine sheen of moisture. Morgan pressed his lips to her forehead. His breathing was shallow.

He felt the tremors that rocked her and touched a finger to the corner of her eye. "Tears?" Immediately he started to draw away. "I have hurt you."

"Nay." She caught him and held him to her. "It is foolish, I know. But I feel like weeping."

"I know, love." He touched his lips to her tears and tasted the salt.

"Oh, Morgan." She clung to him and wept openly, no longer trying to hide the sobs that were wrenched from her. "I know I cannot make up for what happened to you in the past. But if I could, I would erase all the pain from your poor heart."

He went very still, absorbing the shock as her words washed over him. How generous she was. What a wonderful gift he had been given.

Rolling to one side he drew her into the circle of his arms and pressed his lips to her temple. With his thumbs he wiped away her tears. "Do not weep for me, Brenna. Whatever happened before has just been erased for all time."

"But you said you never wanted to marry again. And now you have spoken for me."

He placed a finger over her lips to silence her. "Hush, love. Forget the things I said earlier. I said them to hide the truth from my heart."

She glanced at him, her eyes wide. "What do you mean?"

"Just this." He lifted a strand of her hair and watched through narrowed eyes as it sifted through his fingers. "I love you, Brenna. I think I have loved you from the moment of our first meeting."

She knelt beside him. Her dark hair swirled around her breasts. "You love me? Truly love me?"

"Aye." On his lips was a smile of pure pleasure.

"You are not saying this to soothe me because of what we have just shared?"

His smile grew. Laughter rumbled from deep in his chest. "I love you, my lady. With all my heart and soul."

"And I love you, Morgan." She spoke the words with a hushed reverence. She bent low until her hair spread across his chest like a veil. "Tell me, my lord. When did you first realize you loved me?"

"Ah." He stifled the laughter that threatened. "Why must a woman know such things?"

"It is our vanity." She kissed him hard, quick. "Now tell me."

He propped one hand beneath his head, while his other arm cradled her against his chest. She felt so good there. So right.

"I did not admit it to myself until you had retired for the night. And I realized what I had just done to you." His fingers idly played with her hair. He felt the desire begin anew. God in heaven. How was it possible that he wanted her again so soon? "I feared that I had just dashed any hope of winning your heart."

"So, my lord." She ran a finger across his chest. Feeling his quivering response to her simple touch, she grew bolder. "What were you going to do about this sudden knowledge of your love for me?"

He recognized the gleam in her eye. "Are you teasing me, little one?"

"Nay, my lord. I simply wish to know if you would have ever told me of your love."

His tone grew serious. "I knew I had already caused you enough pain, Brenna. I took you from your home, from all you love, and thrust you among the vultures at court. 'Twas my intention to comply with the queen's wishes and wed you, then return you to your people, where you could live in peace.''

She pressed her hands against his chest and stared into his eyes. ''Are you saying that you love me so much you would live without me?''

''I love you so much I would set you free.''

She surprised him by brushing her lips lightly over his. The heat of desire rose swiftly.

''Then we would never have shared this wondrous act, my lord.''

''Aye.''

Her hands moved lower, causing his stomach muscles to jump.

''Now what are you up to, little one?''

Her eyes danced with a mischievous light. ''It is my intention to store up as many wondrous acts as possible, my lord. In case you decide to send me away soon.''

He threw back his head and roared with laughter. But a moment later, as her hand moved even lower, the laughter died on his lips. With a moan of pleasure he pulled her down on top of him and covered her mouth in a searing kiss.

She sighed and wriggled and moved over him until he felt himself once again slipping over the edge of sanity. Never, never had he known a woman like this one. Some time soon, when he had his wits about him, he would sort out all the changes she had wrought in his life. But not now. Right now he was beyond thought.

With sighs and kisses and little moans of pleasure, they lost themselves in that wonderful place reserved only for lovers.

The steady drumming of rain on the roof of the portico roused him. Morgan awoke slowly. There was a heaviness on his arm, making it impossible to lift it. He opened his eyes to study the beautiful creature who lay facing him. His leg was thrown carelessly across her, pinning her to the length of him. Her eyes were closed, her breathing slow and even.

What a delightful surprise she was. All night they had loved, slept, then awakened each other to love again.

He studied the wide, unlined brow, the lips, so right for kissing. How had he ever thought her cool and haughty? His little ice maiden. She was so generous, so open in her loving. No woman had ever made him ache with such desire. He would never have enough of her. Even a lifetime together would not be enough. His spirit would follow hers even into the hereafter.

He saw the way her lids flickered. Any moment now she would awaken. He was suddenly plagued with a terrible thought. What if, in the cold light of morning, she regretted their night of passion? What if she had given in to her loneliness in a moment of weakness? Or worse, what if she had confused gratitude with love? As her lids opened, he forgot to breathe. His heart missed a beat. Though he had fought hundreds of enemies on the field of battle, this little woman had him terrified.

Brenna lay a moment, feeling the weight of Morgan's leg on her. His breath was warm against her cheek. Even with her eyes closed she knew this man who lay beside her. She knew the touch of him. He had left his imprint on her body. And on her heart. The dark, mysterious taste of him still lingered on her tongue.

She opened her eyes to find him watching her intently. His brow was wrinkled with concern.

"Good morrow," she whispered, reaching a hand to his cheek. Before he could respond she pulled his face close and pressed a kiss to his forehead. "Are you having unhappy thoughts, my lord?"

He felt his breath come out in a slow sigh of relief. She had not blushed nor tried to hide herself. Instead she'd greeted him as if they had always awakened together after a night of loving.

"I was afraid you would awake with regrets, my love."

"I do have one regret."

His heart stopped beating.

Seeing the look on his face she leaned close, pressing her body to his. "I regret that you have a house filled with guests who will expect to be entertained from sunrise to sunset."

His mouth dropped open. Then he roared with laughter. She joined him, a gay, lilting sound that washed away the last of his fears.

"I suppose we shall have to dress and greet our guests." She brushed her lips across his shoulder and began to slip out of bed.

He felt the familiar tingle at her touch and lay very still, allowing the fire to build. As she brushed past him he caught her, forcing her down. His hands tangled in her hair, drawing her face toward his.

"The queen will sleep for at least another hour." He nibbled the corner of her mouth until she gave a little moan and clutched at his waist.

"And how is it that you can be so certain?"

"At this moment, my love, I am certain of but one thing." He rolled over, pulling her beneath him. Already the fire in his loins was raging out of control. "If the queen awakes early, she shall have to find her own entertainment. I have already found mine. Until we can return to this bed tonight, this day promises to be the longest one of my life," he murmured against her lips.

Her laughter died in her throat as he began to work the magic that would tumble them both into a world apart. A world of whispered sighs and endless delights.

Chapter Nineteen

Rosamunde and the servants giggled and chattered among themselves as they prepared a bath for Lord Grey and the Lady Brenna.

Morgan and Brenna seemed unaware of anything except each other. When Rosamunde had finished arranging Brenna's hair, she bowed her way from the room. As she was closing the door she caught a glimpse of Lord Grey standing behind the lady, his hands on her shoulders, his gaze meeting hers in the looking glass. On both their faces was a look of love so intense, so smoldering, it left no doubt in the serving girl's mind. The rumors and whispers had been correct. Lord Grey was truly intent upon pledging his troth to the lady.

But Rosamunde had seen something else that had deeply disturbed her. The Lady Brenna's flesh had been marred by a wound. Though her mistress had insisted that it was merely a scratch, the servant knew better. She had seen enough knife wounds in her young life to recognize one. The question was, who would inflict such pain upon the lovely Brenna MacAlpin? And why?

The same thought was uppermost in Morgan's mind as he escorted Brenna to the refectory. When all were assembled, he intended to study their guests and assorted servants very carefully. One among them was a vicious madman, who would answer to Morgan's sword.

One thought nagged at Morgan. Had the attacker been bent upon harming Brenna, or had he come upon her by mistake? Many of the servants knew that the lady's things had been moved to his room. And in a home such as this, what one servant knew, all knew. Rumors and gossip were a way of life. Still, the nagging thought persisted. Could he have actually been the intended victim?

As they entered the refectory, Morgan noted that Elizabeth and her ladies were already seated at table.

"So, you have finally dragged yourselves from bed." With great care the queen studied Morgan and the woman beside him.

Under the queen's scrutiny, Brenna blushed. Morgan, looking immensely pleased with himself, was unruffled by the queen's perusal.

Glancing around he asked casually, "Where are the others?"

"Madeline and Charles were summoned to Cordell's room early this morning," the queen said. "It would seem that the young Frenchman took a fall down a flight of stairs last night."

"A fall." Morgan's eyes narrowed. "Why was I not summoned?"

"The servants were loath to disturb you, my friend, knowing how you were—otherwise occupied."

At the queen's sly laugh, Morgan felt his temper rising. "Where is Lord Windham?"

"He went for an early morning ride."

"In this rain?"

"He said he had a need to be up and about."

"Did you see him?"

"Nay. He sent word with a servant. Why?" The queen studied Morgan across the table.

He shrugged. "No reason, Majesty. What about my brother?"

"Richard and the young Frenchwoman took a stroll in the garden."

"A walk in the rain." Tossing down his napkin Morgan scraped back his chair. "Now I know that the whole world has gone mad."

"Where are you going?" The queen looked up from her plate.

"To see how Madeline's brother fares."

When Brenna made a move to follow he touched a hand to her shoulder. "Nay, my lady. Stay and visit with the queen. I will return shortly."

"Tell me truly." Richard studied the lovely young woman who sat on a bench beneath the branches of a gnarled old tree. "You do not mind the rain?"

Adrianna's gaze lifted to the man who sat facing her in the wheeled chair. "Nay, my lord. I have often walked alone in the rain in Paris."

"Why would a beautiful woman like you walk alone?"

"Beautiful." She glanced down, feeling her cheeks redden at his unexpected compliment. "I am not beautiful, my lord."

"You think not?" He caught her chin and lifted her face for his inspection.

She blushed clear to her toes. "To a worldly man like you I must seem plain. My eyes are too big, my nose is too small. My hair is so ordinary."

"Ordinary." He allowed his gaze to burn slowly over her until she felt her cheeks flame. "Dear little Adrianna. There is nothing ordinary about you. When I look at you I see hair like burnished copper." He touched a finger to her rain-washed tresses. "Your eyes are greener than the Thames at sunrise. They are big, though." When she lifted her gaze to him he chuckled, low and deep in his throat. "Big enough, I think, for a man to drown in."

She pulled her head away and refused to look at him. "You should not say such things."

"But I must. Or would you have me lie?"

"I did not come here seeking compliments."

"Nay. Nor did I come here to give them away. We both came," he said, turning to glance around him, "to admire the rose garden. See how the flowers lift their heads to drink in the rain."

"Aye. How fresh and green everything looks."

"How fresh you look, dear little Adrianna. You are like a breath of fresh air to these tired eyes."

Again she refused to look at him. "The words roll so easily from your tongue, my lord. I think you find it easy to speak so to every woman."

"You think so?" He reached out, catching both her hands in his. "Look at me, Adrianna."

She glanced up, then away.

"Why will you not look at me?"

When she said nothing his voice deepened. "Are you afraid to look at me?"

She swallowed. "Aye."

He felt his heart contract. He had foolishly set himself up for this pain. All night he had tossed and turned, dreaming of this time alone with such a beautiful lass. And all in vain. She was afraid of him. Afraid of his affliction. And, if the truth be told, probably filled with pity at the sight of him. How could he have been so blind, so foolish? Now he must get through this with as much dignity as possible, and pretend that it meant as little to him as it apparently did to her.

"I am sorry, my lady." He dropped her hands and turned to cup a rosebud between his fingers. "These were some of my mother's favorite blooms."

"I can see why. They are lovely."

He felt the old despair coming over him. How many times would he allow himself to hope, to dream, only to see those hopes and dreams dashed? When would he learn that life was not like those fantasies that played in his mind, teasing him, tormenting him with their promises?

"If you care to push my chair, Adrianna, we can go inside now."

She stood, feeling a stab of pain. She had thought of nothing but this man since their first meeting. She was in such a state of agitation she could hardly breathe. And now he was cruelly dismissing her. Perhaps their little walk had overtaxed him. Still, he had seemed so eager to be with her until a few moments ago. But it had always been this way. She was too shy. Her sister and brother constantly told her so. But clever words and flirtatious behavior were impossible for her to attempt.

"You promised to show me the place where you and your brother played as lads."

Why was she prolonging his agony? Richard pointed toward the row of newly planted trees. "It is over there."

She pushed his chair across the stones worn smooth from generations of Greys who had trod these paths. "There was once a fountain here," he said softly. "Brenna has suggested that the workmen could begin excavating. Perhaps, if my brother agrees, by late summer, there will be a new fountain here."

"It is so lovely." Her voice drifted over him, low, sultry. The soft French accent added a seductive quality. "So peaceful. I envy your mother. 'Twould be a wonderful place to watch children grow."

Children. Did she not know how the knife twisted in his heart? What woman would ever care to have children with a man who could not run and play with them? Or teach them to sit a horse?

"Oh. Look, my lord." Adrianna touched a blood-red rose whose inner petals were touched with palest peach. "How unique this blossom."

"Aye." Despite his glum thoughts Richard felt a rush of pleasure, that she should notice. "I took a cutting from the roses near the hedges and tied them to these stems. And the result is an entirely new strain of rose. This is the first bloom." Without ceremony he plucked it and handed it to Adrianna.

She was stunned at his generous gesture. "My lord. This is a flower like no other ever grown. You should not have picked it and wasted it on me."

His tone was gruff. "It is mine to give. I want you to have it." His tone softened perceptibly. "It suits you, Adrianna. You are a woman like no other."

Oh, why could she not be blessed with her sister's outgoing personality? Or some of Cordell's charm? She played with the sash at her waist while she kept her gaze averted. If only she could find the words.

Again she could not bring herself to look at him. It was further proof to Richard that she had come out here with him only out of a sense of pity.

He watched her for a moment, then said softly, "It is raining harder, my lady. You will soon be drenched. We should go in."

"Aye." She inhaled the fragrance of the rose, then reached for the back of his chair. As she did, her fingers encountered his shoulder. How lean and muscled he was. Her fingers tingled from the contact, and yet she had not the strength to back away.

Richard went very still, feeling the imprint of her touch upon his flesh. How long it had been since a woman touched him. How he longed for that which had been denied him for so long.

"My lord . . ."

"My lady . . ."

They both fell silent.

Adrianna began to push the heavy chair. As they moved past a trellis overgrown with roses, thunder crashed and the sky seemed to open up, drenching them.

"We had better stop here a moment, until there is a break in the clouds."

"Aye, my lord."

They paused in the shelter of the rose arbor, listening to the sound of the rain that pelted. Inside they were snug and dry.

Adrianna lifted her shawl to her face to wipe away the raindrops. As he watched Richard had an almost over-powering desire to kiss each one of them away. This sweet young lass would be shocked to the core if she could read his thoughts.

He glanced around. "I regret that there is no place for you to sit."

"I do not mind standing."

A hint of his old humor returned. "I would gladly ex-change places with you, my lady, if I could."

She laughed at his silly joke. Her laughter was like a soothing balm.

He joined in her laughter. "But, if you would not mind, I would gladly share this chair."

She glanced shyly at him. "There is not room enough for two of us, my lord."

"There is, if you sit on my lap."

"Would I hurt you if I did?"

It would be the sweetest pain he had ever endured. He said simply, "There is very little pain in my legs, Adrianna. Usually there is no feeling at all."

"Oh, my lord." Without any warning she dropped to the ground and wrapped her arms around his knees. Her laughter died in her throat. Tears sprang to her eyes. "For-give me, my lord. I know not why I weep. Nor why I should care so about your pain."

Richard was rendered speechless. While she wept, he could do nothing except sit helplessly and watch her tears fall.

Finally he touched a hand to her damp hair. Such soft hair, he thought. Like a cloud of burnished silk. In a tone low with feeling he whispered, "Do not cry for me, Adri-anna."

"It is not you I cry for."

She looked up at him and he could not help himself. He cupped her face between his hands and at her next words felt his heart leap to his throat.

"I weep because I am too afraid to show you how I feel."

His brows drew together into a puzzled frown. "I do not understand, lass. How do you feel?"

"My tongue is tied in your presence." She touched a hand to her heart. "All the things I have locked inside are bursting to be free. But you are the mighty warrior Richard Grey, devoted friend to the queen, hero known to all of France and England. And I am unworthy—to have such feelings for you."

"Feelings? For me?" He touched a finger to the curve of her cheek, and she moved against his palm like a kitten.

He felt his heart begin to soar and cautioned himself not to hope. But it was too late. Already his blood had begun to heat at the thought that this shy, sweet creature might actually care for him.

"Are you telling me that you are not offended by the sight of me?"

"Offended?" She drew back, aghast. "I am in awe of you, my lord. You are so handsome, so strong."

She thought him handsome? Strong?

"You converse as easily with the queen as you do with the servants. As you do with a foreigner like me."

He was silent for a moment as he studied her. With his thumbs he wiped away the last of her tears. Then, in a voice filled with passion, he whispered, "Talking has always been easy for me. Perhaps it is time I learned to listen as well. Stay here with me, lass. Tell me about yourself, your life, your dreams."

"My dreams are beyond my reach, I fear." She flushed and found herself drawn to open up to this man as she had never opened up to anyone before. "To dwell in a place as peaceful as Greystone Abbey. To awaken each morning to a chorus of birds and the perfume of roses."

He felt his hopes soar to the heavens. "Would there be a place for me in your dreams, lass?"

She gave a barely perceptible nod of her head before turning away with a flush. "You are all I have dreamed of since first I saw you."

"Oh, lass." He caught her hands and drew her onto his lap. With his lips pressed to her temple he murmured, "I pray this rain lasts for hours."

"What is this about a fall?" Morgan strode into Cordell's room.

Madeline sat on the chaise, tying a strip of fresh linen around her brother's hand. Her husband stood beside the fireplace watching.

"It was clumsy of me," Cordell said, glancing up from the dressing. "At first I thought I was pushed. But Madeline has convinced me that it was just my imagination. Who else would have been walking the stairs at that late hour? And why would anyone want to push me?"

Morgan's eyes narrowed. "Perhaps you could tell me more."

"There is little enough to tell. I awoke in need of something to slake my thirst. Rather than wake a servant I thought I would go down to the scullery. But as I paused at the top of the stairs I thought I saw a shadow of someone running toward me."

He glanced at his sister and saw her disapproving look. They were, after all, guests of Lord Morgan Grey and the queen. It would not be proper to suggest that anyone in their host's home would do anything improper.

"I confess it was very dark, my lord. Perhaps, as Madeline has suggested, what I saw was merely a tapestry along the wall, or even a cloud passing over the moon. At any rate, I thought I saw someone or something a moment before I felt a hand shove me as I took my first step. Before I knew what was happening, I had tumbled down an entire flight of stairs."

"A hand shoved you?"

"Perhaps—" Cordell swallowed "—in my confusion, I imagined it."

"The rug at the top of the stairs is loose, old friend," Charles said softly.

Morgan caught Cordell's hand and studied the fresh dressing. "You are wounded."

"A little blood. It is nothing my lord. I must have caught my hand on a splinter. My sister makes too much of it."

"I see you hit your head as well."

"Aye." Cordell touched a fingertip to the tender spot beside his temple. "At the bottom of the stairs I landed on my head."

Morgan's eyes darkened. "Are there any other wounds?"

"Bruises. Scratches. They are minor."

"I am grateful that nothing serious happened beneath my roof." Morgan noted the slight bulge under the Frenchman's tunic. It was obvious that another dressing had been applied to his chest. His tone grew dangerously soft. "I would take it most unkindly if there should be any further mishaps."

"Come," Charles said, taking his wife's arm. "It has been a long night. I would break my fast."

Madeline helped her brother to his feet and twined her fingers with his as they walked from the room.

Morgan trailed at a slower pace, his mind working feverishly.

The villain who attacked Brenna would be aware that she could identify him by the wounds she had inflicted. Could Cordell have faked his fall in order to explain away his bruises?

Morgan felt a momentary stab of guilt. Madeline was one of the finest women he knew. And his friendship with Charles went back to the days of their fathers. Though anything was possible, he could not find it in his heart to believe that either of them would be a party to this. But Cordell was an unknown. He had, after all, been smitten with Brenna when he first set eyes on her. Morgan dismissed the thought. Last night's attack had not been made by a man in love. Only a madman could have attacked Brenna so viciously.

There was, Morgan thought suddenly, something darker, more evil about this attack.

Cordell was an outsider, a loyal Frenchman who would swear homage to Charles IX, king of France. Could it be that this young patriot would go so far as to besmirch his own sister's good name and use her friendship to gain access to the queen? Could Elizabeth be the real target?

As a soldier, Morgan had learned to trust his instincts. And instinct told him that this attack on Brenna was somehow related to the threats to the queen's safety. There was an insidious web of evil being woven around them. And unless he unmasked the villain soon, they could all be ensnared in the ultimate tragedy.

Chapter Twenty

"Well. It seems that at least half of our party is finally at table." After Lord Quigley had given his approval, the queen enjoyed a slice of bread still warm from the ovens, spread with fruit conserve. "It is a pity that you have hurt yourself, Cordell. I pray that it will not keep you from enjoying Morgan's hospitality."

"Nay, Majesty." The young Frenchman seemed embarrassed by all the attention being lavished on him. "I look forward to all the festivities."

"We shall have to..." The queen's words faded as she stared beyond the young Frenchman to the figure in the doorway.

Morgan and the others looked up from the table as Lord Windham strode into their midst. He was bleeding and covered with mud. His tunic and breeches were torn and mud-spattered. The side of his head was badly swollen. He was holding his bloodied hand close to his chest.

"God in heaven." Morgan scraped back his chair. "What has happened to you?"

"My horse stumbled on a slippery bank and before I knew it I was tumbling through the air to land on my head."

"You will need assistance," the queen said, rushing to his side.

"Your Majesty." He glanced around the assembled guests. "You will forgive me if I do not join you until later?"

"Of course," Elizabeth said quickly. "Morgan, summon your servants."

"Aye."

Morgan reached for the cord that would summon a servant. Almost instantly Mistress Leems appeared. When she caught sight of Lord Windham she wrung her hands and hurried away to fetch the servants.

"You are an excellent equestrian, Windham," Morgan remarked, studying the man. Except for his hand, there was little blood. But it was difficult to be certain how badly he was injured under the mud.

"Even the best horseman would find it difficult in this rain. Ah, there you are, mistress." Windham bowed away from the queen and followed the servants from the room. "I will need a bath at once," he bellowed. "And fresh clothes."

"I will send for a physician," Morgan said quickly.

"Nay." Windham whirled. "'Twould be an inconvenience. One of your servants can bind these wounds. They will mend."

"It is no trouble. The queen's own physician can be here before the noon Angelus bells are rung."

"Nay. I insist. I will be fine."

Morgan watched as Windham climbed the stairs behind the cluster of servants.

When he joined the others at table, Morgan allowed the conversation to swirl around him while he sat lost in thought. He had been convinced that Cordell had been the one who had attacked Brenna last night. Now, he was no longer certain. Could Windham have pretended to fall from his mount in order to mask the injuries suffered at Brenna's hand?

His thoughts were interrupted when the door was opened and Richard entered the refectory from the garden. Behind him was Adrianna, pushing his chair. Both of them had smiles on their flushed faces. And both seemed oblivious to the fact that their hair curled damply from the rain and that their clothes were plastered to their bodies.

"Mon Dieu." Madeline got to her feet. "You will catch your death in those wet clothes."

"Oui." Adrianna smiled at her. "Look." She held out the rose that Richard had given her. "Richard has grown a new strain of rose. This is the first bloom."

Madeline stared at her shy little sister. Never before had she seen her look so radiant. Or so animated. "It is beautiful."

"You will excuse our appearance," Richard said, bowing slightly to the queen. "It is raining outside."

"Really? I had not noticed." Elizabeth swallowed the smile that touched her lips. "Not hard, I hope."

"Just a fine mist. A lovely fine mist. The kind of rain one might enjoy walking in." He smiled at Adrianna, then seemed to catch himself. "We must change clothes."

"Of course." Elizabeth lifted her hand in a regal gesture. "I would not want you to stay in those uncomfortable garments."

When the two had left, everyone burst into gales of laughter.

Elizabeth turned to Morgan. "It is as you said earlier, my friend. Everyone has gone mad."

Morgan stared after his brother and the French lass. "So it would seem."

"Come," Elizabeth called to her ladies. "We will retire to the sitting chamber until the rain stops. Brenna, join us."

Reluctantly Brenna joined the cluster of laughing, talking women. She would have rather stayed with Morgan. But the queen's request was a royal command. To refuse was unthinkable.

When they were gone, Morgan sat alone, staring into the flames of the fire, deep in thought.

Dinner with the queen was always a formal affair. Elizabeth and her companions had brought their most elegant gowns and spent hours preparing themselves for the evening.

In their chambers, Morgan and Brenna were grateful for some time alone, away from the prying eyes of the others.

While Brenna allowed Rosamunde to help her into her gown, she was achingly aware of the man who awaited her just beyond the door in the sitting chamber.

"Your hair, my lady."

"It is fine, Rosamunde. Do not fuss so."

"Aye, my lady."

As the servant turned away, Brenna caught her hand. "I did not mean to be short with you." Her eyes danced with unconcealed ardor. "It is just that I . . ."

"I understand, my lady. My Lord Grey awaits you just as impatiently."

With a conspiratorial smile, the servant was gone.

Without even taking time to study her reflection in the looking glass, Brenna opened the door. Morgan turned from the fireplace.

Her gown was deep purple velvet, with a low neckline. The skirt fell in soft folds from the narrow waist to the tips of her pale kid slippers. The sleeves were inset with jewel-encrusted bands.

As she walked closer Morgan reached inside his tunic and removed a velvet pouch. When he handed it to her, she lifted wide questioning eyes to him.

"I noticed that you are the only lady here with no jewelry. I want you to have these, my lady."

Brenna loosened the piece of velvet and caught her breath at the glittering jewels wrapped inside. There was a necklace of diamonds surrounding an amethyst as large as a hen's egg. The matching earrings were clusters of diamonds and amethyst that caught the light of the fire and seemed to glow with their own heat.

"I cannot possibly accept these, Morgan."

"But why?"

She tried to hand the jewelry to him, but he refused to take it.

"I am not yet your wife. It would not be right to accept such a splendid gift."

"But it would make me happy."

"And it would make me very uncomfortable."

His voice grew soft. "Will you tell me why, Brenna?"

She swallowed. "There are those who will think I—sold my favors for a handful of jewels."

"I care not what others say. Nor should you."

She studied the jewels in her hand. "You are too generous, Morgan. These must be worth at least a king's ransom."

"Or a Scots chieftain." He took the necklace from her hand and fastened it around her throat. "These were given to my father by a grateful King Henry. They were my mother's favorite pieces."

Brenna touched a hand to the jewels at her throat. "Then I shall treasure them, my lord."

"Not nearly as much as I treasure the woman who wears them."

"But I would prefer not to wear them until after we are wed."

"And I would prefer to see you wear them tonight."

He brought his lips to her throat and felt the need rising. As she affixed the earrings he allowed his hands to move slowly along the slope of her shoulders.

"How soft you are. How beautiful." He felt her shiver beneath his soft caress. "Would the queen mind if her host was late to sup?" he muttered thickly against her neck.

Brenna laughed. "You cannot be serious."

He turned her into his arms and stared down at her with a look that left her no doubt as to his meaning. "All day I have thought of nothing but you."

He bent his head and nibbled at her throat. With a little sigh she arched her neck, loving the feel of his lips on her skin.

"And tonight I fear the queen will linger below stairs long into the night. Unlike us, she has no reason to hurry to her bed."

"Though the evening will be unbearably long, what can we do about it?"

"This." His hands moved to the buttons of her gown.

"Morgan." As he slid the gown from her shoulders, she stifled a gasp. "The queen will be furious if we keep her waiting."

"Aye. But we will be so happy, love. And we will only be a little late."

When he scooped her into his arms and carried her to the bed, she pressed her lips to his throat to stifle her laughter as they once more tumbled into a world of exquisite pleasure.

"I am jealous," the queen said, staring at the jewels that adorned Brenna's throat and earlobes. "Your jewelry outshines even mine."

"I am told they were a gift from your father." Self-consciously Brenna touched a hand to her throat as she took a seat beside Morgan at the table.

"Aye. And though I have heard about the splendid Grey jewels, I have never before had occasion to see them. They are magnificent. You must please Morgan very much," the queen added slyly.

Brenna felt the heat rise to her cheeks.

To cover her embarrassment, Morgan said, "Brenna did not wish to wear them tonight. She thought them too opulent for her taste. But I persuaded her to wear them for just this one night to please me. Then they can be put away until our betrothal."

Across the table, Lord Windham studied Morgan and Brenna through narrow, hate-filled eyes. It was obvious that these two had become lovers. They flaunted their intimacy in his face. In the face of everyone in the room. How he hated Morgan Grey. All his life he had had everything he had ever wanted. The most beautiful women. The most exotic jewels. This fine estate. But the day was soon coming when Grey would see everything in his life turn to ashes.

"I am disappointed by all this rain," the queen was saying. As they enjoyed a late supper, she stared out at the gloomy sky. "I had hoped to hunt."

"The weather is the one thing in England that does not obey your command," Morgan said.

"Her Majesty will find a way to bring even that errant subject to its knees," Charles said with a laugh.

"Would that I could." Elizabeth tasted the tender young duckling and felt her mood lighten. "If we cannot hunt, then we must find another means of entertainment. Richard, did I not see a chess set in the library?"

"Aye, Majesty. You did." Beside him, Adrianna sat quietly, content to have her hand held firmly in his. They thought that the table linens hid their hands from view. But everyone at the table was aware of the way they sat, shoulders brushing, gazes darting at one another.

"Then I challenge you to a chess match after we sup."

"I accept your challenge. But be prepared. Though I am your loyal subject, I will not deliberately let you win."

"If you did, it would be no challenge. But I warn you, my handsome friend, I do not know how to lose."

Richard's eyes crinkled with a smile. "Perhaps tonight you shall have your first lesson in losing, Majesty."

"Rogue." The queen sipped her tea. "What of you, Madeline? What is your pleasure?"

"You know my pleasure. And my weakness. Cards, Majesty."

"Ah, yes. The gaming tables." Elizabeth glanced across the table toward the man who sat scowling. "Windham, are your wounds causing you pain?"

"Nay, Majesty. They will quickly heal." He seemed to catch himself. He had been brooding about the weather. All of his plans had centered around a hunting accident. It would have been so easy to hide himself and aim an arrow that would bring down the throne of England. But what if the damnable rain continued and they never got a chance to hunt? "I would prefer cards to another night of dancing."

"And you, Cordell? Are you feeling well enough to join us for the games?"

"I would not miss it, Majesty."

"I fear Madeline's brother possesses the same weakness as my dear wife," Charles said with an exasperated sigh. "Neither can resist a game of cards."

Windham brightened. "Then we shall play for money rather than just the challenge?"

"But of course," Madeline replied. "What fun would it be to play without a bet?"

Windham's evil smile grew. He loved nothing better than to gamble. Especially if he could find a way to sway the cards in his favor.

When they had finished their meal, the queen stood and the others followed.

"Perhaps this will be even more challenging than the hunt."

Everyone in the company brightened. The rain had not ruined this trip to the country after all. There were still many ways to test one's skill.

The cozy library was the perfect place for the queen and her party to relax. A cheery fire burned in the fireplace. Small tables had been set up for the various games to be played. A side table groaned with trays of sweets. Crystal decanters of wine and ale gleamed in the light of the fire.

"Do you play cards, my lady?" Lord Windham asked Brenna.

She backed away from his touch. Though he was aware of her reaction, his only indication was a tight-lipped smile.

"Aye, my lord. But it has been a long time since I have tested my skill."

"Splendid. Every game needs a sacrificial lamb."

Morgan held a chair for Brenna at a small game table. Cordell, Madeline and Lord Windham took the other seats.

"Beware, my lady," Morgan muttered loud enough for the others to hear. "There is talk of heavy wagers being made on the cards lately. Your cohorts at table do not play merely for sport."

"Truly?" Brenna cast an innocent glance around the table. "You would not take advantage of a stranger in your midst, would you?"

Madeline and her brother exchanged wicked chuckles.

"*Cherie*. We are all friends here. What can be the harm of a friendly wager?"

"What harm indeed?" Brenna picked up her cards.

"You will need money for wagering," Morgan said. He placed a large sum of money in front of her, which the others studied with greedy pleasure.

"How much is here, my lord?"

"The equivalent of fifty gold sovereigns."

"Fifty..." Brenna glanced around the table. "Did you not say this was to be a friendly wager?"

"For fifty gold sovereigns, my lady, we will be very friendly," Cordell said with a laugh.

Across the room, the queen and Richard set up their chess pieces and began their match. Brenna glanced at them and suppressed a smile. Adrianna sat beside Richard, drinking in every move he made. The queen, determined to win, studied her opponent with all the skill of a general.

Some of the queen's ladies sat on cushions on the floor, listening to the haunting music of a lute played by the queen's musician.

Servants scurried around with trays of goblets filled with ale and wine. In this relaxed atmosphere, even the queen enjoyed a second serving of ale.

Like a good host, Morgan moved between the tables, watching both the chess match and the card games.

"It appears that I have won," Brenna said excitedly as the last card was played.

"You were indeed lucky," Cordell said with a little frown. "This time I wish to double my bet."

Brenna scooped up the money she had won and matched his bet. "What about you, Madeline?"

Grudgingly the Frenchwoman reached into her pocket for more money.

Across the table, Lord Windham studied his cards, then agreed to bet.

When the cards were played, Brenna won again.

"I have never seen such luck with cards." Madeline turned to her husband, who stood watching the chess game. "Charles, I need..." She saw the disapproving frown on his face and bit back her words. She stood, scraping back her chair. "I have already overspent my limit."

"So have I," Cordell said with a laugh. "But I cannot allow myself to be beaten by a lowly female." He and Lord Windham shared a laugh. "One more hand, my lady, and we shall see who ends up with all the gold."

"Aye, Cordell. 'Tis only fair that the lady give you a chance to win back your money lost." Windham's words taunted. "Shall we double the bet again?"

"I would not advise it." Brenna glanced at the young Frenchman, hoping to discourage him.

"But I insist." Cordell tossed in his last coins.

Windham followed suit. Reluctantly Brenna did the same.

The cards were dealt and Brenna scanned them quickly, then made the first move. The others followed. When the hand was over, she scooped up a pile of money from the center of the table. At her yelp of laughter everyone looked up.

"Will you loan me the money to play again?" Cordell asked softly.

Brenna gave him a pitying glance. "'Twould be folly for me to allow you to sink into debt for a mere game."

"Ah, but it is not a game to me, my lady. I am compelled to try again. I know this time I can win. Will you loan me enough to at least make a wager?"

Before she could respond, Lord Windham said, "I will loan you the money, my young friend."

Cordell bowed his head. "I am most grateful."

"As for you, my lady." Fingering a gold coin, Windham turned to Brenna. "Your luck must end. We will play another hand, if you are willing. This time the wager will be two hundred gold sovereigns."

"Two hundred..." Brenna saw the greedy look in Windham's eyes. But she also saw the way Cordell studied her gold. The money was, after all, theirs before she won it. "Aye. You both deserve a chance to win back some of your gold."

She watched as Windham dealt the cards.

Morgan strolled across the room and stood behind Brenna as she played out the hand. When the last card was played, Brenna had again won.

"I believe the wager was two hundred gold sovereigns, my lord." Brenna's eyes danced with laughter.

"Aye." Lord Windham's face was expressionless as he counted out the money. But his eyes mirrored his anger.

"And two hundred for me," Cordell said.

Lord Windham counted out another sum, then spoke curtly to Cordell. "I shall expect your payment on the morrow."

"Aye, my lord. I am grateful for your generosity. Though in this instance, I fear the lady's advice was sound. I should not have made the final wager."

Morgan studied Brenna as she calmly collected the money. "I do not believe this is your first experience with gambling at cards, my lady."

Brenna gave him a demure smile. "My father would have been shocked to learn that my sisters and I were taught the fine art of gambling by my old nurse, Morna, and our keeper of the door, Bancroft. Often, on a winter's eve, my sisters and I would sneak into the servants' quarters to while away an hour or two." Her smile grew. "Old Bancroft showed no mercy toward us, despite the fact that we were the MacAlpin's bairns. The only way we could win was to best the old man. And best him we did. Eventually.''

"Cordell," Charles called to his brother-in-law. "It would appear that you and Lord Windham have been taken in by this innocent-looking female.''

The others burst into gales of laughter, and as Morgan joined them, he felt a grudging respect for the woman who sat calmly counting her money. There was so much about her he did not know. But he would learn. His smile grew as the wonderful thought struck. Aye. He would learn. They would have a lifetime to learn everything there was to know about each other.

Brenna turned to Morgan. "I believe this money is yours, my lord.''

"You won it, love. It is yours to keep.''

"I have no need of it.'' She thrust it into Morgan's hands.

Across the table, Lord Windham's lips curved into a smile as he watched the woman who had charmed everyone. The magnificent jewels at her ears and throat caught and reflected the light from dozens of candles.

A plan was growing in his mind. A plan that could bring down the Crown, Morgan Grey and everyone around him. And in the process, Windham would wind up with the woman.

It was brilliant. And if handled correctly, he could not lose.

The Frenchman's weakness could prove to be the key to everything.

Chapter Twenty-one

"Two hundred gold sovereigns, or the equivalent." Lord Windham glanced out the window at the gray mist.

"Aye, my lord." Cordell felt a trickle of sweat beneath his tunic. "As I said, I am a man of my word. I do intend to pay my debt. But if you could give me a few days..."

"You agreed to payment on the morrow. It is a new day, my foolish young man. And I expect payment, or I shall have to approach the queen about—" Windham paused for dramatic effect "—debtor's prison."

"My lord, I am a guest in your country. My resources are at my home in France."

"Your sister is married to a very wealthy man. I am certain that if you went to her..."

"Nay." Cordell held up a hand to interrupt him. "I cannot go to Madeline and Charles. As you know, my sister has run up gambling debts of her own, many of them to you. I sense that Charles is very unhappy with what he considers her weakness. Their marriage is happy enough, but I think that this could prove to be too much of a burden." Cordell paced the room, his hands locked behind his back. "If you would permit me to give you a note of indebtedness, I will be happy to send you the funds by courier when I return to France within a few days."

"Do you think me a fool?" Lord Windham's face was a sudden mask of fury. "You will pay your debt, my young man. Or you will pay in prison."

Cordell crumpled into a chair and buried his face in his hands. "Please, my lord. I cannot bring this scandal to my family. My sister has made a good life for herself here. She desperately loves her husband."

"Love." Windham gave a cruel smile. "It is such a fragile thing. It can so easily turn to hatred." His voice frosted over. "Have you no friends?"

"I am a stranger in your land."

Windham looked out the window, calculating how long before the young man would sink into despair. In silky tones he said, as though speaking to himself, "I suppose the tenderhearted young Scotswoman might be willing to come to the aid of anyone facing such bleak prospects as prison."

Cordell looked up. "Do you think the Lady Brenna would settle my debt?"

"You saw the jewels our host has lavished upon her. And the ease with which he gave her the money to gamble. Two hundred gold sovereigns would be a paltry sum to her."

Cordell brightened. "And the lady could be trusted to be—discreet."

"Aye." Windham watched the transformation in the Frenchman. "The lady seems your best hope." He walked closer, pretending to be deep in thought.

He saw the frown of distaste etched on Cordell's face at the thought of baring his soul to the beautiful Brenna, and added hastily, "Best of all, your family's good name will not be marred."

Cordell thought about Madeline, whose husband enjoyed a position of such importance with the queen. She would be devastated if any scandal touched him. And dear sweet Adrianna. The look in her eyes each time she was with Richard Grey left no doubt. She was in love for the first time in her life. She would be shattered if her brother's gambling debts created a scandal.

"Do you really think the Lady Brenna would help me?"

Windham chose his words carefully. "The lady has sisters of her own. If you are completely honest with her, and tell her your fears for your sisters, I have no doubt that she will come to your aid."

Cordell nodded. "I will speak with her immediately."

"I would wait—" Windham touched his arm as he opened the door to his chambers "—until you can speak with her privately. Morgan Grey may not be as sympathetic to your cause as the Lady Brenna."

"Aye, my lord. I will choose my time carefully."

When he was alone, Lord Windham walked to the window and stared out at the prosperous lands of the Grey estate. When the new king of England was crowned, perhaps he would settle Greystone Abbey upon the one who had been responsible for the downfall of Elizabeth.

It was all so easy. Everything in life was a gamble. But it helped if one saw to it that one were dealt the right cards.

"Another day and still it rains." The queen greeted the others in the refectory, then flounced to the windows to stare morosely at the leaden sky.

In an attempt to tease her out of her dark mood, Richard said, "I could beat Your Majesty at chess again today."

He sat beside Adrianna at the table. He was achingly aware of the young lass who looked as fresh and sparkling as a spring day. Last night, after all the others had retired to their chambers, she had sat talking with him until almost dawn. She had even permitted him several chaste kisses before hurrying off to her bed as the first pink streaks had colored the sky.

"I have some news that should brighten your day, Majesty."

Morgan placed a scroll before her on the table. "The people from the village have proclaimed this as a day of festivities in your honor."

He saw the light that came into the queen's eyes. It was no secret that Elizabeth loved all the pomp and ceremony that accompanied her wherever she traveled. There were even those who whispered that the reason the queen moved from palace to palace throughout the kingdom was to meet the people. In every hamlet and village in which she passed the citizens turned out to pay homage to their monarch. Their outpouring of love delighted her. And though she often complained in private about their long-winded orations, in public she was the benevolent monarch.

"Have you responded?" Elizabeth looked up from the scroll.

"Nay, Majesty. A messenger just delivered this from the village dignitaries. They await your decision."

"How delightful." She glanced around at her ladies. "If we cannot hunt, at least we can join in the feasting and celebration." With a flourish she affixed her signature to the scroll and handed it to Morgan.

At the far end of the table, Lord Windham watched the queen's reaction with great interest. He had come here for one reason—to find the right moment to do the deed for which he had been recruited. There had been a good chance that at some time during their hunt, he would find the queen unescorted. After all, he reasoned, Morgan Grey could not spend every minute at the queen's side, guarding her royal flank. It would take but a minute to aim and shoot the arrow into her heart, then to hide himself in the forest. No one would ever learn the identity of her executioner. And the one who would ascend the throne would owe Windham a great debt.

The weather was forcing him to change his plans. He would simply have to find some other way to get the queen alone. Alone. Aye, that was the problem. He must find a way to eliminate Morgan Grey. And, he thought with a sense of elation, he had come up with the perfect plan.

It was not riches alone that Windham coveted; it was the power. No longer would Morgan Grey hold sway over the throne of England. It would be Lord Windham to whom the new monarch would turn in times of crisis. And it would be Windham who would be admired throughout the land.

"The thought of a village feast does not please you, Lord Windham?"

He composed his features and chose his words carefully. "I came here to Greystone Abbey for one reason—to bask in the glow of your radiance, Majesty. But of course I had hoped to join you in the hunt."

"Aye. It is what I promised you." Elizabeth gave him a happy smile. "But the people wish to show me how much they love me." She shrugged. "How can I deprive them of their pleasure?"

As always he ingratiated himself with the queen. "I can understand their devotion, Majesty. It pleases me as it pleases all your subjects to convey our love and devotion to our beautiful queen."

From his place at the table Morgan listened to this exchange with a sense of disgust. Could the queen not see through Windham's shallow flattery?

He thought of Elizabeth's words at court. Even a woman as powerful as the Queen of England desired honeyed words at times. Even if they masked the truth.

"Then it is decided."

At the queen's nod, Morgan rang for Mistress Leems, who directed the servants to begin serving the queen and her company. "After the noon Angelus chimes we will leave for the village."

The villagers of Greystone Abbey were fiercely proud of their legacy of devotion to the Crown. In preparation for the visit of their monarch, the village square was hung with flags and buntings and banners proclaiming this the queen's day. A feast had been prepared by the village women. Tables set with fine linen and crystal had been placed in the village square beneath tents to protect them from the rain.

A gift was hurriedly prepared. A tax had been collected to fill a wooden coffer with gold. When Morgan had heard, he'd insisted upon adding to the gift, so that the villagers would not be forced to sacrifice their meager funds. He had also donated several deer from his larder to round out the feast.

When the carriages from Greystone Abbey arrived in the village, the inhabitants crowded around for their first glimpse of the queen. Many in the crowd held their children aloft. When Elizabeth stepped from her fine carriage, arrayed in a royal velvet gown and matching cape lined with ermine, and wearing a diamond tiara in her hair, there were shouts and cries of joy. The church bells rang out, filling the air with their happy sounds for nearly ten minutes. Then, as the queen stood, proud and haughty before them, the assembled crowd grew abruptly silent as they bowed and curtsied, awaiting her benediction.

The queen studied the silent, respectful crowd. The men and women were dressed in their finest clothes. The children, plump and pink-cheeked, were on their best behavior as they stared unblinking at the red-haired woman who looked every inch the queen.

"Majesty." The village elder was led forward, pale and trembling in the presence of his queen. "Words cannot express the love your people feel for you. Unworthy though we be, we are grateful for your visit to our humble village."

Seeing the way his hands shook, the queen blessed him with her sweetest smile. "It is I who am grateful." Her voice rose above the crying babies and the sighing of the wind in the trees. "Grateful for the love and loyalty of good people like you."

As she began to move among the villagers, Morgan stayed close by her side. His men, having been carefully instructed, mingled with the people, watching to see that no one who came near the queen could be concealing a weapon. Though Morgan knew the perils, he had been unwilling to deny his villagers this chance to see their ruler. Yet he also knew that he would not relax his guard until this day was ended, and the queen was safely at his home.

The village elder led the queen to the green, where the feast awaited her. As she took her place at the head of the table, Elizabeth knew from experience that she would have to endure endless speeches before she was allowed to enjoy the food. Lord Quigley sat alone, already tasting every morsel that the queen would be permitted to eat.

When everyone had taken their places at the rows of crude tables, the lord mayor of the village bowed low before the queen and began his prepared speech. His voice quavered in a most unbecoming fashion. His knees trembled. His beard shook. But though he appeared terrified, he continued speaking until the queen was forced to stifle a yawn.

After the lord mayor came the sheriff, who proved to be a fine orator. So fine that he talked until he spied the village elder's head nodding. Reluctantly he turned to the village recorder, who would also make a speech before presenting the queen with the village gift.

When at last Elizabeth was presented with the coffer of gold, she stood regally and declared, "I am most grateful. But all that I have ever desired were the hearts and true allegiance of my good people."

Then, handing the gift to Morgan, she asked that the feasting begin.

Seated beside her, Morgan swallowed his laughter. Despite all her denials, he noted, the queen did not return the gift of gold. Nor would she when the feasting was done. She may desire their hearts and allegiance, but she enjoyed their gold as well.

When the last morsel had been consumed, the queen and her guests were treated to a great pageant. Thespians performed a play in which the queen was likened to the Greek gods. Musicians from the village played while young maidens, clad in their finest gowns, performed ancient dances. And finally, the brightest young lad was brought forth to recite a poem praising the queen's beauty and integrity.

When darkness fell there were fireworks. And when at last the queen and her company were assisted into their carriages, the church bells tolled, filling the night air with the sound of celebration.

"What think you, Morgan?" the queen asked as the carriage rolled along the road toward Greystone Abbey.

"I think, Majesty, that the villagers will speak of this for generations to come. Mothers will tell their daughters, and they will speak of it proudly to their children, until this grand visit of yours has become a legend."

"Aye," Brenna said with a sigh. "'Tis the stuff of legends, Majesty. Never have I seen such an outpouring of love."

The queen leaned her head back and closed her eyes. What need had she of a consort? This love was what fed her soul. With love like this, how could she have ever believed for a moment that her life was in any danger?

Brenna awoke from a deep sleep and listened to the insistent tapping on the door of the sitting chamber. For a moment a chill passed through her as she was reminded of her nighttime attack.

The tapping continued. She chose to ignore the sound. If one of the servants desired entrance, they would have to come back in the morning.

Morgan lay against her back, his arms wrapped protectively around her. Their legs were tangled in the bed linens. They had spent a long, leisurely night of lovemaking. Her body still hummed from his caresses.

The tapping sounded again. Her lids opened. Judging by the darkness of the room, Brenna knew that it would be hours until dawn. Who would seek her out at such a time? Certainly not her attacker.

Her heart skipped a beat. Perhaps Madeline. Or an emissary from the queen. Could one of them be ill?

She slipped soundlessly from bed and snatched up her dagger from the bedside table. She slipped it into her waistband, then pulled a shawl around her shoulders and padded barefoot to the other room.

When she pulled open the door she was stunned to find Cordell standing with his hand poised in the air, about to knock again.

"My lady," he whispered, "I must speak with you."

For a moment she could only stare at him. Then, as she began to close the door she whispered, "On the morrow..."

"Nay." He caught the door, holding it open. "This cannot wait until morning."

Brenna's eyes widened. "Is it Madeline? Or Adrianna?"

"Nay, my lady. The problem is mine. Will you come with me below stairs where we may speak without detection?"

Brenna hesitated. But the imploring look on his face, and the urgency of his tone, persuaded her. She closed the door behind her and walked beside him until they reached the deserted great room.

Brenna crossed the room to stand before the fireplace. Even though the fire had long ago burned down, the hot coals chased away the chill. She turned.

"What is so urgent, Cordell, that you would rout me from my bed at this late hour?"

"It is my gambling debt to Lord Windham," he began.

"What of it?"

A chilling voice sounded from the far side of the room. "He promised payment on this day," Windham said, stepping from the shadows.

Brenna felt the ice curl along her spine. Her hand instinctively moved to the hilt of her dagger.

"It will soon be the dawn of another day, and still this Frenchman has not paid his debt. Unless this thing is settled now, I will be forced to go to the queen and demand that Cordell be confined to debtor's prison."

"That would seem a harsh measure, my lord." Brenna glanced from Windham to Cordell. "What has this to do with me?"

"I had hoped, my lady," Cordell said, his face pale, "that you might be willing to buy my debt from Lord Windham."

"Buy your debt?" She glanced at Windham. "Would you be willing to sell it?"

"Aye, my lady. For the amount due. Two hundred gold sovereigns."

Brenna shrugged. "I will speak with Morgan."

"Nay, my lady." Cordell stepped forward until she could see his eyes by the light of the coals. They were round with fear. "My little sister, Adrianna, seems captivated by Richard Grey. I cannot allow his brother to think unkindly about my family, else I could shatter Adrianna's heart. And Madeline and Charles are two of Morgan Grey's dearest friends. A scandal like this could come between their friendship." His voice pleaded. "All I ask is that you pay Lord Windham two hundred gold sovereigns. In return, I shall send you the sum of two hundred fifty gold sovereigns when I return to France."

Brenna caught his cold hands in hers. "Two or two hundred, it matters not to me. I have no money of my own in this land. I am completely dependent upon the generosity of Morgan Grey."

Her words were like a knife in Cordell's heart. With a stricken look he turned to Windham.

"My lord. You have heard the lady. How can I persuade you to allow me more time?"

"Your time is up." Windham paused, then said softly, "Unless..."

"What is it? Please," Cordell urged, feeling a glimmer of hope. "I will do anything."

Windham glanced beyond Cordell to study Brenna, as though the thought had just struck him. "I might be persuaded to accept something of value until the debt can be paid."

Cordell was puzzled. "I have nothing of value, my lord."

"Perhaps the lady has." Windham waited, becoming aroused as his sense of power began to grow. They still did not understand. But in a few moments they would be caught in his web.

"Nay. I have nothing," Brenna said. "I was brought to England with nothing but the clothes upon my back."

"You have jewels." Windham deliberately kept his tone soft, to veil his mounting excitement.

"They are Morgan's jewels," Brenna said patiently. "They have been in Morgan's family for generations."

"The necklace you wore last night is yours." Windham glanced at Cordell for confirmation. "Did you not hear Morgan Grey say as much?"

"Aye," Cordell affirmed. "But they are worth far more than the two hundred gold sovereigns that I owe you, my lord."

"True. This would seem a paltry sum for one as wealthy as the Lady Brenna. But I would be willing to hold the jewels until you can return to France and pay your debt to the lady."

Brenna felt the protest rise in her throat. She turned to Cordell. "I cannot do this without Morgan's permission. I would feel that I had somehow betrayed his trust."

"I understand, my lady." Cordell turned to face the man who would be judge and executioner.

Windham's voice was pure silk. "Of course, if the jewels mean that much to you, my lady, that you would refuse to help a friend, I understand, too." He sighed, as if the matter were finished. "I regret that I will be forced to go to the queen." His voice purred. "I regret that Madeline will be shamed before her husband. And of course, a young woman as sweet and shy as Adrianna will never again be able to face Richard Grey. She is young, though extremely vulnerable. He, of course, has already been severely damaged. The scandal could shatter their lives."

Brenna paled. She thought of her own sisters, and the fierce pride they had in their family honor. And then she thought of the first woman who had befriended her in this land. Madeline. And what of Adrianna and Richard? No one deserved love and happiness more than they.

"You will only hold the jewels, my lord? And when Cordell's debt is paid you will return them to me?"

"Have I not said as much?"

Brenna hesitated for a moment longer, seeing the light of hope that flickered in Cordell's dark eyes. She had not the heart to extinguish his last hope.

She started toward the door, determined to do the deed quickly, before she changed her mind. Within minutes she had returned with the velvet pouch containing the necklace and earrings.

"You will breathe not a word of this," she said, placing the pouch in Windham's hands.

His eyes glittered as he opened the pouch and felt the warmth of the diamonds and amethyst in his palm. "My lips are sealed."

"And you," she said to Cordell, "will give me your word that you will never again gamble."

"I swear it, my lady." He fell to his knees and brought both her hands to his lips. "I am your devoted servant for the rest of my life."

As Brenna made her way to bed, she felt a heaviness around her heart. This had all happened too quickly. In her tired, overwrought state, there had been no time to reason her way through this, and now her mind was reeling.

There would be no sleep for her this night. As she settled herself beside Morgan, she drew close to him, hoping to absorb his warmth, his strength. She had helped a friend, but it gave her little satisfaction. She could not shake her eerie feelings about Windham. The man was evil. And she had the frightening feeling that there was more to this than a gambling debt.

Chapter Twenty-two

"You look tired, lass." Richard's head came up from the rose he was tending.

"Aye. I did not sleep well last night." Brenna glanced around. "Is Adrianna not with you?"

"Nay. She and her sister are visiting with the queen. I thought you would be with them."

"I sent my regrets. I have been searching for you." She licked her lips. "You once said that if I desired to talk, you would be here to listen."

Richard placed the shears in his lap and leaned forward in his wheeled chair. "What is it, lass? What troubles you?"

"Oh, Richard."

He saw the tears that welled up in her eyes.

"I cannot tell you without betraying a confidence. But I fear I have done a terrible thing. If Morgan learns of it, he will never forgive me."

"You, lass?" Richard took her hands in his and stared into her eyes. "You are the best thing that has ever happened to my brother. You have brought back all the love, all the laughter, that had been buried beneath so much pain. Because of you, Morgan has learned to live again, and laugh again. And what is more important, trust again."

Trust. Brenna felt as if her heart would break from the pain. "By helping a friend I may have destroyed his trust forever."

Richard leaned forward and touched a finger to her lips to silence her. "Listen to me, Brenna. I had not thought it possible that Morgan would ever recover from the pain of his youthful marriage. What you have done for him is nothing short of a miracle."

"I do not understand. Why was he left so bitter and angry?"

"When a man is young and honorable, he believes that the whole world is the same. It is shattering to discover that some people are so shallow, or so cruel, that they have no regard for anyone but themselves."

Richard leaned back, feeling the sunshine warm upon his face. "My brother was hardly more than a lad the first time he went to his marriage bed. No more than twenty. And she but ten and five."

"What was her name?"

A slight frown furrowed Richard's brow. "She was the queen's cousin, Catherine Elder."

The queen's own cousin. Timidly Brenna asked, "Was she very beautiful?"

"Beautiful enough to turn the head of every man at court. She had hair the color of a gold sovereign, and a full, ripe figure." Richard's frown grew. "But Morgan was not the only man in love with her. There were many men who paid her court."

"But of all the men who sought her, Morgan was the one who won her hand."

"Aye, lass, but the price he paid was not worth the prize."

"I do not understand."

"Morgan may have won her hand, but another won her heart. She came to her marriage bed carrying another man's child."

"How horrible."

"Aye. Other men would have had her put away. But Morgan was too tenderhearted for his own good. He reasoned that he would save the lady's honor, even though everyone already knew she was sullied. The other man had refused to do the honorable thing. So Morgan endured the humiliation. But within weeks of their marriage, she fell once more under the spell of her former lover.''

"Did no one know his identity?'' Brenna asked.

"Nay. She refused to tell even her family who the man was.'' Richard shrugged. "At the time, we thought she was simply so in love, she could not bring herself to speak of him. But later, when it was too late, we realized that she had been warned by this man not to reveal his identity under threat of death.''

"How could he claim to love her and still threaten her life?''

"Catherine was too blinded by passion to ask that question, lass. She simply wanted to believe that the rake loved her. But he was merely using her. He coerced her into stealing from Morgan's considerable fortune. This went on for several months, and may have gone undetected even longer had not the man become greedy.''

Picturing a youthful, noble Morgan, Brenna felt the sting of tears. She quickly blinked them away. Though it pained her to hear of Morgan's past, she was now compelled to hear all of it.

"In the library Morgan discovered a strongbox opened. The contents were missing. When he confronted Catherine, she admitted that she had given them to her lover. Morgan flew into a rage and ordered her to tell him the name of the man who had dragged her to such depths.''

Brenna sat very stiffly, twisting her hands together until the knuckles were white from the effort. In her mind's eye she could see the young, honorable Morgan being consumed with rage and allowing his heart to harden forever. "What happened then?''

"Catherine must have feared Morgan's rage more than her lover's. She agreed to fetch the contents. She was gone so long that Morgan sent servants out into the countryside to search for her. Late that night she was found along the road, bruised and bloodied beyond saving. She had been run through by a sword. With her last breath she begged Morgan's forgiveness, then told him she had once truly loved him, but she had been persuaded to give in to the lustful desires of another. She admitted that she had wanted a father for her child, and had hoped that she could be a good wife to him. But her lover's hold on her was too strong to break. With her last breath she begged Morgan's forgiveness. In her hands she clutched the contents of the strongbox.''

Brenna felt her throat go dry. She suddenly knew without asking what the contents of the strongbox were. Running her tongue over her lips she whispered, ''Tell me, Richard. Did the box contain the Grey jewels?''

''Aye, lass. The Grey jewels. Including the pieces Morgan gave you the other night. When I saw you wearing them, it was the first time they had been out of that box since that terrible night.''

God in heaven. What had she done? Brenna felt a wave of nausea. Windham had coerced her into doing the one thing Morgan could never forgive.

With her hand to her mouth she let out a cry and bolted from the garden.

''I must speak with Lord Windham.''

As Brenna entered Windham's chambers a servant looked up from her chores. ''Lord Windham is gone, my lady.''

''Gone? Where?''

''He said he had urgent business at the Crooked Tree Inn in the village.''

''When is he returning to Greystone Abbey?''

''He is not, my lady. He took all his things with him, in preparation for his departure to London.''

London. Brenna felt a wave of panic. He must not be allowed to take the jewels to the city. She must get them back before it was too late.

Hurrying to her room, Brenna pulled on a traveling cloak and called to Rosamunde, "Order a groom to saddle a mount."

"But my lady..."

"Now, Rosamunde. Hurry. There is no time to explain."

Minutes later Brenna flew down the stairs and out into the courtyard, where a groom stood holding the reins of a horse.

As Brenna pulled herself into the saddle Rosamunde called, "If my lord Morgan Grey should ask, where should I say you have gone, my lady?"

"Tell him I have gone to retrieve something of value. And when I return I will explain everything."

She urged her mount into a run. And as they covered the miles to the village, Brenna's heart matched the thundering tempo of the horse's hooves. What had she done? God in heaven. What terrible thing had she done?

Though it was early afternoon, the public room of the Crooked Tree Inn was filled with the laughing, raucous voices of tradesmen and travelers.

Brenna stood just inside the entrance, uncomfortably aware of the curious glances from some of the patrons. A serving wench whispered in the ear of a big coarse man dressed like a sailor. He laughed, then pulled her down on his lap and kissed her soundly. With a playful slap at his shoulder, she looked up, straightened her skirts and made her way to Brenna.

"Yes, miss. What would be your pleasure?"

"I am looking for Lord Windham. Recently arrived from Greystone Abbey."

"Aye. A fine, fancy man with golden hair and eyes that undress ye every time he looks at ye?" She seemed to assess Brenna for a moment, then gave her a conspiratorial smile. "His lordship said there'd be a fine lady along soon."

Her words caused Brenna to blink. Had he arranged a tryst with someone? He would not take kindly to her interruption. She would have to beg his pardon and conclude her business quickly.

"His lordship's having a meal in his room. Second floor."

"Thank you."

Brenna climbed the stairs, rehearsing the things she would say to Windham. She would appeal to his honor as a gentleman and as a friend of the queen. She would remind him of the hospitality shown by Morgan while Windham was his guest. And if all else failed, she would beg him to return the jewels and she would agree to sign a document attesting to her debt on Cordell's behalf.

She knew that she was taking a dangerous risk. But she no longer had anything to lose. If she tried and failed, she would lose Morgan. But if she did nothing, she would still lose Morgan. One desperate thought echoed in her mind. If she succeeded, she would have everything her heart had ever desired.

She paused outside the door, then lifted her hand and knocked.

"Enter."

Brenna stepped inside.

Lord Windham sat before a cozy fire, enjoying a sumptuous meal. His smile was dazzling.

"My lady. Come in. Join me in a celebration feast."

"Forgive my intrusion. I will be but a moment."

"Nay." His evil smile grew. "You are a part of the celebration."

She felt a sudden chill at his words. "What are you celebrating, my lord?"

"A new era for England. A time of great wealth and power for me."

"Wealth." She misunderstood his meaning. "You mean the Grey jewels. About those jewels, my lord . . ."

"These?" He held up the little pouch, and Brenna took a step closer.

"Aye. I came to ask that you return them."

"Of course you did."

"You do not mind?"

He threw back his head and laughed. "Mind? My lady, it is exactly as I had planned it."

She paused, puzzled by his words. "I do not understand."

He lifted a goblet of wine to his lips and drained it. Scraping back his chair he stood. "Come closer, my lady."

When she hesitated, he caught her roughly by the arm and dragged her close.

His voice, which only seconds ago had been jovial, was now low and deadly. "When I give an order, you must comply immediately. Do you understand?"

She felt the sting of his hot breath and was reminded of the man who attacked her in the night. Her eyes widened. "It was you. That night in Morgan's room. It was you."

He gave her an evil smile. "Do you remember the lesson I taught you?"

Without thinking she touched a hand to the scar on her arm.

He pulled out a chair and ordered her to sit. When she refused he brought his hand across her face, slapping her so hard it snapped her head to one side.

"Now," he said, as quietly as if nothing had happened, "you will do as I order. Sit down."

It was as she had known the night of her attack. Only a madman could behave in such fashion, one minute calm, almost serene; the next vicious.

Her hand went to the knife at her waist. As if reading her mind, Windham twisted it viciously from her hand and gave her a crashing blow to the temple.

Stunned, Brenna sank into the chair and watched as Windham pulled out a scroll and began writing. When that note was finished he wrote a second, then tugged on a cord. A few minutes later the serving wench stood at the door. Windham handed her the notes and several coins, then gave her detailed instructions on how the notes were to be delivered.

He sat down at the table, filled his goblet and drank.

"We should not have to wait too long." His eyes glittered with a feverish light. "Then everything that was once Morgan Grey's will be mine. Including you, my lady."

The queen read the note that had been delivered, then gave a little cry of pleasure. "What a perfect ending to my visit at Greystone. Morgan says that the weather is improving." She lifted her skirts and rushed to the window. "Aye. Though it is still quite misty, I can see the sun breaking just beyond those trees." She tossed down the missive and turned to her ladies. "We must hurry and change into suitable clothing. We are going on a hunt."

Morgan looked up from the ledgers as Mistress Leems entered.

"There is a messenger here from the village, my lord."

"Show him in."

Morgan waited until both messenger and housekeeper had gone, then unsealed the scroll. Something fell from the scroll and dropped to the desk. An earring, Morgan realized as he picked it up. His eyes narrowed. An earring made of dazzling diamonds and amethysts.

He read the words with a growing sense of revulsion. For long minutes he stared into the flames of the fire, reliving all the shame and pain and horror of his past. With a savage oath he tore the message into small pieces and dropped them one by one into the flames. Then he strode across the room and picked up his sword.

This time they were not dealing with some pink-cheeked lad whose head was filled with noble thoughts. This time he would dispose of the lady himself. And her lover.

As he raced from the room the words of the message rang in his mind.

"I have once again seduced the woman you love. And this time she has brought me your treasure even before the wedding. I have enclosed proof of her loyalty."

Through a haze of pain Brenna watched as Windham calmly continued eating his meal. Her head still swam from his blows. She struggled to clear her mind. Somehow she had fallen into a trap. He had said he was expecting her. But why? And what had the jewels to do with all of this?

So many pieces to a puzzle. But until they were all in place, she was left with only questions. She must bide her time. And watch for a chance to escape.

"So you came for the jewels?" He broke off a joint of fowl and began to eat.

Brenna was instantly alert. "Aye."

"Has Morgan missed them?" He washed down his food with a swallow of ale.

"Nay."

"So." He grinned. "Your conscience has gotten the best of you."

"Aye. I had no right to give away what was not mine."

"And what about that which is yours to give?"

His gaze roamed the bodice of her gown, making her feel soiled. She thought about the serving wench's description of Windham. His eyes were undressing her.

She gauged the distance to the door. She would never make it. But if she were to find some way to distract him, she might be able to run to safety.

"I am not loose with my favors." She struggled to hide the revulsion she felt at the thought of this man's touch. "And your own queen has decreed that I am to be betrothed to Morgan Grey."

"You are not yet betrothed. Besides—" he smiled and dropped the linen napkin on his plate "—if Grey were dead, you would be free to wed another."

Dead? Morgan? Was this what it was all about?

Lord Windham scraped back his chair and strolled to the window. He watched as a horse and rider moved up the lane in a cloud of dust. There could be but one man who would whip his mount into such a frenzy. He felt a curl of excitement begin deep inside him.

He heard the slight swishing of skirts and turned just in time to see Brenna racing toward the door.

As her hand closed over the door pull, Windham caught her by the hair, yanking her head back with such force that tears stung her eyes. He slammed her against a wall, then pinned her there with both hands firmly against her shoulders. When her eyes could focus, she realized he was holding her knife, the knife Morgan had given her, to her throat.

His face was inches from hers. His eyes blazed with fury.

"Little fool. Did you think I would get this close to my goal and let it slip through my fingers?"

"It is Morgan, isn't it?" Brenna felt herself very close to hysteria. "That is what you scheme. To somehow lure Morgan here and kill him."

His shrill laugh sent a new wave of fear coursing along her spine.

"Your lover is already here. Any minute now he will step up to meet his death. But Grey is only half of the plot. The other half is even better."

Brenna felt the cold steel of the blade as it was pressed to her flesh. She was certain that nothing could cause her more pain than the thought of Morgan's death. But Windham's next words caused her to freeze in absolute terror.

"When Grey is eliminated," he muttered, "the queen will be without her protector. And the future of England will be in my hands."

Chapter Twenty-three

The serving wench directed Morgan up the stairs, then watched as he took them three at a time. How she wished she could see the faces of the two lovers when this one burst upon them. His features were distorted with rage. His hand was already on the hilt of his sword.

Morgan had been unable to think, to reason, on his journey from Greystone Abbey. The only thought that drummed in his mind was that this could not be happening again.

Even now Morgan could not believe that he would find Brenna with Windham. Despite the message, despite the horse at the railing that he knew to be from his stables, he harbored the glimmer of hope that it was all some horrible mistake. The woman who had shared his bed, the woman he loved more than life itself, was incapable of the deed Windham had described. But in some small corner of his mind remained the knowledge that it had happened to him before. And it was happening to him again.

He did not bother with the formality of knocking. With a booted foot against the door he sent it crashing inward. He strode inside, his sword drawn, then stopped in midstride.

Windham stood across the room, holding Brenna captive in his arms. With one hand he held her arms behind her back. His other hand held a dagger to her throat. Morgan's own dagger.

"You came so quickly, Grey." Windham's voice was strangely high-pitched with excitement. "I hardly had time to prepare." He laughed, high and shrill. "I'd hoped to have the lady lying in bed with me, just to add to your discomfort. But alas the lady would not cooperate."

Morgan's eyes narrowed as he studied the scene before him. From Brenna's disheveled appearance, he knew that she had put up a brave battle. But she would be no match against the cruel Windham. Still, it was enough to know that she was not a willing party to this.

"Why are you here, Brenna?" Morgan's voice was calm. Too calm.

Brenna recognized the terrible control he was exerting on his temper.

"I persuaded the lady to pay Cordell's gambling debt."

Morgan ignored Windham. "You have no money, Brenna."

"Aye." Her voice was unnaturally subdued. "But Lord Windham said that unless the debt was paid by midnight, he would send Cordell to debtor's prison. I knew that would bring shame to his sisters. And so I agreed to allow Lord Windham to hold the jewels until Cordell could arrange to pay his debt." Her voice began to break, and she knew that the tears were starting. She quickly swallowed them back. "Today, when Richard told me about your first marriage, I knew that I had to retrieve the jewels before you discovered what I had done. And so I came here to plead my case. Alas, it was what Lord Windham had expected."

"Let the lady go, Windham. This is between the two of us."

"If I let her go, you will run me through with your sword." Windham gave an evil smile. "But unless you lay down your sword, I intend to run the lady through with this knife." He paused, seeing the fury in Morgan's eyes. "Which shall it be?"

Without a word Morgan let his sword drop to the floor with a clatter.

"That is very wise, Grey. We would not want the lady to end up like the last one."

Morgan went very still. His eyes blazed. "How would you know how Catherine died unless…" His tone hardened. "It was you. God in heaven. All those years ago, it was you."

At the stunned expression on Morgan's face, Windham said, "She did not fight as well as the Lady Brenna. Perhaps it was the baby that slowed her down. Or perhaps she had already lost her will to live. At any rate, I realized she would be of no further use to me. And I feared you would persuade her to reveal my name."

Morgan's voice was barely more than a whisper. "She took her secret to the grave. Why would you risk the truth now?"

"Because I have nothing to lose. You will never leave this room. My secret dies with you."

"There were so many beautiful women, Windham. Why did you choose Catherine?"

"Why did you? We were both young and eager to taste the nectar of all the flowers in the realm." His eyes narrowed. "But you always seemed to have everything I wanted. The finest estate. The most precious jewels. And then, the most beautiful woman I had ever seen. I could not let you win again. I vowed to have the woman, and to make you suffer."

"But you are a wealthy man. You did not need my gold or jewels. Why did you force her to steal?"

"She was a proud woman. The queen's own cousin. It pleased me to see her humbled like a beggar. And I knew how much it would shame you. Aye. You are a sore that has festered upon my soul since we were lads."

Brenna saw the pain etched on Morgan's face, and heard it in his tone.

"Then the fight is between us." Morgan forced his tone to remain even. If it took every ounce of his willpower, he would keep Windham from exploding and perhaps harming Brenna. "Let the woman go. And I will face your wrath without a weapon."

"I intend to keep the woman." Windham's tone grew sharper. "And as for you, you are no longer a threat to me. You are doomed."

"Why this elaborate plot, Windham? Why now?" Morgan studied the distance between them. Somehow he had to get to Windham and wrestle the knife from him before he could use it on Brenna. For now, he would keep him talking. "If you wanted me dead, why have you gone to such trouble to bring me here? The deed could have just as easily been done at Greystone Abbey."

"I tried that. And came upon the lady in your bed. Besides, I needed you away from your home today."

Morgan tensed. "Why?"

Windham gave another shrill laugh. "I need you as far away from the queen as possible."

Morgan felt his blood freeze. "What has this to do with the queen?"

"At this very minute Elizabeth is preparing herself for a hunt. But what she does not realize is that she will be the one hunted."

"Elizabeth will not go to the forest without me."

"She has already received a note from you telling her that you have been called away on urgent business, but that you want her to accompany me and the others."

So his instincts had been correct. Morgan felt a rush of self-loathing. Though he had known of the queen's peril, he had allowed his own troubles to blind him. "You are the one who caused those mysterious accidents."

"Accidents. Aye. And each time I have been thwarted in my efforts. But not this time. Today the gods smile upon me, Grey. Today the monarchy will be brought down by my hand." Windham chuckled, enjoying the feeling of importance. "The queen is dead. Long live the king."

"Who has bought your loyalty, Windham?"

Never before had Windham dared to reveal his allegiance. But with success so close at hand, he was feeling expansive.

"Norfolk." He spoke the name like a deity.

"He is the queen's own cousin. Surely he would not give the order for her murder."

"He covets the throne. And Elizabeth gives no indication of abdicating or of dying of natural causes."

"Then he is mad. The people will not rally round him when they learn what treachery he employed."

"The people will never know. Elizabeth will die this day of a hunting accident. Her subjects will grieve. And Norfolk will lead them in their mourning."

Morgan watched the slight fluttering of the curtains at the window. If he were to fling himself at Windham, the momentum might carry them both through the open window. But if he were not quick enough, Windham would have time to cut Brenna. It was a calculated risk. There was a time when he would have easily risked it. But now, his love for Brenna changed everything. He was not certain he could risk her safety.

"What will you gain from all this?"

Windham tugged on Brenna's arms, causing her to gasp in pain. "A grateful new king will grant me any request. My first may be marriage to the lady who has stolen your heart."

"I would die first," Brenna hissed. "And I would tell everyone what you did this day."

Morgan felt a little thrill at the way Brenna, even now, would stand up to this coward.

"Careful, my lady. If you should become tiresome, I will see that your wish is granted." Windham went on as though he had not been interrupted. "My second request will be your lands and titles, Grey."

"My brother, Richard, is next in line to inherit. He would fight you."

"After the queen's accident, Richard will have to suffer a fatal attack. Perhaps I will have him fall from his chair onto a well-placed knife."

Morgan felt a fresh wave of hatred at this monster who calmly planned the deaths of all the people close to his heart. His hands clenched at his sides. There was no time left for strategy. He leaped forward, catching Brenna by the arm and casting her aside.

Windham caught him with the sharp blade of his knife, tearing his flesh from shoulder to wrist.

Before Morgan could pull back, Windham lunged forward. "Prepare to meet your maker, Grey."

Brenna watched in horror as the knife plunged into Morgan's tunic above his heart. When Windham pulled it out, blood streamed from the gaping wound, soaking the front of Morgan's clothes.

Morgan's face was ashen. But despite his wound, he struggled with Windham and brought him to the floor where the two men writhed and thrashed and fought for control of the knife.

Brenna picked up Morgan's sword and turned just as Windham scooped up the knife and knelt over Morgan. As he moved his hands in a downward stroke, Brenna thrust the blade of the sword, aiming for Windham's heart. At the last moment he turned, taking the blade in his shoulder. With a shriek of pain Windham rolled away. Before Brenna could strike again Windham lifted the knife and again plunged it into Morgan's body.

"Now, my lady," Windham said with a sneer, "I fear you must join your lover in death."

He towered over her, lifting the knife for the fatal plunge. As the blade came crashing down, Brenna felt it tear through her flesh and scrape against bone. Pain engulfed her. The sword dropped from her hand and she crumpled to the floor.

"I leave you to watch your lover's lifeblood spill on the floor of a lowly tavern. And yours with it. As for me, I have an appointment with destiny."

From some distant part of her mind, Brenna heard his booted footsteps cross the room and descend the stairs.

With a cry of pain and rage Brenna forced herself to crawl until she was lying across Morgan's still form. All the tears she had kept locked inside now spilled forth, mingling with the blood that spilled from his wounds.

Thick, impenetrable clouds of mist shrouded the waters of the Thames. Morgan struggled to keep his head above water, but each time he came up for air, the mist closed in, choking him. When he struggled to the surface, shafts of pain crashed through him. His lungs ached, his arm, his shoulder. The pain was too great. He longed to slip once more beneath the waters and drift until his life slowly ebbed. In death there would be relief from the pain.

He heard Brenna's voice from a great distance. Brenna. His beloved Brenna. To see her face once more, to hear that voice, he would risk the pain. But only once more. Then he would give up the battle.

Setting his teeth against the pain he struggled to the surface. Her voice was close now. He could hear her calling his name. His eyes opened and were assaulted by blinding lights. Hundreds of candles blazed, burning his eyes. He quickly blinked, then tried again. This time, though the light was too bright, it did not blind him. He moved his lips, but no words came out.

"Morgan. Please, Morgan. You must try."

Swimming? he wondered. Did she want him to swim? He could feel the water, all around him, warm, sticky. He gazed down at his arm and saw that the water of the Thames had turned to blood red.

Blood. He was not in the water. He was bleeding. And though Brenna was frantically tearing strips of her gown to stem the flow, the blood was seeping through the dressings.

He watched in horrified fascination as Brenna tightened a bandage on his arm until the blood slowed to a trickle. Working quickly, she applied another dressing, then moved to the wound in his chest.

By the light of the candle she saw the glazed look in his eyes and knew that the pain was unbearable. "Fight, Morgan. You must fight the pain and stay alive. The queen needs you."

The queen. He struggled to remember. As Brenna bound him tightly, he clamped his mouth down on the oath that sprang to his lips. With the pain came remembrance. Windham was on his way to kill the queen. He had to be stopped at all cost.

"Help me to stand."

"Aye." Brenna draped his arm around her shoulder, then slowly helped him to his feet.

"My sword."

She slipped it into the scabbard at his waist.

With her help he walked to the stairs. Each step brought a knife thrust of pain, swift, sharp, cutting off his breath. But at last they had managed to descend the stairs. When he pulled himself into the saddle, Brenna saw the way his lips whitened. But he caught up the reins and led the way as she struggled into the saddle and urged her mount to follow.

He noted that she held her arm at an odd angle. "You are wounded."

"Aye. Windham thought he had killed us both." Her gaze met his. "It is what saved us. Else he would have stayed to finish the job."

"My brave little Brenna. Forgive me for the pain I have caused you."

She brought her horse close to his. "I pray you will forgive me for lending Windham your jewels and falling into his trap."

"Hush, love. There is still work to be done. We must find the queen's party," Morgan rasped.

"Aye. But they could be anywhere in the forest."

"I know these woods. Richard and I have explored them all our lives. I will find her."

Brenna saw the beads of sweat on Morgan's forehead as he urged his horse into a run.

Ahead the forest loomed. And as they entered the thick wooded area, Brenna felt her heartbeat begin to race. Somewhere very near, the queen was being stalked by a vicious killer.

"There, Majesty. A fine buck."

"Aye, Lord Windham. I see him."

The queen drew back her bow and took careful aim. The arrow sang through the air. At the last moment the buck lifted his head, as if sensing danger. But the arrow found its mark. Leaping high in the air, the buck executed a graceful death dance, then sank to its knees.

"A perfect kill, Majesty."

The queen acknowledged his compliment with a slight nod of her head.

"If you hurry, you can have another trophy, Majesty. I spotted a second buck just slipping off to yonder woods."

"I did not see it, Windham. Are you certain?"

"Aye."

The queen glanced around toward the rest of their party, who had fanned out on either side of them. "We will lose the others if we do not tell them where we are heading."

"I will slip back and tell them which direction to take. You follow this trail around to the other side of those trees, Majesty. And I will show you where the buck is hiding."

The queen hesitated. "My groom . . ."

"He is tending to your kill, Majesty. Hurry. Else we will lose the finest buck I have ever seen."

"Truly? How large?"

Windham's voice took on a note of excitement. "At least ten points, Majesty."

"I must have him." The queen urged her mount forward. "Wait until Morgan sees what I have brought down."

"Aye, Majesty. He will be impressed."

"I do not care about impressing him. I want him to regret missing this perfect day."

Windham turned away. On his face was a smug smile. He waited until the queen disappeared beyond the line of trees. Then he carefully studied the others to be certain that no one was watching. With a flick of the reins he urged his horse into a thicket. He pulled an arrow from the quiver he had stolen from Morgan's room. By the time the queen reached the appointed place, he intended to be ready for her.

By sheer force of will Morgan was able to sit his horse. He could feel his strength ebb as he ducked in the saddle to escape low-hanging branches.

A short distance away Brenna, unmindful of the briers that snagged at her hair and raked her flesh, peered through the brush.

"I see a movement, Morgan." Her voice was a soft whisper.

"Where?"

She pointed. He brought his mount closer. There was a sudden flash of color, then it was gone. He nodded then took the lead.

This had been his favorite part of the forest. Thickly wooded, it was strewn with boulders and pockmarked with small burrows where wild animals took shelter. He felt the sweat form a river along the small of his back at a sudden thought. It was the perfect place for a man to hide himself from view if he were stalking game.

Signaling to Brenna to follow his lead, Morgan dismounted and tied his horse. Walking as quietly as a deer, he moved through the shadowy forest until a movement caught his eye.

He stepped behind a tree and pointed. Brenna came up beside him and studied the area carefully, then nodded. Some distance away the figure of a man could be seen standing perfectly still behind a tree. His bow and arrow were at the ready, the bowstring drawn tautly. Following the direction of the man's gaze, Morgan caught his breath.

Just stepping into the man's line of fire was the queen astride her horse.

Morgan and Brenna assessed the situation and realized that they were moments too late. Before Morgan could cross the space that separated him from Windham, the arrow would be fired.

If they were to shout a warning, the queen would hesitate, allowing Windham the time he needed to get her into his sight and release the fatal arrow.

Though they spoke not a word, they were of one mind. Morgan raced toward Windham while Brenna sped toward the queen.

Lifting her skirts Brenna dodged fallen logs and the sharp edges of half-buried rocks. As she ran she blessed the training she had received in the company of her father's men. With a last burst of speed she leaped high into the air and caught the queen in a great hug, knocking her cleanly from the saddle. Both women fell in a tangle of arms and legs and billowing skirts.

Elizabeth was outraged. "How dare you!" As she struggled to sit up, her famous temper boiled over. "Scotswoman, you have sealed your fate. It is not marriage to which I condemn you—'tis the hangman, for causing bodily harm to the queen."

"Forgive me, Majesty."

Brenna regained her feet, then offered a hand to the queen. Elizabeth refused to accept her offer. Instead, she slapped away the offending hand and lumbered to her feet.

"Hanging is too good for you. I should have you..." The queen's gaze was arrested by the arrow imbedded in the tree. She glanced at Brenna, then back to the arrow. She guessed that it was just about where her head had been when she was on her horse.

"Was that intended for me?"

"Aye, Majesty."

"Who..." Turning, she saw two men locked in a desperate struggle. "Morgan? Lord Windham?"

"Aye, Majesty. Morgan and I discovered Windham's plot to kill you. We feared we would not find you in time."

As they watched, Morgan's sword slipped from his hands and clattered among the rocks. With a valiant effort he lunged at Windham. But the wounds suffered at the inn had taken their toll. Windham evaded his grasp and with a vicious kick sent Morgan stumbling to his knees.

Windham seized Morgan's mount and pulled himself into the saddle. As he disappeared among the trees, Brenna and the queen hurried to Morgan's side.

"You are safe, Majesty?"

"Aye. Thanks to you and Brenna. But you are badly wounded, my friend."

"My wounds will heal. But we must find Windham."

"Let your soldiers find him. We must get you back to Greystone Abbey and have those wounds tended."

"Greystone Abbey." As a sudden, terrible thought struck, Brenna turned to the queen. "Who is left at Greystone Abbey?"

Elizabeth thought for a moment. "Besides the servants, only Richard and Adrianna."

"God in heaven." Brenna stared down at Morgan, who had come to the same conclusion and was already struggling to his feet. "We must mount and ride. And pray we make it in time."

Chapter Twenty-four

Richard sat alone in the rose garden, snipping ruthlessly at the thorny stalks. When he had finished pruning he realized that he had cut away too much of the stem. Poor flower, he thought with a trace of remorse. This was not a day for delicate work. He was far too agitated. He let the pruning shears drop to his lap.

He had ordered a servant to bring him out here where he could sort out his thoughts. But the more he thought, the more confused he became.

He had been without a woman too long. In his loneliness he had begun to spin fantasies. All of that was well and good, as long as he could distinguish fantasy from reality. But ever since Adrianna had arrived, he had begun to believe in miracles.

She was everything he had ever wanted in a woman. She was quick of mind, sweet-natured and a delight to be around. Despite her natural shyness there was a vitality about her that lit up a room. And though she appeared docile, she had learned to stand alone against her overbearing brother and sister. Aye, she was all he could desire. But what about her desires?

His hands curled into fists and he slammed them against the arms of the chair. This hated chair. When Morgan had devised it, it had offered Richard freedom. The freedom to move from room to room, and even out into the garden. But it had also become his prison. It teased him and tantalized him into thinking that he could be free once more. But he was free only to watch. He could no longer participate in life. In this chair he could only sit and stare at the world passing by.

His thoughts returned to last night. Adrianna had come unbidden to his sleeping chamber. She had stood beside the bed, wearing a night shift of gossamer and lace, looking as beautiful as any bride. Gazing at her from his bed he had felt his passions rise and knew that what she offered was the sweetest, most generous gift anyone had ever offered him.

How much courage must it have taken, for the shy, virginal Adrianna to come to him? Could he show any less courage? Though his basest instincts were to take what she offered and feast on what he had so long been starved for, he knew that she deserved better. If he gave in to his desires, she would be forever sullied in the eyes of other men. Who would marry a girl who had given her virtue to another?

Adrianna had pleaded with him to reconsider. She swore she loved him and wanted only to stay with him. How his heart had soared at her words. Dear God, how he wanted her. But he knew that her good and generous nature was blinding her to the truth. How could she possibly love him for a lifetime? When their passion cooled, she would realize what a difficult path she had chosen. A man who could not walk would become, in time, a burden. And so, though she thought Richard had chosen a nobler route, the truth was, he was saving her from herself. Holding his passion in check, he had sent her away and told her to save herself for someone who would truly deserve her.

He felt the pain, sharp and swift. On the morrow Adrianna would leave with Madeline and Cordell. His life would be as before, only worse. From this day on he would be tormented by what he had been forced to give up. Even in his dreams he would see her, breathe her in the perfume of the roses, taste her in every drop of honey that passed his lips.

With a scowl he looked up to see the object of his thoughts moving toward him along the garden path. As always the desire rose in him, swamping him with need. He carefully banked his feelings and composed his features.

"Mistress Leems said you were out here." Adrianna continued walking until she was standing directly in front of him.

He shifted uncomfortably. "Aye. I have much work to do. I have been neglecting my roses."

He picked up the shears and made an attempt at a stalk. He snipped off a perfect bloom. It fluttered to the ground. Taking no notice he snipped another and another, until an entire row of rose bushes had been shorn of their blooms.

"Perhaps I should leave you," she said softly, "before you destroy your beautiful rose garden."

"Aye. I believe we said everything we had to say last night."

"About last night..." Adrianna saw the way he flinched at her words and paused. Then, licking her lips, she forced herself to go on. "I do not regret what I did, my lord. I know it was brazen of me, and I know that I have shocked you. But I do not regret it. My only regret is that you refused me."

He wondered if she could hear the wild thundering of his heart. God in heaven, how much should a man have to take? In a voice trembling with passion he said, "We will speak no more of this."

"*Oui.* We will never again speak of it. And I will go back to France only because you will not permit me to stay with you. But know this, my Lord Richard. You cannot command my heart. That stays here with you. I love you. I will always love you."

"That is the child in you speaking. You think you love me out of some noble need to help the less fortunate. But when you return to your home, you will be grateful to me for setting you free to love the way you deserve to love."

For a moment the fire inside her raged out of control. "The child in me? Nay, my lord. It is the woman in me who speaks. I will be grateful for having known you, my lord." Her voice caught in her throat. "But I will never thank you for sending me away."

She turned, but not before he saw the tears that filled her eyes. Without thinking he caught her hand and folded it between both of his.

In a voice filled with pain he whispered, "For God's sake, Adrianna, leave me. Now. Before I weaken."

"How—touching."

Richard and Adrianna looked up in surprise at the sound of Lord Windham's caustic tones.

Seeing his torn and bloody tunic, his dirty breeches, Richard commented, "It would seem you've taken another nasty fall, Windham."

"Aye." Windham's lips twisted into a cruel smile. "A fall from grace."

"I do not..."

Windham took his sword from the scabbard and studied it. "All my life in my climb to power I have been thwarted by one man." He looked up and fixed his gaze on Richard. "Your brother."

"Morgan? What are you talking about, Windham?"

Lord Windham took a step closer. His eyes narrowed. "Morgan Grey thinks I am a beaten man. But he has not yet won. There are still some things I can do to hurt him."

Instinctively Richard shoved Adrianna roughly aside. In a sharp commanding tone she had never heard before he said curtly, "You will go inside at once, Adrianna. And you will not look back."

Windham's cruel smile grew. "You would spare this sweet child the sight of your death at my hands?"

Adrianna sucked in her breath. "What are you saying?"

"Go, Adrianna." Richard caught at the wheels of his chair, turning it so that he placed himself between the woman and Windham. "I command you. Go now."

"Nay, my lord." Though her face had gone pale and her voice trembled, she did not move. "I obeyed you last night. And I was wrong. I should have disobeyed you and stayed as I wanted. But now you cannot command. If you must die at this man's hand, I would rather die beside you than live without you."

"There is little enough challenge here," Windham said, lifting his sword. "One with no legs, the other with no courage."

Richard recalled the way his blood had always heated just before the battle. His heart would race, his palms would sweat, and he would feel the kicking, churning juices deep inside begin to pump as the battle began. He felt that way now. It was as if he had never been away from it.

He glanced down at the shears in his lap. They were his only weapon. But he would do what he had to. Adrianna's life depended upon it. As for his own, it mattered not.

As Windham thrust the sword, Richard ducked and waited until his opponent moved in closer. Then, slashing out, he managed to cut Windham's arm. With a savage oath Windham dropped his sword and clutched at his bloody arm.

"For every wound you inflict on me, I shall inflict a dozen upon you and the woman. Before I finish with you, you will beg me to kill you."

They heard the sound of horses' hooves, but neither man was willing to take his gaze from the other long enough to see who was riding toward them.

Windham's voice grew shrill with growing rage and frustration. "You will pay for this, Grey. You and your brother. I will see you both destroyed."

As he bent to take up his sword, a dainty foot pressed down over the jewelled hilt. With his mouth open, Windham looked up to see the young Frenchwoman facing him, her eyes blazing.

"You will not harm Richard."

"Harm him?" Windham gave an evil laugh. "I will kill him. And you as well, little fool."

"Toss me the sword, Adrianna." Richard watched in horror as Adrianna and Windham struggled for control of the sword.

But when Lord Windham lifted his hand and slapped her, knocking her to the ground, Richard's horror turned to fury.

"No!" As Windham lifted his sword above Adrianna's head, Richard gathered all his strength and lunged from his chair, taking Windham with him.

From their positions on their horses, the queen, Brenna and Morgan watched helplessly as the two men collided, their fists raised, their voices muffled in grunts of pain.

For long, agonizing minutes the two men lay very still. Around them no one spoke. No one seemed able to move. All who watched were paralyzed in fear. At long last Richard lifted himself up on his powerful hands and stared down at the man beneath him.

Lord Windham lay, faceup, the pruning shears buried in his chest. His tunic was stained crimson. His mouth was twisted in a soundless cry of rage. His eyes stared, lifeless, vacant, fixed on some distant pinnacle he would never reach.

Adrianna fell into Richard's arms, sobbing against his chest, "Oh, my beloved. Never, never will I permit you to send me away again."

He clutched her to him. Against her hair he murmured, "Nor will I try. When I thought I might lose you, I realized just how much I love you. I can only pray that I will bring you half as much happiness as I know you will bring me."

Though she rejoiced in their triumph, a terrible weakness seemed to have taken over Brenna. She turned to Morgan, her head swimming. Her relief turned to shock when she saw the blood seeping from him in half a dozen places. His face had lost all its color. His lips moved but no words came out. His eyes rolled back in his head. And without a sound he slid from his horse and fell to the ground.

With a cry she dropped from the saddle and clutched him. If it took her last breath, she would see to his needs.

Morgan came awake slowly, as if from a long, drugging sleep. Sunlight streaming through the balcony windows stabbed at his eyes and he had to blink several times before he could bear the light. He glanced around the suite of rooms that had been his since boyhood. The familiar surroundings brought him comfort.

He felt a stirring beside him on the bed and turned his head. Even that slight movement sent pain crashing through him.

Brenna lay curled on her side, facing him. He drank in the sight of her.

Bits and pieces of his tormented dreams still clouded his mind. In each of them, his beloved Brenna had suffered at the hands of demons. He studied her carefully. Except for a dressing on her arm, she seemed unharmed.

He watched as her lids flickered, then opened. At the sight of him a smile touched her lips, animating all her features.

"At last you have returned to me." She knelt and placed a hand on his forehead, then gave an audible sigh. "Oh, my beloved." She felt her lips tremble as tears filled her eyes. During the long days and nights of her silent vigil she had held all her dark fears at bay. Now, when the danger was over, she gave in to a bout of weeping. "I was so afraid I would lose you."

"How could I give up my life now, when there is so much to live for?" Morgan drew her against his chest and wrapped his arms around her, offering her his quiet strength.

That was how the queen and her servants found them. Flustered, Brenna tried to draw away, but Morgan caught her hand, forcing her to stay by his side.

"So, my friend," Elizabeth said as she strode across the room and paused beside his bed. "You have rejoined the living. Your wounds were grave. You had us all alarmed. But Brenna never gave up."

With a tender smile Morgan turned to the woman beside him.

"When my physician insisted upon bleeding you, Brenna chased him from your chambers and took over your complete care."

At that, Morgan threw back his head and roared. "You dismissed the queen's own physician?"

"You had already lost too much blood. I feared if he had his way you would have no blood left."

"The lady is truly your champion," Elizabeth said. "She has not left your side. She even took her meals here in your chambers. Such devotion is rare indeed."

At the queen's praise, Morgan watched the color rise to Brenna's cheeks.

"And you, Majesty?" Morgan studied the queen. "Are you unscathed?"

"Aye. Thanks to you and the Scotswoman. And to show your queen's gratitude," Elizabeth said regally, "there will be a ceremony here in the abbey as soon as you are strong enough. You and Richard will receive your country's highest honor. And Brenna MacAlpin may ask any favor from a grateful queen."

"That is not necessary, Majesty. It is reward enough to know that you are unharmed."

"It is my desire that all of England will know of your brave deeds." Elizabeth touched a hand to Morgan's cheek, and Brenna was certain that she saw tears in the queen's eyes.

"Rest now, my brave rogue," Elizabeth murmured. With a rustle of skirts she was gone.

Morgan stood in a small antechamber of the abbey, awaiting Brenna's arrival. Rosamunde had insisted that she be allowed to fuss over her mistress's hair and clothing before the ceremony. After all, it was not every day that the titled lords and ladies of the realm came to the humble abbey at Greystone to bask in the presence of their queen.

Morgan moved to the door and peered at the crowd of beautifully dressed men and women. How ironic, he thought, that they should come here this day to honor him and his brother. He would have much preferred the simple gratitude of his queen. But Elizabeth had insisted upon this ceremony. He and Richard would be knighted here in the abbey of Greystone.

The original abbey had been built nearly two hundred years earlier. When one of his ancestors had successfully defended the monks against an attack, his reward from a grateful king had been a gift of the abbey and all the surrounding villages.

Morgan thought about the many ancestors whose blood flowed through his veins. How many battles they had fought. How many victories they had enjoyed. But the sweetest victory of all, he knew, was the victory of the heart. With Brenna at his side, he could do anything. Without her... He thought about all the bleak years when he had hardened his heart against love. Brenna had been the one to unlock the door, freeing him to love again.

He heard the trumpets blare and knew that the queen had arrived. Opening the door, he watched as Elizabeth moved along the center aisle, lifting her hand in a blessing as she walked toward the altar. The women curtsied, the men bowed as she passed.

When she was seated upon her throne, she signaled for the ceremony to begin. Morgan glanced toward the rear of the abbey and saw Richard seated in his chair. With quick steps he joined him.

"Sir Morgan," Richard said, winking at him.

"Aye, Sir Richard." Morgan clapped a hand on his brother's shoulder, then stepped behind the chair and began to push.

Together the two men moved up the center aisle toward their smiling queen.

The ceremony was brief and moving. Elizabeth cited her two noble warriors for risking their own lives for the life of the queen. With gleaming sword she touched their shoulders and spoke the words that would forever set them apart from other men. They were exalted knights, whose glorious deeds would be recorded for posterity.

A hush fell over the crowd and Morgan turned expectantly. He saw Brenna standing at the back of the abbey. As she began to move up the aisle, he thought again about the woman who had refused to leave him until his wounds were completely mended. Day and night she had stayed by his side, tending him, ministering to him with that same quiet dignity he had come to love.

He watched her now, looking every bit as regal as the woman who sat upon the throne. No one in this assembly would believe that she could fight like a wildcat and wield a sword like a soldier. Nor would they believe how the woman could love.

He felt a warm glow. Last night their lovemaking had taken on a fierce, passionate nature that had left him breathless.

Brenna bowed low before the queen, then lifted her head.

"Brenna MacAlpin," Elizabeth said in tones that carried throughout the abbey. "Though not a citizen of this land, you risked your life so that I may live. I proclaim to all assembled that a grateful queen offers to grant your most fervent desire."

Elizabeth looked at the young woman who stood humbly before her and was reminded of the proud, rebellious young Scotswoman who had stood before her so defiantly on their first meeting. "What is your request, Brenna MacAlpin?"

Brenna felt her heart thundering. She'd had several days to contemplate this. Since the queen had first informed her of this celebration, she had pondered. The queen had assured her that gold, titles, land, were all hers for the asking. But she had known from the first that there was only one thing she desired.

She loved Morgan. Loved him with all her heart. But she would come to him freely, of her own choice. He would understand. He was a man who valued his own freedom.

Beside her, Morgan beamed. He had no doubt as to what Brenna would choose. She loved him. He loved her. She would choose to stay with him forever.

"Freedom, Majesty. I would return to my people a free woman."

Morgan caught his breath as a pain as sharp as a dagger pierced his heart. This could not be happening. She would not ask such a thing. Leave him? Return to Scotland?

As the queen spoke the words granting Brenna her freedom, Morgan felt all the joy of this day turn into ashes.

From the choir loft came organ music, swelling dramatically as Brenna made her way down the aisle. From her position in the first pew Adrianna rushed forward and hugged Richard.

Morgan spun on his heel and bowed before Elizabeth. In hushed tones he said, "I was told that Alden has assembled an army to ride to Wales."

"Aye." The queen looked puzzled.

"I would ride with them."

"You? Morgan, you have barely recovered from your wounds."

"I have been away from the battle too long, Majesty. I am weary of lolling about like an old man. Give me your blessing."

The queen stared beyond him to where Brenna waited in the back of the abbey. "This has to do with the lady's request for freedom, does it not?"

"It has to do with my freedom, Majesty. The lady has earned her freedom. I will not hold her. I freely choose to go to war."

Elizabeth placed a hand on Morgan's shoulder and brought her lips to his ear. "You know I cannot refuse your request, my friend. But I fear this time you go too far. She loves you. But how long can she be expected to wait while you work out your demons?"

"Have I your permission to go to Wales?"

Elizabeth gave a long, expressive sigh. "Aye, my dear friend. You may go. So long as you promise to stay alive."

He kissed her hand and turned away. Then, steeling himself for the final confrontation, he made his way down the aisle and stopped before Brenna.

Her bright smile nearly shattered his resolve.

"I must bid you goodbye, my lady."

Brenna stared at him, uncomprehending.

"The queen is sending me to Wales to put down a rebellion."

"Wales. For how long...?" Brenna tried again. "I had thought that you would accompany me to my home."

"I will send several of my most trusted men."

"I had so hoped you would meet my sisters."

"As you can see, my lady, it is an impossible request. My duty to the queen must come first."

"Aye." Brenna felt her lower lip tremble and bit down hard. Had he not made it plain a long time ago that he did not wish to marry again? What had he said? "I would rather face a horde of invaders without a weapon." She had been warned. But like all women from the beginning of time, she had foolishly thought her love could change everything. "I shall miss you, Morgan. Will you come to Scotland when this—rebellion is put down?"

Morgan looked away, unable to meet her gaze. "If I could but see the future, Brenna."

He forced himself to take her hand and lift it to his lips. He felt the jolt and took a deep breath. For a few minutes longer he must be strong.

"Farewell, Brenna."

"Goodbye, Morgan. God go with you."

"And with you, my lady."

He turned away and squared his shoulders. Behind him Brenna leaned against the cold stone wall of the abbey and prayed her legs would continue to support her. The pain around her heart was so terrible, she feared she would embarrass herself by bursting into tears.

From her position at the altar a compassionate queen watched with keen interest. And when Morgan and Brenna turned away from each other, she felt their pain as if it were her own.

Chapter Twenty-five

Morgan leaned a hip against the balcony and stared out over the vast lands of his estate. Always before, Greystone Abbey had brought him peace. After each battle he had returned eagerly to this place so that he could refresh his mind, his soul, his body. But that was before Brenna. Now he could find no peace at Greystone. Perhaps, he thought darkly, there would never be peace for him again.

Everywhere he looked he saw Brenna. In the cheery rooms that had once been so somber. In the refectory, where Mistress Leems still served the foods that Brenna had introduced to her. In these very rooms, where the air was perfumed with the dried flower petals that lined the chest and wardrobe. In the rose garden, where a new fountain bubbled beneath the gnarled old tree where he and Richard had played as lads.

He glanced down. In the rose garden below he watched as Adrianna settled herself on Richard's lap and brought her arms around his neck. Morgan turned away, feeling like an intruder.

He had returned from Wales in time for their wedding. The celebration had been a moving one, causing more than a few tears among the guests. But though most of the guests had long since left, the queen remained.

She had been badly shaken by Windham's attempt on her life. It reminded her, Morgan knew, of her mortality. And though she would soon return to London, she put off the journey as long as possible, desiring to store up the peace of the country for the long days ahead.

At the knock on his door he turned.

"Enter."

Elizabeth swept in alone.

"Where are your ever-present ladies, Majesty?"

"They await me in my chambers. My musician is entertaining them."

"Sit, Majesty. I will send for a servant."

"Nay." Elizabeth caught his arm. Then, in a playful gesture, she ran her hand along the muscles of his arm. "You are so strong, my friend." Her tone became brisk. "Perhaps too strong."

"What does that mean?"

She paused, carefully choosing her words. "Have you heard from her?"

"Who?"

"You know." She watched the way his eyes narrowed. "Brenna."

"Nay. There have been no messages between us."

"Why?"

He shrugged, hating the feeling that came over him at the mere mention of her name. "We have made our choices. Our lives move in different directions."

"Perhaps, if you loved her more, you would go to her."

"If she loved me enough, she would have stayed."

"She is the MacAlpin, Morgan, the leader of her people. When you brought her here against her will, she left many important things undone. It was her duty to see to her responsibilities."

"Aye. And I have responsibilities, as well." He turned blazing eyes on the queen. "Or would you have me walk away from you, from all that I hold dear, and crawl to her."

"You, Morgan? Crawl?" The queen laughed. "It is unthinkable."

"Aye. So where is the solution? She has her life in Scotland—I have mine in England."

The queen took a long, deep breath. "Brenna is a proud woman. I can understand that. I am also a proud woman."

"What about my pride?"

"Aye. There is that." The queen studied his firm profile. The merest hint of a smile tugged at her lips. "My proud savage, I would ask a favor."

"Anything."

She arched an eyebrow. "You make this easy."

"I am at your command, Majesty. You know that."

"There is talk of a rebellion on the Scottish border."

His eyes narrowed as he studied her. "I have heard no talk of a rebellion."

"The news was just brought to me." She paused. "Take your most trusted men and look into this."

"I will not see her while I am there."

"I would not ask it."

He nodded. "I will leave at dawn."

Elizabeth brushed her lips across his cheek. "Hurry back. Your queen needs you."

Morgan had forgotten how green the land was. And how blue the sky. Little villages were tucked into the folds of hills strewn with sheep. As the horses clattered over a stone bridge, he caught sight of the distant turrets of MacAlpin Castle.

He had searched this idyllic land for signs of a rebellion against the queen. He had found none. Instead he had found the peace he had not found since Brenna left. Everywhere he looked he saw proud young lasses with windswept curls and laughing eyes. And all of them tugged at his heart, reminding him of the one who had captivated him from the first moment he had seen her.

Alden wheeled his mount and raced past the long column of men to where Morgan's horse stood.

"Across yonder river there are over a hundred men assembled. At last I think we have found our rebellion."

Morgan forced his attention to the task at hand. "Tell the men to prepare their weapons. Send two of your best men to ride ahead and ascertain the enemy's strength and number."

"Aye." Alden urged his horse into a gallop.

Morgan touched the dagger at his waist, then pulled his sword from the scabbard.

The day was so perfect. The sun shone from a cloudless sky. The slightest breeze ruffled the leaves on the trees. It was not a day for spilling blood.

Morgan rode hard until he reached the front of the column of men. Alden turned in the saddle just as the two riders returned.

"They insist it is no rebellion, my lord. They say they are celebrating a wedding. But they are dressed as if for battle. And there are Highlanders among them."

"Highlanders?"

"Aye, my lord. Giants, they are. In full battle dress. Barelegged heathens, with legs as big as tree stumps. They carry broadswords and longbows as well as swords and daggers."

"And they say it is a celebration?"

"Aye, my lord. There is one among them who said we were invited to join them."

Morgan's eyes narrowed. What sort of ploy was this?

Turning to Alden he said, "You will stay on this side of the river with half the men. I will lead the other half across. If we are in need of your help, we will signal."

"Aye, my lord." Alden watched as Morgan hastily assembled his men.

Taking the lead, Morgan started across the river. On the other side he faced the rows of Highlanders who watched in silence as he and the others rode slowly through their midst.

"Welcome to our wedding feast," one of them called.

Morgan turned. The man had russet hair that fell across a wide forehead. He was taller even than the others, and his shoulders were as wide as a broadsword.

"We do not wish to intrude upon your celebration." Morgan reined in his mount. "We have been sent by Queen Elizabeth to look into rumors of a rebellion."

"Our queen, Mary," the man said, his eyes showing no sign of anger, "has asked that our people live in peace with yours."

"Aye. I have seen no sign of discontent. But your assembly caused us to inquire." Morgan glanced at the Highlanders, who began laughing and talking among themselves. Though all wore their weapons, they seemed more interested in feasting than fighting. "Forgive our intrusion into your celebration. We will leave you to it."

"Nay," the Highlander said with a laugh. "Join us."

"It would not be right."

A beautiful woman crossed the expanse of lawn and stood beside the Highlander. In her arms was a cooing infant, whose chubby fingers curled around a strand of her mahogany hair. The warrior put his arm around the woman in a protective manner. When she looked up at Morgan, he felt his heart stop. Though he had never before seen her, he knew she had to be Brenna's sister.

"You are Meredith. And you," he said to the Highlander, "are Brice Campbell."

"Aye." Meredith gave him a warm smile. "And you are Morgan Grey. Brenna told us all about you."

"She spoke warmly and lovingly about you, as well."

His gaze moved beyond her to the lass who strolled toward them. Megan, the youngest sister, was wearing a flowing gown of gold that matched her golden hair. In such formal attire she looked incongruous with a bleating lamb slung across her shoulders. She moved catlike across the lawn. When she spied him, her eyes narrowed and he saw the way her hand went to the dagger at her waist.

"I come in peace, Megan." Morgan swallowed a smile at the way she boldly studied him.

"Brenna boasts that the Queen's Savage is fine and noble," Megan said. "And though I remember only an arrogant English soldier, I will not argue with my sister on this special day."

"So you are to be wed?" Morgan said.

"Nay. Not I." She tossed her head and again Morgan had to stifle a smile. "There is not a man alive who would own my heart."

"Then who marries this day?"

Megan cast a glance at her sister, then back at Morgan. "I thought you knew. It is Brenna's wedding day."

Morgan felt his heart stop. He gripped the reins until his knuckles were white. And though the talking and laughter swirled around him, he heard nothing.

Brenna's wedding day. He felt the stab of pain and gritted his teeth. He would not mourn. She was not worth it.

Anger replaced the pain of a moment ago. Wild, surging anger. She had not loved him. She had never loved him. If she had, she would have not found another lover so soon. She had merely used him. Used his friendship with the queen to secure her freedom.

"I hope you will give the Lady Brenna my best wishes."

"You can give them to her yourself," Meredith said gently. She had read the pain in his eyes. Her heart went out to this Englishman. He was so fierce. And so wounded. "Brenna has gone to a favorite place to be alone before the wedding."

"It does not matter, my lady. I must rejoin my men on the other side of the river."

"Aye. I understand," Meredith said softly. "But Brenna would wish to see you, to thank you for all you did for her."

"I need no thanks from her."

"Brice will show you the way," Meredith said as if he had not even spoken.

Morgan watched as the Highlander pulled himself onto a horse and took off at a run. And though he had no intention of following, Morgan found himself doing just that.

The Highlander never paused, never looked back. His mount raced across the rolling hills, then began a steep upward climb. They crossed a farmer's field, and the Highlander waved to the man and his family before disappearing into the woods. Morgan followed. When they finally left the forest, they stepped out into a field of heather.

Morgan stared out at the sea of blue. In the gentle breeze, the blossoms waved and nodded, giving off their wonderful perfume. He breathed it in, filling his lungs. It seemed appropriate that he should come upon her again in this field of Highland heather. For it was here that he would always see this haughty, regal woman. His mind went back to the first time he had been here. He could still see Brenna, looking so small and alone as she bravely tried to outrun him. What an amazing woman she was.

He glanced around. The Highlander was nowhere to be seen. Shielding his eyes from the sun, he stared out at the expanse of blue. In the middle of the field stood a figure, gowned in white.

His heart began to race. Urging his mount forward he drank in the sight of her. How beautiful she was, with the proud, haughty lift of her head, that cool demeanor.

"Brenna."

At the sound of his voice she turned slightly. Her lips parted in a smile. "Morgan. The queen said you would come."

"The queen." A little frown touched his brow. "When did you see the queen?"

"She arrived only hours ago."

"Here? She is here in Scotland?"

"Aye. She came for my wedding."

His eyes narrowed. How could she speak so lightly of something that would tear out his heart? "You did not wait long, my lady."

"I waited too long. But my lover was away, putting down some unrest."

"He is a soldier?"

"Aye." She stepped closer, and he watched the way the white gown fluttered about her ankles.

"I never knew you were such a cruel woman, Brenna."

"If one is to lead her people, she must harden her heart to many things. Your queen told me that."

"Elizabeth is a remarkable woman. But I would not have her for a wife."

"I would hope not, my lord."

He glanced sharply at her. She was making no sense.

"A man can have but one wife. And you are already spoken for."

"I? Nay, I have no wife."

"But you shall very soon."

He saw the curve of her lips as she gave a delighted laugh. And then he understood. Still, he had to be certain.

He slid from the saddle but did not make a move toward her. "What are you saying, Brenna?"

"It was important for me to return to my people a free woman. And it was equally important to be able to choose my own husband. It is the way of the MacAlpins."

The relief he was beginning to feel gave him renewed courage. The light of teasing laughter came into his eyes, warming his voice. "What if this husband you choose does not return your ardor?"

"Ah, but he does, my lord. I would not be foolish enough to choose a mate who would not want me."

"Perhaps he has had a bad experience that has left him embittered."

"I would heal his heart."

"Perhaps his duties will take him far from his home."

"I will wait for him. Unless, of course, he wishes me to accompany him."

"Perhaps he swears allegiance to a queen other than yours."

"Then I will swear my allegiance as well."

"To his queen?"

"Aye." Her voice lowered. "To all that he holds dear."

"And what of your people?"

"There will always be the MacAlpin. In this case, Megan."

"You would entrust the care of your people to that little firebrand?"

Brenna laughed, and the sound of it skimmed across his nerves. "Aye. She will be a fine leader. And if there is ever a rebellion in our land, she will stand at the head of it."

He took a single step toward her and reached out a hand to her cheek. The moment he touched her she felt the weakness spread through her limbs.

"It would seem that you have thought of everything, my lady."

"Aye. Everything but one."

He waited, loving the way her eyes danced.

"The man who holds my heart has not yet agreed to wed me."

"Ah." He took a step closer and cupped her face between his big hands. With his thumbs he traced the outline of her lips. He felt the rush of heat. She was the only woman who had ever made him burn like this. "How could any man resist such a tempting offer?"

Her lips curved into a radiant smile. "You will marry me, Morgan?"

"Since the celebration has already begun, I see no reason to waste the day."

"Is that the only reason you agree?"

"Should there be another?"

"Aye." She brought her arms around his neck and drew herself close until their bodies were touching. "You should whisper sweet words of love and tell me that your heart would break if we could not be together for a lifetime."

He closed his eyes, loving the feel of her in his arms. "Oh, my haughty little ice maiden. How the thought of you has tormented me."

"That is better," she whispered against his lips. "Whisper more love words."

"I missed you more with each passing day." He pressed his lips to her temple and felt the need begin to pulse and throb. "I love you more than life itself."

She sighed and brought her lips to his throat. "More, my love. Tell me more."

His lips roamed her eyelids, her cheek, the corner of her mouth. "I need you as a starving man needs food." He glanced down at her and saw the soft glow of love that seemed to surround her with a halo of light.

"Then come with me now to the meadow where the others are waiting. We will lead them to the kirk where we will pledge our love forever."

"Nay, my love. I fear I cannot go."

Her eyes widened. Her mouth opened, but no words came out.

Morgan nibbled her earlobe. "I cannot go anywhere until you lie with me here in the heather."

"But the others are waiting."

"Brenna. Take pity on me. I have been to far-flung lands on a mission for my queen." His hands moved along her spine, igniting little fires. "But now I have come home to your arms. The Queen's Savage has been gentled by your touch."

They dropped to their knees in the heather and he breathed in the wonderful fragrance that would always remind him of her.

"Wherever you go, Morgan Grey, I go, too. In your arms I have found my home."

Home. From this moment on, home was in her arms. He lost himself in her kiss.

As his lips and fingertips began to move over her, Brenna gave herself up to the pleasure of his touch. Her heart was nearly bursting with the love she felt for this man. Her gentle savage. One lifetime, she decided, would never be enough to show him how much she loved him. But considering how far they had come, it did not seem unreasonable to believe that they would follow one another, even into the hereafter. Where they would spend an eternity loving, as they did now.

*   *   *   *   *

Coming in March from

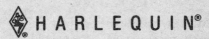

◈ H A R L E Q U I N ®

LaVyrle Spencer's unforgettable story of a
love that wouldn't die.

LAVYRLE SPENCER

SWEET MEMORIES

She was as innocent as she was unsure . . . until a very special
man dared to unleash the butterfly wrapped in her cocoon and
open Teresa's eyes and heart to love.

SWEET MEMORIES is a love story to savor that will make you
laugh—and cry—as it brings warmth and magic into your
heart.

"Spencer's characters take on the richness of friends, relatives
  and acquaintances." 	—*Rocky Mountain News*

Harlequin romances are now available in stores at these convenient times each month.

Harlequin Presents **Harlequin American Romance** **Harlequin Historical** **Harlequin Intrigue**	These series will be in stores on the 4th of every month.
Harlequin Romance **Harlequin Temptation** **Harlequin Superromance** **Harlequin Regency Romance**	New titles for these series will be in stores on the 16th of every month.

We hope this new schedule is convenient for you. With only two trips each month to your local bookseller, you will always be sure not to miss any of your favorite authors!

Happy reading!

Please note there may be slight variations in on-sale dates in your area due to differences in shipping and handling.

HDATES

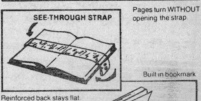

Coming soon
to an easy chair near you.

FIRST CLASS is Harlequin's armchair travel plan for the incurably romantic. You'll visit a different dreamy destination every month from January through December without ever packing a bag. No jet lag, no expensive air fares and *no* lost luggage. Just First Class Harlequin Romance reading, featuring exotic settings from Tasmania to Thailand, from Egypt to Australia, and more.

FIRST CLASS romantic excursions guaranteed! Start your world tour in January. Look for the special **FIRST CLASS** destination on selected Harlequin Romance titles—there's a new one every month.

NEXT DESTINATION:
AUSTRALIA

 Harlequin Books

JTR3